Dear

MW00800618

Small Town Affairs

I hope you enjoy
the Book.
Best Wishes
Joyce
Brennan

Cover by Susan Schetter
15302 Lakeview Parkway
Findlay, Ohio 45840
419-423-2468
http://www.inspiringimagesbysusan.com
Cover model, Sarah Spangler

Copyright © 2007 Joyce Brennan
All rights reserved.
ISBN: 1-4196-2833-X

To order additional copies, please contact us.
BookSurge, LLC
www.booksurge.com
1-866-308-6235
orders@booksurge.com

JOYCE BRENNAN

SMALL TOWN
AFFAIRS

2007

Small Town Affairs

To My Husband Tom, And Our Children, Tommy, Elizabeth, Tim And Elia.
Thanks To Jeanne Cooper For Hours Of Editing, Connie Berreth And D.j Perkins For Additional Grammar And Spell Check. Also To Shelly, Bill, Jerry, Roger And The Gang For Their Help And Encouragement.

ONE
MANHATTAN, NEW YORK CITY, NEW YORK

O h my God." Olivia's hands flew to her face and the papers she carried scattered around the room like oversized confetti. She didn't expect to find anyone inside the dimly lit copy room, especially Brian Mercer.

"Damn, Olivia, what the hell are you doing here? I thought you'd left for the day." Shaken from the surprise interruption, Brian loosened the grip on the girl he had stretched across the desk, and allowed her to roll with an awkward thump onto the floor.

"You, you tramp," Olivia screamed as she recognized the flashy secretarial clerk. The girl had become the topic of off-colored office gossip. With her over-endowed figure and long brassy, bleached-blonde hair, she wore enough gaudy eye make-up to give the appearance of a common street walker.

The girl didn't speak, but smirked at Olivia as she fumbled around to find Brian's shirt to cover herself. With the rest of his clothes out of reach, Brian defiantly focused his stare on Olivia.

"You bastard, how could you?" Olivia said as her eyes swept the windowless room. Shoes danced across the floor followed by a long string of rumpled clothing. An empty champagne bottle lay on its side at the edge of the copy machine as two paper cups bore witness to the scene.

Olivia should have become suspicious when she found the key in the lock instead of hidden away in the top drawer of the file cabinet, but the urgency to copy documents for Monday's staff meeting had distracted her. Brian's father, CEO of Mercer Advertising, Inc., constantly warned the staff about the danger of corporate espionage, almost to the point of paranoia. Since security became top priority, the copy room, located in a small office off the file clerk's cubicle, was always kept locked.

Olivia's emotions spiraled from shock to disbelief. Raw anger took over and she bent down and snatched one of Brian's handmade Italian loafers to throw at him. She glared at the two of them for a moment then turned, slammed the door shut and locked Brian and his playmate inside.

Olivia fought hysterics as she rushed down the hallway to her office. This couldn't be happening. Her fiancé, Brian Mercer, with that bimbo. The scene flashed in her head. The sight of the girl's lacy red thong dangling from the back of a chair and the smell of her cheap perfume mixed with Brian's aftershave caused the sour taste of nausea to burn in the back of her throat. She couldn't wipe the image from her mind.

She gathered a few personal items from the desk and stuffed everything into a tote bag. She grabbed her coat and snapped off the main overhead light switch, which she spitefully remembered darkened the rest of the offices including the copy room. She locked the main door with her set of executive keys, and still shook with anger as she made her way to the elevator.

Olivia jabbed the down button, paced the hall and waited. It seemed to take forever for the elevator to reach the fourteenth floor. She heaved a sigh of relief when the doors opened to an empty car. No one had to witness her rage as she unleashed her temper and called Brian every name that came to mind during the ride down to street level. Olivia's frantic pace toward the subway, turned into a run as she attempted to suppress the fury that boiled inside her.

When Olivia searched the tote bag for a subway token, she noticed Brian's loafer. She fished it out, held it shoulder high as if it were the remains of a dead skunk, and dropped it in a garbage bin, relieved to get that and any other reminder of Brian Mercer out of her sight. She pushed through the turnstile and boarded the train.

The subway car was crowded and she edged her way down the aisle until she found an open seat. She had to contain her emotions...regain composure. Olivia closed her eyes and inhaled deeply to quell the overwhelming resentment that simmered inside her. What a fool she'd been not to take heed of the rampant office rumors about Brian's skirt chasing.

"Silly gossip," he said when she mentioned it. "Those days are completely in the past. Every young man sows his wild oats but once I met you, I became a changed man. Don't ever doubt my love."

She believed him. They made plans for the future, but Brian obviously had another agenda. *How could I have been so stupid?*

Rage gave way to disappointment as the incident played over and over in her mind. Passengers began to stare as tears splashed down her face. The car seemed to be closing in, squeezing the breath from her. Humiliated and trapped, she couldn't escape the prying eyes.

She reached into her coat pocket for a tissue and fingered the metal key. When she locked the boss's son and his lover in the dark copy room, she not only left her fiancé, but abandoned any hope for a future in advertising. Brian wielded enough influence in the industry to blackball her career. Her life was crumbling into irretrievable pieces.

The day's events blurred her mind. Olivia scarcely remembered leaving the subway or the two block walk to her apartment. She unlocked the door, mumbled a quiet 'thanks' that her roommate hadn't arrived home, and dropped the tote bag and her coat on a chair. At least she wouldn't have to recap the entire office scenario until she had the opportunity to gather her thoughts. She needed time to sort out what was left of her life.

She mentally calculated her options when the phone interrupted her thoughts. Olivia's first impulse was to let it ring. What if it was Brian? Would he dare call?

She lifted the receiver and whispered, "Hello." She felt relieved when she recognized the voice coming from the phone. "Aunt Etta, how nice to hear from you," Olivia said with all the confidence she could muster.

"Livie dear, it's been ages since we've talked and you've been on my mind all afternoon. Are you okay?"

The sound of Etta's voice brought out all the emotion that welled inside and caused the tears to fall again. Between sobs, Olivia told her aunt that she was temporarily out of a job, stressing the 'temporarily' part. She didn't reveal the entire sordid story. "I don't know what to do."

"Do you have money for air fare?"

"Yes."

"Then come home, Livie. Come back to Ohio and we'll figure it out. As soon as you know what flight you're on, call me and I'll pick you up. Toledo or Dayton, it doesn't matter."

Later, when her roommate entered the apartment, Olivia gave a sanitized account of the situation.

"What do you want to do about the apartment?"

"I hadn't thought that far ahead," Olivia said.

"I'll check around. Maybe one of my friends knows someone who is waiting to move to the city."

They made a trade. In exchange for Olivia's furniture, her roommate agreed to pack and ship the remainder of her possessions to Rexford, Ohio. Olivia hoped a new tenant would be found before the end of the following month, when her rent came due.

Olivia e-mailed her letter of resignation to Mercer Advertising, citing personal reasons, put the office keys in an envelope for her roommate to mail, and caught the morning plane to Dayton. She felt like an escapee. Free from facing Brian's betrayal, their broken engagement and the office gossip that she knew would spread like a bad case of the flu. Everyone who worked at Mercer Associates would have their own version of the story by Monday, adding facts they couldn't possibly know.

Olivia hadn't slept Friday night as she rehashed the office episode over and over again. In the quiet atmosphere of the plane the next morning, she closed her eyes and didn't awaken until she heard the, 'prepare for landing' announcement at the Dayton airport.

Olivia couldn't wait to see Aunt Etta and stretched to peer over the crowd as she waited her turn to go through the security gate. She broke into a smile when she caught a glimpse of her aunt standing on the other side, running her fingers through soft gray hair.

"Aunt Etta."

"Livie, you look more like your mother every day, God rest her soul. How are you?"

"Better now," Olivia said as she threw her arms around the aunt that raised her.

"You'll be fine. Let's get your luggage and go home. We've so much to catch up on."

A myriad of memories piled one on top of another as they made the eighty-plus miles to Rexford. The Ohio countryside hadn't changed, but after New York City the sky seemed bigger and the fields a brighter green. Open space, miles and miles of open space seemed to free her heart.

Aunt Etta avoided the interstate and took the longer route following the less traveled country roads.

"I don't trust driving I-80. The trucks come up behind you and almost push you off the road," Etta explained.

Olivia enjoyed the scenery beside the two-lane highway that ran through farmlands and a string of small towns. Different names, but similar neighborhoods. Communities where people knew each other. Olivia sighed, wondering how she could have left this tranquility. College and dreams of becoming a success in advertising were her goals then.

"Livie?"

"I'm sorry."

"I asked if there was anything special you wanted to eat. We could stop at the grocery."

"Whatever you have on hand will be fine."

Etta pulled into the driveway and stopped the car. "We're home."

"You can't imagine how comforting that sounds."

Etta picked up a small bag while Olivia grabbed the rest of her luggage from the car and brought them to the front door of the three-story house where she was raised. It hadn't changed. The porch that followed the contours of the house held wicker furniture and a swing attached to a beam in the ceiling.

Urns of geraniums sat at the entrance. Fancy trim fringed the eaves and around the windows. A large turret rose from the porch to the original slate roof, complete with octagon shaped stained-glass windows. As a child, Olivia used to call it her castle. She closed her eyes and reminisced. Those were carefree times.

"Go on in, Livie," Etta's voice brought her back to the present.

Then she recalled Aunt Etta never locked the house. Simple things. Simple lifestyle. Her thoughts were interrupted by a voice coming from the shadow of a hanging fern.

"Etta, I thought we agreed you weren't to drive."

Olivia turned to find a scowling man clad in a white shirt, tucked into Levis that seemed to be pasted on his hips. He wore sneakers and had a Phillies baseball cap pulled down on his forehead. His arms were crossed and the tone of his voice commanded attention.

"I suppose you're the cause of this," he directed his remarks to Olivia. "Everyone thinks Etta runs a free taxi service."

"I beg your pardon," Olivia's face reddened, almost to the color of her hair.

"Don't mind him, Livie. Mitch thinks he can control my life."

"Someone should be in control," he shot back. "If I see that car out of your garage again, I'll have the sheriff remove your license." He stomped off the porch, climbed into a mud-spattered Jeep parked at the curb and sped off.

Olivia arched an eyebrow. "Who on earth…"

"Mitch James, the new doctor in town."

"Aunt Etta, are you ill?"

"A few dizzy spells, dear. Nothing to worry about."

"He seemed worried and very rude. I might add he didn't look like any doctor I've seen before."

"Don't mind him. He's new generation, and a very intense young man. He runs a clinic for the migrant workers in Worthville on Saturdays, and stops on his way back to check on me. He's upset because I won't go to the hospital for tests."

"If that's a sample of his bedside manner, I don't know how he keeps his practice."

"Come on, let's have lunch and get you settled in. We can discuss Mitch James later," Etta said.

Over homemade soup and iced tea, Olivia felt more relaxed than she had been in a long time. How she missed Aunt Etta's spotless and well organized kitchen. It brought back so many memories. Like the first time she baked cookies or her attempt to make pie dough. What a mess that turned out to be. She managed to spread flour all over the counter and the floor.

"You have a smile on your face, Livie. What are you thinking about?" Etta asked.

"Oh, I remembered the time I made an anniversary dinner for you and Uncle Fritz. The roast was tough and the mashed potatoes lumpy, but I felt so proud of my cooking. You both ate it without a complaint."

"Those were good times. Your uncle Fritz loved you as if you were his own."

Olivia cleaned up the lunch dishes and then brought her luggage into the spare bedroom. "My room hasn't changed. You've kept everything the same as when I left it."

"It will always be your room, Livie. This is home."

Olivia experienced a surge of guilt. It had been years since she'd been back to Rexford. In the past, she and Aunt Etta took yearly trips together, but they always met in New York and left from there. Lately, phone calls became their only means of communication.

Olivia put her suitcases on the bed and Etta helped her unpack. While Olivia placed folded clothes in the same dresser she used as a child, Etta hung blouses and slacks in the closet. When Etta turned to reach for one of Olivia's suits, she fought to keep her balance and grabbed the door for support.

"Livie."

Olivia looked up to see her aunt's face drained of color. "What is it?"

"I'm a little light-headed. I believe I need to lie down a bit."

Olivia's bed was piled with luggage and clothes. She helped her aunt down the hall to the master bedroom.

"Lie still and I'll bring a damp cloth."

Etta didn't protest.

Olivia returned and put a cool compress on her aunt's forehead. "What was that doctor's name?

"Mitch James. His number's next to the phone in the kitchen."

"I'll call him." Olivia rushed to the kitchen where she found Dr. Mitchell James, written on a card along with his office and home telephone number. She tried his home first since it was late Saturday afternoon.

"Doc James," he answered on the first ring.

Olivia didn't bother to introduce herself, only said that Etta Anderson had fainted. Before she could finish, he said, "I'm on my way."

TWO

Olivia chewed on her lower lip as she stood in the foyer and waited for the doctor. Concern about Aunt Etta's dizzy spell, allowed different scenarios to darken her mind. The front door flew open and snapped her back to reality. Dr. James didn't speak, but went directly to Etta's bedroom. Like an obedient child, Olivia trailed behind.

"Well, Miss Etta. What's going on? Seems I can't leave you alone for a minute." He checked her heart. "Are you from Home Assistance?" he addressed Olivia.

"Mitch, I want you to meet my niece, Olivia. She came from New York to visit me. Livie, this is my doctor."

"I believe Dr. James has already vocalized his opinion regarding my transportation here." A frosty tone coated Olivia's words.

Dr. Mitch James raked his fingers through his jet black hair. "Oh, you were here at noon. Sorry, I didn't recognize you. I called Home Assistance when I returned to the office and I thought..."

He turned his attention back to Etta. "How are you feeling? Any pain, blurred vision?"

"No, out of breath...tired."

"That's to be expected," he said as he gave her an injection. "This should relax you. If you have any of those symptoms, have your niece call me. I'll stop by in the morning."

"It's her heart," Dr. James told Olivia when she followed him to the foyer. He opened his medical bag and handed her two medicine bottles. "Give her these. The directions are on the labels. If she has pain or vomiting call me immediately."

Before she could ask any questions, he hurried out the door.

"Is he always so abrupt?" Olivia asked when she returned to sit with her aunt.

"Livie, he has the only family practice in town. Most certainly he's overworked, but he's quite personable when you get to know him and he's dedicated to his patients."

Olivia's mixed opinions about the doctor were interrupted by the door bell.

"How can I help you?" Olivia asked.

The woman standing in the doorway wore slacks pressed with a knife-edge crease, a crisp white smock, and had her salt and pepper hair pulled back into a loose bun.

"I'm Sarah." I'm here to tend to Miss Etta. Sorry I'm so late, but my car wouldn't start." Her smile warmed the room.

"I can do that," Olivia said.

"Please, it's my job. I can't afford to lose a client. The doctor called me at noon to come and check on Etta. I told him I'd make time to stop between appointments. Then he called again and said she had a spell with her heart. He wanted me to take her vitals and tomorrow, I'll help her bathe. I do the usual housekeeping chores. Doc said Miss Etta's to have complete bed rest for the next few days."

Olivia showed Sarah to Aunt Etta's bedroom and made the introductions. She left them to become acquainted and went back to finish unpacking. Alone in the quiet privacy of her room, she began to comprehend the full impact of her previous actions. Olivia pressed her hands to the side of her head. *"What have I done? My career is ruined."* When she left New York, she left her only source of income. She had never before done anything so impulsive but, under the circumstances, what choice did she have? The overwhelming reality came crashing down. Could she ever get another job after walking out of Mercer Associates without proper notice?

First things first, she decided. Taking care of the aunt she loved, became top priority. She'd stop feeling sorry for herself, attend to pressing responsibilities and then worry about the future.

"Miss Olivia, do you have a minute?"

"Be right there," Olivia said as she walked to foyer.

"I've changed the bedding and cleaned Miss Etta's room," Sarah said.

"Thank you. I appreciate your help."

Sarah picked up her purse from the table in the hallway and started for the door. "I'll be coming every day for the next week or two, but since you're here and I'm running late, I'll go on to my next client. I'll see you between noon and one tomorrow."

"Thank you. We appreciate your help. I'm sure I can handle it from here."

After Sarah left, Olivia sat with her aunt. "Is there anything you need?"

"Only for you to tell me what's really bothering you. It's more than me you're worried about."

"We'll talk about it when you're feeling better. Meanwhile, what would you like for dinner?"

"Something light. I'm not sure what's left in the refrigerator, but there's plenty in the freezer. Maybe Monday morning you could go to the grocery for some fresh fruit and vegetables."

Olivia managed to put together a meal and then settled Aunt Etta in for the evening.

Dr. James arrived at 7:30 Sunday morning. "Sorry," he said after he rapped on the door and then entered without waiting to be let in. "I'm not used to seeing anyone here but Etta. Did she rest well last night?"

"She seemed to. I set my alarm and checked on her every three hours." Olivia handed him a detailed list of the times she gave her aunt medication. "I wanted to ask you what she should be eating."

"Anything and everything. She's underweight and needs to build up her strength. And by the way, you'll need your rest. If you wear yourself out, someone will have come to take care of you both."

Olivia noticed a trace of a smile creep across his face before he went into Etta's room. A few minutes later, he rushed past her and out the door, not bothering to speak.

"That man's more than rude." Olivia's unpleasant thoughts of Dr. James ran longer than the grocery list she compiled. Olivia waited until Monday morning, when Sarah arrived to take care of Aunt Etta, to shop for groceries.

In Rexford, there were three traffic lights, a railroad crossing and more bars than churches. The newspaper Olivia's grandfather had established stood tall on the corner of Main and Belmont Streets. Groceries, drug stores and a smattering of small shops for clothing, computers, hardware and gifts dotted the main part of town.

A dry goods store looked new, or at least newly painted. The post office, gas stations, a bank and restaurants planted themselves on the side streets. The elementary school Olivia had attended now sat beside a new high school.

Olivia passed the city park. It seemed much larger than she remembered. A bronze sign embedded in a stone monument at the entrance explained the picnic shelter had been donated by

Harvey Webber, owner of Harvey's Department Store, located at the end of East Elm Street.

Situated on the outskirts of town were stores for farm machinery, feed and lumber and a new and used Ford car dealership.

Rexford also sported a paper factory, built adjacent to the railroad siding, which manufactured and printed business forms. Most of the residents either worked there, in the adjoining cities, or were retired farmers.

"I'd know you anywhere," the grocery clerk said when Olivia brought her basket to check out. "You look like your mother when she was young."

"I've been told that," Olivia said.

"How's Miss Etta? I heard the doctor was there yesterday."

"She's doing much better, thank you."

"Tell her Jenny at the Food Mart says hello."

"Small towns," Olivia mused as she left the grocery. "I've been here one day and already people remember who I am, where I'm staying and that Aunt Etta isn't feeling well."

Olivia stopped at the bank to arrange the transfer of her accounts from New York. She rummaged through her purse to find the necessary information as she waited her turn in line.

"Next, please."

"Robyn, Robyn Gleason? Is that you? I had no idea you still lived in Rexford."

"I'm still here." Robyn's smile took over her face. "It's good to see you, Olivia. Someone mentioned this morning that you were in town. Gosh, it's been over seven years. Are you here to visit your aunt?"

"I didn't realize it had been so long. It's good to see you." Robyn hadn't changed since high school, still small, bubbly and quick to laugh. Best friends growing up, they had lost touch with each other over the years. The bank wasn't busy and it gave them a few minutes to talk.

"I'm Robyn Martin now. I married Greg Martin from Lima." Robyn kept a picture of Greg in her teller station and turned it around to show Olivia. "I don't believe you know him. He's with the Marines stationed overseas."

"Good-looking guy. Do you have children?"

"We decided to wait until his military stint is over. Meanwhile, I manage to stay busy. It makes the time go faster."

Another customer took his place behind Olivia. "I don't want to hold up your line. Let's get together for dinner some evening. We have so much to catch up on," Olivia said.

"I'd like that. I finish working at five."

"Why don't we plan for tomorrow night? I'll check with Aunt Etta to see if she feels well enough to stay by herself a few hours. What's your phone number?"

"I'm living with mom while Greg's away. It's the same number we always had."

"Good, I'll call you there." Olivia smiled at the gentleman behind her and hurried out of the bank.

The next evening, Robyn brought her mother along to the Anderson house. Mary Margaret Gleason visited with Etta while Robyn and Olivia went to the Steak Grill for dinner.

Robyn knew the hostess and asked for a quiet table in the corner of the restaurant. After they ordered, they fell into a conversation as if time had stood still. No awkward moments came between the two of them as they talked over their high school days and the town's latest gossip.

"Tell me about the doctor. I find him extremely rude," Olivia said.

"Mitchell James? He's handsome, isn't he? When old Doc Bailey retired, Dr. James took over the office. I don't know too much of the story, but when he first came to Rexford he brought a new bride with him. Evidently, his wife couldn't stand our small town. After more than a few trips back to Philadelphia to visit her family, she stayed there. I don't know if they're divorced or if the marriage was annulled. There are conflicting versions of his personal life. At any rate, Dr. James no longer wears a wedding ring and never mentions her name."

"I see."

"He's an excellent, caring doctor," Robyn continued, "but he won't allow himself to get close to anyone. He's become very cynical."

"With his personality, I can't imagine who would want him," Olivia said.

"Believe me, there are plenty of girls in this town who would like to get their claws into him, especially Victoria Gillette. You might remember her—three years behind us in school."

"Tall, blonde, blue eyes, and had that annoying habit of conversing in baby-talk?"

A mischievous grin appeared on Robyn's face. "Now she's twenty-three and has graduated to teen-age slang. Her father is a retired judge. He headed a committee to bring Dr. James to Rexford. I heard they made some arrangement to pay part of his student loan if he agreed to stay. There are as many stories about it as people who tell them."

"I found him brash and overbearing, but Aunt Etta seems to like him and I could tell he's genuinely fond of her."

"All of his patients love him now, but it was a tough sell at first. His casual dress put some off. After his wife left, he seemed to live for his practice. He makes house calls and has spent more than one night at the hospital when someone's critical. He knows his stuff."

"I guess that's more important than his attire."

"People appreciate dedication and he's dedicated."

Olivia asked Robyn about old schoolmates, town politics, her job at the bank and everything else that came to mind before she noticed the time. "I had better get home to check Aunt Etta."

"It's been great to get together again," Robyn said as they went to the cashier to pay their bill.

"I can't thank you enough for bringing your mom to stay with Aunt Etta. I hate to leave her alone, although she tells me she's feeling fine. She's very independent."

"Mom enjoys visiting with Etta. It's a break for her to talk with someone other than me."

"Let's stay in touch," Olivia said. "I enjoyed catching up and I need a friend."

"How long do you plan to stay?"

"I'm not sure, at least until Aunt Etta recovers."

"While you're here, we could get together once a week. You're not the only one who needs someone to talk to."

They made plans to meet at the restaurant every Wednesday at six.

Etta Anderson recuperated from her heart spell over the next few weeks. Olivia insisted Etta eat well and spend time in the fresh air every day.

They were sitting on the porch swing, watching the cars pass down Main Street, when Etta looked her niece in the eye. "Don't you think it's about time you told me what's going on in your life? A few months ago, you told me you were engaged to a man in New York, but you haven't once mentioned him. I expected to plan that wedding we always talked about, but instead, you're free to nurse me back to health. I don't recall phone calls from anyone but your roommate in New York and your friend Robyn. You've changed your mailing address from New York to here, and last week all of your belongings came by UPS. Just how temporary is this job loss?"

"Aunt Etta, I've messed up my life big time." Olivia told her the full story about her job, including the scene in the copy room.

"I can't believe you locked them in a dark room." Etta snickered.

"I was furious and not thinking straight. I allowed my temper to cloud my judgment. On the plane trip here, it occurred to me that Brian probably used his cell phone to call someone to come to the office and unlock the door. I can't imagine what excuse he came up with, but the way the office grapevine operates, he'll have a lot of explaining to do to his father." Then she added, "I'm sure the loafer I threw in the dumpster had to be worth a fortune. Brian wears nothing but the best. It's a shame I didn't think to grab his pants instead of a shoe."

"Livie, it sounds like this Brian person is the one who messed up. If he carried on with other women while engaged to you, he probably would have done the same after you married him. You would have had a miserable life."

"I realize that now, but leaving the way I did destroyed my career. I left my job without giving notice, other than a quick e-mail. My reputation in the advertising field is ruined. I don't know what I'll do when I leave here."

"Livie, you don't have to leave. I'm sure we can find a spot for you at the Press. Howard Benson has been at the helm since your Uncle Fritz died and has talked about retirement for the past five years. His wife wants to move to Florida while they can still enjoy the outdoors. I don't have anyone with any experience to take his place. I feel certain you'll fit in."

"The family newspaper? I don't have that kind of experience. I'm not sure I'm capable."

"Nonsense, you worked for a major firm in New York City. You know the ins and outs of selling advertising space, and you majored in English at college. Besides, you could breathe new life into our small town paper. I know Howard will be happy to show you the ropes."

"Would that be fair to the other employees?"

"If one of them were qualified to take it over or even wanted to train for the job, he would have left last year. Bring me the phone and I'll arrange a meeting. If it's not a satisfactory arrangement for either of you, we've lost nothing, but maybe you'll both be pleased. I know I'll enjoy having you back home."

Olivia brought the phone to Aunt Etta and while she called Howard Benson, Olivia leaned on the porch banister and gazed out over the tree lined street. She had never considered staying in Rexford.

After a short conversation, Howard agreed to come to the Anderson house in the morning for the initial interview.

"It's settled. You'll like Howard. He's from the old school of newspaper editors," Etta said.

Olivia wondered if that was good or bad.

Dr. James stopped by the Anderson house. This time, he knocked before entering.

"I didn't expect you today Mitch," Etta said.

"I'm on my way to Lima General to see a patient. Thought I'd stop a minute and check on you. She giving you any trouble?" he directed his comment to Olivia.

Those were the first civil words he uttered to Olivia during the entire time she'd been in Rexford. She bristled at his smug tone. "Aunt Etta is an ideal patient. Doesn't she look well?"

Mitch seemed unaware of Olivia's cool sarcastic demeanor as he took Etta's pulse and listened to her heart. "Sounds good. I want you to start walking a little. Go up and down the street. Nothing too strenuous, but try to do it every day. I'll stop by next week." He gave Olivia a half smile and went back to his Jeep.

"Humph. I don't think Mitch dropped in to see me this time. I do believe he came looking for you."

"I hope not. I've had my fill of men, especially those as rude as your Dr. James. Let's try that walk."

After Etta retired for the evening, Olivia went up to the attic and dragged out a box containing past issues of the Rexford Free Press. For a town of thirty-five hundred, they produced a decent weekly paper with well written, although not too creative, advertising copy. She enjoyed the everyday news events of the community most of all. The Press contained a personal touch that only a small town paper could achieve.

Could she be content living here again and working at the Press? She felt sure Howard Benson agreed to interview her as a favor to Aunt Etta. Well, she had nothing to lose. She'd give it her best shot. She went back to her room to update her list of qualifications.

THREE

When Howard Benson arrived at the Anderson house, Olivia led him to the den. She decided it would be better to hold their interview in private, without her aunt's input. She handed Howard a prepared résumé and waited while he looked over her qualifications.

Howard, a short, balding, overweight man, and well past the age for retirement, pulled wire-rimmed glasses from his shirt pocket. He took his time looking over Olivia's list of accomplishments.

"I'm impressed with your job history, but I can't imagine why you would leave a high-paying position in New York City. What prompted you to come to Rexford?"

Olivia made eye contact with him and gave a thumb-nail recap of her situation with Brian, omitting the explicit details. "It would be impossible for me to stay on with the Mercer Company after he broke our engagement and dated another employee. I didn't believe I could do my best work if I had to face them everyday. Taking care of Aunt Etta gave me the opportunity to rethink residing in the city. I have experience and I believe I can do a good job for you."

"Miss McDougle, I'm sure you can do a good job in place of me. The operation is pretty straight forward, now that we use computers. My assistant runs things for the most part, but she doesn't want the responsibility or the long hours. Come down to the Press tomorrow and let me show you around. You realize your salary will be nearly half of what you're used to earning. Are you prepared for that?"

"If you knew the cost of living in New York, you wouldn't ask that question. Aunt Etta insists I live here. I'll do quite well, that is, if it won't cause a problem with the other employees."

"Don't give that a second thought. You'll find them very receptive." Howard went over the day by day operation of the Press, covering the job description Olivia would have along with the responsibilities of his staff.

"Does that mean I have the position?"

"Miss McDougle, you are the new editor of the Rexford Free Press. It's a pleasure to have you on board." Howard smiled and shook Olivia's hand. "I want to have a few words with Etta before I return to the office."

"Livie, I'm so pleased," Etta said after Howard left. She wrapped her arms around her niece. "You can't imagine how much I wanted you to stay here. I know I'm being selfish, but I feel more comfortable with you in the house."

"I hope I can live up to everyone's expectations. Also, it's great to be home again."

Etta's health had improved enough to stay alone. Sarah came once a week instead of daily and Etta's friends visited often. Olivia felt secure in her decision to return to work. The next morning she chose a plain green suit and a white shell, opting for quiet sophistication. She caught her long auburn hair in a clip at the nape of her neck and after a quick appraisal in the mirror, drove Etta's car to the Press office for the tour and orientation.

The outside of the building hadn't changed for as long as Olivia could remember. A bronze plaque above the door read: "Freedom of the Press. All Opinions Welcome." For the first time, it took on a new meaning for Olivia. She would be in charge of some of those opinions. She smoothed her skirt before entering the front door.

Howard Benson greeted Olivia and ushered her into his private office. He pulled in a bent metal chair from the hallway for her to sit on.

Howard's office resembled something out of the fifties. An old fashioned wood chair, with a large spring, was situated behind a battered oak desk. The chair gave a mournful squeak when Howard sat down. Aside from scratched and dented metal file cabinets that lined part of one wall, no other furniture filled the room. Boxes jammed with miscellaneous papers and magazines stacked haphazardly in the corner and the back wall added to the chaotic and disorganized appearance.

The only adornment in the office was an oil painting of snow covered mountains, their image reflecting in a clear stream. The peaceful scene looked out of place as it hung behind the desk on a plain brick wall.

The room reeked of cigar smoke and printers ink although Howard no longer smoked and computers had been used at the Press for years. The dirt between the floor planks probably dated back to the time the office first opened.

Howard could put his finger on folders and records, although most weren't labeled. He gave a running commentary on his filing system. Olivia clenched her teeth as she surveyed the clutter. She couldn't imagine how he found anything in the jumble.

Howard assembled the employees, and took his time to introduce each one to Olivia. They all performed multiple duties and seemed to work well together. It became apparent to Olivia that everyone had been employed at the Press for a long time.

Evan Henner, the photographer, ran a private studio on the side to supplement his income. He took crime scene photos for the Rexford Police Department and also contracted to do the annual school pictures.

Julius Mendon wrote articles on special interests, crime and local politics. He attended court hearings whenever a Rexford resident was scheduled to appear. Both Julius and Evan worked part-time.

Millie Jeffers copy-edited staff pieces and articles submitted by locals. She served as Howard's assistant as well as receptionist/file clerk. In spite of Howard's casual approach to business, Millie ran an efficient office.

Frank Wills designed the layout of the paper and put it to print. He also created invitations, announcements and posters among other printed paper products. He and Millie were full time employees. Olivia considered their experience and knowledge a definite plus. She made a mental note not to make any changes until she felt completely accepted and comfortable.

Howard assured her he would stay on as long as necessary. "I'll be around town for awhile. If you have a problem, give me a call. You can depend on the staff. You'll find them more than helpful."

With little fanfare, Olivia McDougle took over as Editor of the Rexford Free Press. Everyone seemed pleased. Olivia remained the only one who harbored any doubts of her ability to run the operation.

FOUR

Olivia couldn't wait to tell Robyn the news when they met on Wednesday at the Steak Grill. She held off until they started dinner.

"What's going on with you? You look like a diamond thief in a jewelry store," Robyn said.

"I don't know about that, but I have news. I'm staying in Rexford."

Lines crossed Robyn's forehead. "Isn't Etta feeling better?"

"She is so much better I'm going to work here. Robyn, I have a job."

"Give, Olivia. What are you talking about?"

Olivia went into great detail about Aunt Etta's suggestion that she work at the Press, the interview with Howard Benson, and her new position as editor.

"Do you think I can handle it?"

"I know you can. Olivia, I'm so excited for you. You'll be a great asset. It's time the community had a fresh slant on the news. The Press tends to put a conciliatory spin on every story. They never take a stand."

"I'm not sure I'll do anything controversial, but with my advertising background I can certainly add zing to their ads. When I read back copies of the Press, I noticed their lack of imagination in the advertising copy. The right choice of words can make a world of difference."

"Think of the other possibilities. You could promote new youth programs. The kids in this small town have nothing to look forward to."

"I remember that from years back. We had to make our own fun," Olivia said.

Robyn wrinkled her nose and giggled as she recalled the past. "On a hot summer day, we would sit on your front porch, eat popcorn and drink ginger ale, while we made up stories about every carload of people that drove down the street."

"And then we'd jog to the other side of town to get ice cream."

"Mom always worked, but your Aunt Etta kept us occupied. Lots of kids here don't have an Aunt Etta. They're latch-key."

"I know. It's a sign of the times."

"A sad sign."

"Robyn, I didn't come here to take care of Aunt Etta. A turn of fate brought me back to Rexford."

"What do you mean?"

"Aunt Etta didn't become ill until after I arrived. She called New York on Friday night to check on me. That phone call couldn't have come at a more perfect time." Olivia told Robyn all the sordid details about surprising Brian and his plaything.

"How did you happen to find them in the copy room?" Robyn asked.

"Brian came into my office about 5:30 on Friday afternoon. That day will be imbedded in my memory forever." She told Robyn the entire sordid story.

"Hi darling." Brian kissed Olivia on the cheek. "I thought you'd be gone by now."

"Just finishing up. I'll be on my way home in a few minutes."

"There's a party at the country club Saturday evening and then we'll stay the night with my parents. I'll drive over to pick you up between nine and ten tomorrow morning. Bring something special to wear. Everyone who's anyone will be there."

"Formal or cocktail?"

"Cocktail. Wear that sexy black dress, the one with the low cut neckline."

"Not too racy for the country club set?"

"It's perfect. It shows off your auburn hair, not to mention your figure. Go on home. I'll turn out the lights and lock up when I leave."

"Brian returned to his office. I cleaned off my desk and reached for my coat when one of the assistant managers asked if I'd look over the advertising copy he had prepared. We went to the art room to discuss the ad and agreed there should be a cover letter to send to our clients. After we compiled the text, he left for the day while I went to make copies for the Monday morning staff meeting."

"And that's when you caught them. Olivia, you must have been devastated."

"That, and all of the other emotions you can imagine. I still get flashbacks of them lying stark-naked across the desk."

"I wondered if you had another reason to stay here so long, but I didn't want to pry. Did you really love this Brian character?"

"I thought I did. Once I returned to Rexford, I did some serious soul-searching and realized the idea of marriage and a sense of belonging is what I longed for."

"Believe me, I can relate to that."

"New York is a romantic city," Olivia continued. "And Brian, a handsome, charming man, escorted me to Broadway shows, the best restaurants and trips on his family's yacht. I got caught up in the excitement, the parties, and the celebrities Brian introduced me to. My engagement with him became a whirlwind of adventure, not to mention, I had the job of a lifetime.

"Brian's father groomed him to take over Mercer Advertising, Inc. and encouraged our relationship. He wanted to make sure Brian was emotionally settled before he handed the reins of the company to his only son.

"After I recovered from the shock of finding Brian with another woman, especially the tramp of the office, I realized he would never be dependable. You know, once a playboy always a playboy.

"He liked to show me off to his friends. What do they call it, eye candy? For awhile, I thought he might be gay. I mean, he didn't pressure me for sex. It stopped at kisses and hugs. Later after we became engaged, I took that to mean he respected me." Olivia made a face. "I couldn't have been more wrong. I always considered myself urbane and sophisticated. The harsh reality, I was terribly naïve."

"From what you told me, that man gave big-time rats a bad name. He wanted you for a showpiece and other women for his sexual pleasures. Be glad it happened, Olivia. Be glad you discovered his two-timing ways before you married him."

"That's what Aunt Etta said. In spite of everything, the situation bruised my ego."

"You'll get over that a lot quicker than you would a bad marriage."

"I know you're right. I couldn't imagine what I would do with my life after I left New York. When Aunt Etta suggested the family newspaper, I jumped at the opportunity. I hope I can do a good job and live up to her expectations. At any rate,

I'm here to stay." Olivia settled back in her chair. "Would you believe it? I'm the new editor of the Press."

"I have a selfish reason to be happy you're staying. I really need a friend. At my age, living with mom can be a trial...you know, two adult females living in the same house. And a very small house, at that. I have trouble talking to her. If I have a problem, she feels it's her duty to solve it, instead of simply listening."

"Your mom had a difficult life."

"She did. She always worked and saw to it that I had everything I needed, but she never allowed me to grow up. She still believes she should make all of my decisions."

"That's tough, but you know she means well."

Robyn sighed. "That's true, but you can't imagine how much I need to be with someone my age. There are lots of things you can't discuss with your mom. I treasure our Wednesday nights."

"Don't you have other friends here?"

"Not since I eloped with Greg. I joined him in North Carolina after he finished boot camp. When he received orders to go to Korea, I came back here. We've spent less than six months of our married life together. All of my former friends are either married, have left town, or both."

"I had the same situation in New York, with friends I mean. I worked long hours. Once in a while I stayed in the city if Brian had reservations for someplace special, but as a rule, by the time I took the subway to my apartment, I was too tired to go anywhere. My week-ends were spent with Brian and on rare occasions, his family."

"This will be a great change. Gosh, you can leave work here and be home in five minutes. That gives you plenty of time to plan for the evening."

"And I can keep an eye on Aunt Etta. Robyn, this is the best of both worlds. I hope it works out."

"Me too, Olivia."

"You said you lived with your husband a very short time. How did you meet him?"

"I mentioned that I went to a business school in Lima. After I graduated, I found employment at a mortgage company. Greg worked as an assistant manager of a fitness center on the same block. He brought free passes to our employees and a few weeks later he asked me out. We had dated for six or seven months when he told me his job was going nowhere and he considered enlisting in the Marines. He said they had an excellent continuing education program and he couldn't afford college on his present salary. By the end of that week he signed up, and we flew to Las Vegas to be married."

"Gosh, Robyn, how did your mother react to the news?"

"You can't imagine the argument we had when Greg and I told her. Livid doesn't begin to describe her reaction."

"That explains a lot. No wonder you need a friend."

"She's come to terms with the situation, but it was so difficult to move back home."

"I understand. Will you look at the time? They'll close the restaurant around us if we don't leave."

Robyn hugged her friend as they paid their tabs. "I'm so glad you're back. See you next Wednesday."

FIVE

Dr. Mitch James spent the night in the ICU at Lima General Hospital stabilizing one of his critically ill patients. By the time he left, his office hours back in Rexford were about to begin. In spite of being overworked, and more often than not, exhausted, he loved his practice.

Mitch felt fortunate to inherit Maxine Plumber when he took over the office from retiring Dr. Bailey. Maxine, his nurse/assistant, processed and submitted insurance forms, handled appointments, collected fees and advised him how to cope with the most difficult patients. He found her to be indispensable.

Mitch and Dr. Bailey had shared the patient load for the first six months after his arrival in town. It took that long before he felt accepted in Rexford and confident to hang his shingle over the office door.

Mitch liked the small town, the people and his patients. His practice exposed him to every kind of illness and situation, from farm accidents to teen-age pregnancy. He found himself thrust into the role of marriage counselor, and on many occasions had to console family members as they dealt with a life threatening diagnosis for themselves or a loved one.

He had been kissed, screamed at and punched by patients. He held hands with survivors when their spouses passed on and had more than one cigar thrust into his mouth after the birth of a baby. The hours were terrible, and some patients were slow to pay, but he wouldn't trade it for any other career.

Mitch had never heard of Rexford, Ohio when a committee approached him at the hospital in Philadelphia, where he completed his last year's residency. Their offer answered his lifelong dream. The overwhelming student medical loans would be paid, if he agreed to stay in Rexford for five years. His long term goal had always been to set up practice in a small town, much to the dismay of Lily, his ex-wife.

Lily and Mitch met at the Philadelphia hospital where he worked long hours and struggled to make ends meet. He was aware that Lily's family doted on their attractive daughter and lavished her with anything she wanted, but she portrayed herself as the girl next door. She told Mitch material things didn't mean anything to her but the attention she paid to fashion was important for her career.

Lily worked for a company that arranged fund-raising events for the hospital auxiliary, among other charities. Some of the perks of her job were free concert tickets, plays and restaurant comps. Mitch and Lily spent as much time together as Mitch could manage. Before he proposed, he made sure she understood their income would be limited until he became settled in his own practice. Lily assured him that she would be content with the simple things in life and support him completely. They married after six months of dating.

Mitch knew immediately he had made a mistake. Lily's aspiration to become a doctor's wife quickly faded when he accepted Rexford's offer. He found his income would be further limited because of the necessity to purchase new equipment to update Dr. Bailey's office and it might take a while before patients felt confident to make appointments with the new doctor in town.

To add to her displeasure, the small town bored Lily. She found the lack of culture appalling and had little desire to volunteer or become part of the community. She had had no understanding of Mitch's commitment to his practice and his long hours were a constant annoyance. She referred to his patients as country hicks. Far removed from the lifestyle she had envisioned, Lily didn't bother to hide her discontent.

When she attempted to manipulate him into moving back to Philadelphia, by arranging a position with a prestigious medical firm without his knowledge, Mitch could no longer ignore how ambitious and very shallow she had become. Lily told him, in no uncertain terms, if he didn't take the job in Philadelphia, she'd go back alone. Mitch regarded her threat as a gift. She returned home to her parents and attempted to get an annulment. When that failed, she petitioned for a divorce. He didn't contest the action.

Looking back, Mitch realized he hadn't put a lot of thought in his past life decisions. He wanted a wife, family and the house with a picket fence and all the comforts he didn't have growing up. Instead of searching for a compatible match, he took the easy way out by convincing himself that a wife would provide the contented lifestyle he craved. He became so busy with his practice, he allowed himself to be controlled to a degree. In the process, he disregarded the most important ingredients in a successful marriage, love, honesty, respect and mutual goals.

After his wife left, Mitch gave up their rented house and moved into the living quarters behind his office. If his practice grew, those rooms could be used for expansion, but for the present, they provided the ideal bachelor pad.

Mitch glanced at his watch. He could spare a few minutes to drop in on his favorite patient, Etta Anderson. Maybe her niece would be there. She intrigued him. Her auburn hair enhanced the unsettling color of her green eyes. Her cream-colored skin glowed, allowing a few freckles to dot an otherwise flawless complexion. She didn't fall all over him like most of the local girls. In fact, he seemed to annoy her. That made him smile. She aroused inner feelings in him that he thought were permanently suppressed.

He pulled into Etta's driveway and walked to the front porch. "Etta, it's Mitch," he said as he tapped on the door before walking in.

"You look like the devil," she said as a greeting. "Have you been up all night?"

"Yeah, Bill Sarpy had a spell. I sat at the hospital with him until I was sure he'd pull through. Let's talk about you. How are you feeling?"

"I'm doing fine, Mitch. Walking everyday like you told me and Livie makes sure I eat right."

Mitch looked around the house.

Etta laughed, "She's not here. She's working at the Press."

His face reddened. "I wasn't..."

"Sure you were. You can't fool an old lady."

He grinned at Etta. "I guess I was looking for her. You say she's working here? Does that mean she's going to stay awhile?"

"Permanently, if I have my say. I enjoy her company and she breathes life into this old house."

"That's good to hear. You need someone to look after you. You don't follow orders too well."

Etta put her hands on her hips and glared at him.

"Now don't get your dander up. I'll check on you later," he said as reached for the door knob. "I have to get to the office."

When he returned to his Jeep, a grin stretched over his handsome face. So Olivia McDougle is staying in town. He drove down the street, whistling an off-key tune.

SIX

April's weather turned pleasantly warm and although Olivia had the use of Aunt Etta's car, she opted to walk to the Press office. As the morning sun seeped through the trees, touching branches formed graceful arches over the sidewalks, creating a lacey tunnel. The six block trek provided exercise in the morning and gave Olivia a chance to unwind on the way home at night.

The newspaper operation ran without complications. Each staff member had their own section of expertise and knew exactly how to handle their assignments. They automatically preformed their responsibilities and, when together, entertained each other with inside office jibes and jokes. The climate at the Press reminded Olivia of a close family. She hoped she'd fit into the mix.

Cleaning Howard's dark, stuffy office became her immediate challenge. Olivia wasn't sure how to get rid of the intense musty smell, or where to start to clean out the files and cartons.

"Millie, does this open?" She pointed to the only window in the editor's office.

"Howard never wanted it open."

Olivia picked up an undertone in Millie's voice. "I believe we need to let in some fresh air. Do you know if it's been sealed?"

"I don't know. I've never seen it open in all the years I've worked here."

Olivia gave it a push. "It's no use. It won't budge. It must be painted shut. Do we have any tools in the building?"

Millie held her head a little too high as she walked to the back room and returned with a toolbox. "There might be something in here you can use." She set the box on the desk.

Olivia selected a screw driver and slowly edged it along the lower edge of the window, tapping it lightly with a hammer. "It's moving. Give me a hand."

Millie hesitated before she walked to the window to assist Olivia. Pressure from the two of them persuaded the window to inch open.

"The fresh air smells good. Now, let's tackle the rest of the office," Olivia said.

"What do you have in mind?" Millie stood back with her hands on her hips.

"I'll need trash bags. I'm going to clear out these cardboard boxes and go through the files to discard anything we don't need."

"Howard keeps all his important papers there. I don't think you should..."

"Millie, I hope I can do as good a job as Howard has done at the Press, but I can't work like this. I need order. Please help me sort through this. I value your opinion on what's necessary to keep."

Millie's attempt to preserve a bland look on her face, failed. "I'll find the trash bags."

Olivia frowned as she thought about her assistant. Tall, thin and clearly set in her ways, Millie looked to be in her middle to late fifties. Olivia found her very professional in her work performance, but realized Millie could become a challenge to work with. Olivia would have to be careful not to hurt the lady's feelings.

Millie returned to the office and shook a trash bag from the box. "Here," She said and handed it to Olivia.

Millie took her time to read every paper before deciding to put it in the 'file' or 'discard' pile. Olivia set a box aside with folders to label anything to be kept. They filled two trash bags before the space began to show any sign of organization. By the end of the day, they had everything labeled, filed and all the trash removed.

During the next week Olivia hired a crew to paint all but the brick wall. She had the floor carpeted and brought furniture from Aunt Etta's attic to improve the area. She replaced the window with one that opened and closed easily, and added blinds and tailored drapes. She had thought to replace the painting until she noticed her Grandfather Anderson's name signed in the corner. When she finished, the room had an updated, modern decor.

"What do you think?" Olivia asked as she showed Millie the finished project.

"It's very nice. I guess you big city folks are used to plush surroundings."

"I worked in a small cubicle but the Mercer offices were decorated with taste. Because of the clientele, the reception area did have the best of furniture and appointments. The firm enjoyed a multi-million dollar business, and it wouldn't serve well if our clients weren't comfortable."

"This must be small-time to you, working for the family newspaper and all."

Olivia bit the inside of her lip to keep from saying something she might regret. Instead, she calmly told Millie about the rest of her plans. "I'm going to have the wall taken out that separates your office from the entrance. Then we will have an open reception area. I'll do it over the week-end and try to have it painted on Monday. Why don't you take Monday and Tuesday off? It will be impossible for you to get any work done in the middle of the mess."

Millie's rigid posture became apparent. She put her hands on her hips and glared at Olivia. "Do you realize what you're suggesting? I have to be here. Who will man the phones?"

Olivia couldn't ignore the look of defiance that took over her assistant's face. She chose her words with care. "Millie, I hope I haven't started off on the wrong foot. My objective is to make the office more receptive to people who visit the Press. Please enjoy a few days off with pay. I promise to take care of the phones and call you if I run into any problems."

Before she left work for the day, Millie placed her letter of resignation on Olivia's desk.

Olivia went forward with her renovation plans. She had Millie's desk refinished, purchased a leather office chair and replaced the ancient stacked metal file drawers with new wide oak cabinets. Their low tops provided an extra work area. Two upholstered chairs, a table and a lamp completed the outer office. The cramped cubicle behind bars, where Millie previously sat caged like an old fashioned bank teller, had been transformed into a large attractive upscale reception area.

Wednesday morning, Olivia drove to Millie's house and rapped on the door.

"What can I do for you, *Miss* McDougle?"

She overlooked the obvious sarcasm. "Please call me Olivia. Before I accept your resignation, may I ask for your indulgence? Allow me to drive you to the Press. I promise not to keep you too long."

Millie stared at Olivia for a few seconds before she made the concession. "I'll get my sweater."

Olivia didn't speak as the two of them rode to Rexford's business district. She parked the car in front of the office, and before she entered the building, opened the door with an exaggerated gesture allowing Millie to enter first.

"Oh my," Millie said when she took in Olivia's remodeling efforts. She ran her finger over the refinished desk and slid open the file cabinets. She walked behind the desk and sat in the new chair, rolling it back and forth on the plastic floor mat.

"I'm sorry if you thought I overstepped the bounds. I didn't want to change how we do business. I wanted to create a more pleasant work environment. I hoped you would be more comfortable in an open space. I felt as if you were held captive behind those bars. Now our office creates a more appealing atmosphere. Would you reconsider your resignation? I don't believe I can run the Press without you."

Millie's face reddened. "I don't know what to say. If you really need me..."

"I absolutely need you. I depend on your knowledge of the newspaper and of the town."

"Well, if you put it that way, I guess I could stay on. I know you'll need a liaison between the residents and our office. I've lived here much longer than you, and a lot happened in Rexford during the time you were in New York." She stressed the words, New York as if she was referring to a foreign country.

"I appreciate your experience, Millie. I think we'll work well together." Olivia provided her assistant the opportunity to save face.

Howard made one last visit to the Press. "Good God, what happened here? I heard through the rumor-mill you had some construction going on, but I never imagined this." He spread his arms as he tried to comprehend the major renovation. "It looks, ah, modern or something." He took his time scanning the new reception area. He rubbed his hand over Millie's leather chair. "Place looks bigger. You've done a good job, Olivia."

"Thank you."

"I need to talk to you in private." He followed Olivia into the refurbished office.

Her face tightened. "Have I done something wrong?"

"Nah, nothing like that. Close the door, there's something I need to give you."

He waited until they were alone before he walked behind the desk and removed the painting from the wall. "Thought I had better get this before you had the room papered in some fancy flower print and then I wouldn't be able to find it." Howard grimaced as he looked around the neat, but feminine décor that once housed his disorganized office. His eyes darted toward the door again before he removed two loose bricks from the wall and set them on the carpet. His arm disappeared up to the elbow before he extracted a large worn book from the cavity. "Your Uncle Fritz gave this to me when I took over the operation. Your grandfather started the record. Fritz and I have added to it over the years, now it's yours. I hope you never have to use it."

"What on earth?"

"It's a log kept on all the public officials and prominent citizens of Rexford. Most of what's written here would have little impact on our town, but if push comes to shove and something happens to pin you in a corner it might come in handy."

"I don't understand."

"You will once you've read it. Keep it someplace safe. I'm the only one who knows about this book. Now it's your responsibility. Don't let anyone get their hands on this information." He left her holding the large, dusty black journal.

She quickly stuffed the log back into the hiding space, replaced the bricks and re-hung the scenic oil painting.

"What was that all about?" Millie asked.

Olivia's face reddened slightly. "Howard wanted to see what I've done with the place. He liked your reception area but he seemed uncomfortable with his old office. He said I made it too feminine for his tastes. He wondered what I had done with all of his boxes."

"I bet he did. Organization wasn't one of his strong points but he could put his finger on anything in that room at a moment's notice. And his memory of dates and events never ceased to amaze me."

"I wish I had that trait. I have to rely on notes and calendars."

Millie softened. "I hear you."

"Was Howard easy to work for?"

Millie made a face. "Easy, yes, but I carried more than my part of the load." She paused to stress her point. "You must remember, Frank and I are the only ones who work full time. My plate is full."

"I understand. I hope you'll let me share part of your workload."

"I'll say this for Howard," Millie continued. "When I needed time to take care of my husband after his surgery, Howard did it all. He insisted I stay home as long as necessary."

"Who made the sales calls for the Press?"

"Gosh, Miss McDougle, ah, Olivia, we've never made sales calls. We're a small town. If anyone wants to advertise, they come to us."

"That's interesting. I believe I'd like to take a different approach. I intend to meet as many business owners as possible, whether they advertise in the Rexford Press, or if I solicit them to support a community project. Once I make contact, I'll have an 'in' to sell advertising space in our newspaper."

"I have some work to finish," Millie said. Before she returned to her desk, she sucked in her lower lip to keep from commenting further. She had a new resolve to make this arrangement work. Miss McDougle had a lot to learn about the politics of the community. She would need all the help she could get. Millie clicked her tongue. She had to be there to smooth things out and pick up the pieces when her over-zealous editor got in too deep.

SEVEN

Millie's lack of enthusiasm at the suggestion to rework the advertising methods at the Press, didn't escape Olivia. She realized old habits were hard to change, but it was time to take a more aggressive stand and make the Rexford Press a more profitable undertaking.

Olivia had always been an overachiever. She took a hard look at the books over the next few days and decided now was the opportune time for the Press to expand. Once she formed a plan, she pulled a chair along side of Millie's desk.

"I have an idea to bounce off you. What's your opinion about going outside Rexford for advertising?"

"We currently carry a few ads from Lima."

"I'm considering running a promotion to encourage other small towns around the area to participate and report news to the Rexford Press. I thought we could begin by giving extra coverage of local events like the annual Corn Roasting Festival in Millsburg. When I looked through our past issues, I noticed small articles appear in the Press every August. What if we send Evan there this year to take pictures and give them extra coverage? Maybe we could raffle gift certificates from some of our local shops."

"And our gain would be?"

"Two-fold. First we could lure business's to advertise in the Press, and second, sell subscriptions. If Millsburg is receptive to my promotion, we could devote a few weekly columns to their town. If it proves successful, we could expand it to a full page. I'm sure there's a budding writer in Millsburg who would submit something on a regular basis. It shouldn't be hard to fill with church events and school news, local marriages, births, death notices. The ads we sell would be placed on that page."

"This sounds like a huge undertaking. Who will approach them and how?"

"Advertising is my field of expertise. If you agree my plan has merit, I'll arrange to talk to the mayor and the city council. I'll ask Frank to design a mock-up page for them to review and explain the importance to keep the communication open in towns similar to ours. If they're receptive, I'll prevail upon our staff and their families to attend the festival. I'm sure I can convince some of Aunt Etta's friends, as well as Robyn Martin and her mother to make the short drive to Millsburg."

"Sounds like you've put a lot of thought into this."

"I have. The small amount of space allotted to another column or two would more than pay for itself if we sold more papers and a few ads."

"How do you plan to approach our local merchants?" Millie's voice fell flat with skepticism.

"I'll use the same method. If their ads reach out to neighboring towns, their advantage will be more sales. A lot of people don't like to go to the city to shop. They're reluctant to take the time and fight the traffic.

"Take Harvey's, for instance. He sells almost everything and his store is located within a few miles of Millsburg. I'm positive he'll be the first to offer something for the raffle."

"I guess it's worth a try if you're willing to put in the time and effort."

"It's important we start now if we want to set this program in action. I'll need to make sales calls as soon as I get feedback from Millsburg."

Millie shook her head as Olivia returned to her office to work out a sales presentation.

Over dinner that evening, Olivia told Aunt Etta about her plans.

"Livie, it's going to take a lot of work to make your plan successful. Are you up for the challenge?"

"I thrive on it. I'm used to working ten to twelve hour days. I love a challenge. Besides, down the road I can see the Rexford Press sponsoring other events for the small towns around us. I think it will bring more buyers into our market. I perceive it as a win-win situation."

"What else do you have in mind?"

"How about swim meets at our community pool or essay contests sponsored by the paper or an arts and craft fair?"

"You've put some preparation into this, Livie."

"Do you think it's too ambitious?"

"I think it's just the poke this tired old town needs. Let me know how I can help."

"I plan to start with the Corn Roasting Festival. We'll see how that goes."

Armed with a mock-up newspaper and oral agreements from many Rexford merchants, Olivia, along with the Press photographer, Evan Henner, made the short trip to Millsburg the next day to present her proposal to the mayor. Olivia, careful not to overdress, chose dark slacks and a white blouse. While Olivia attended the meeting at the Millsburg Town Hall, Evan used the time to wander about town photographing the local business establishments and asking questions.

Millsburg was a town frozen in time. The population, fewer than 1,700, varied little over the years. A factory which manufactured machine parts sat on the outskirts. Small businesses lined the main street. Large wooden planter boxes filled with flowers were situated in front of the stores. Evan learned that Lowell Lumber and Hardware store built the containers and members of the Millsburg Ladies Club filled them with flowers and took care of the maintenance. Evan also was told that Millsburg couldn't support a newspaper but the grocer included some local events with his weekly ads which were hand delivered in town.

Millie had warned that local business owners might think of Olivia's overtures as a threat but the contrary prevailed. The mayor invited the Millsburg business owners to sit in on their meeting and they welcomed Olivia with handshakes. They listened as she outlined her advertising strategy. Olivia stressed the benefits to Millsburg, both through personal communication and business sales.

"Miss McDougle, anything that brings people to our town will bring business. We depend on the Corn Roasting Festival each year to attract farmers to spend a day in town and purchase goods from our merchants," the mayor said.

"If advertising in your newspaper gives us more coverage, my business will profit," the owner of a small restaurant told her.

Others at the meeting quickly agreed and the mayor gave Olivia the agenda for the festival. There were races and contests planned, plus the crowning of The Corn Roasting Queen from entries of local high school girls.

"The main street of town is blocked off for the event. Hamburgers, hot dogs and of course, roasted corn will be on sale, plus an assortment of cold drinks. The ladies of the church will have a stand to sell home-made desserts. The fun day will end with bingo at the school auditorium," the mayor said.

"I'm impressed," Olivia told them. "The Rexford Press will help get the word out, and as a special introductory offer, the weekly newspaper will be given free of charge to all town residents for the entire month before the event. I'll need someone to send me your local news, births, deaths, etc. and I'd like to feature your merchants on that page as well." She showed them the mock-up. "I'm excited about this project. I believe everyone will benefit."

As if on cue, Evan arrived and snapped photos of the mayor and Olivia shaking hands. The owner of the local grocery became the first business to take out an ad. "We're in the food business, not printing. Your newspaper has a much better way to get our advertising to the public." He contracted for three months of ads with an option to pick up the rest of the year at the same price provided enough of the locals subscribed.

On the way back to Rexford, Olivia outlined the plan to Evan. "We'll have to find someone to deliver the papers. I'll have posters made to place in the windows of local merchants and check with the grocer to see who delivered his weekly ad. I'll call the school and see if they have any events going on this summer. Maybe the superintendent will recommend someone."

Evan smiled and nodded in agreement as Olivia continued to think out loud.

"To be successful, we have to convince the locals it's worth their while to subscribe to our newspaper. I hope, when the local grocery ads appear, more merchants will advertise."

As soon as they returned to the office, Olivia called a staff meeting to outline her plans. In spite of herself, Millie got caught up in her editor's enthusiasm and added her input. They all agreed it would take extra time and more work but the end results would be satisfying. Until they found delivery people, the Press would be placed at all of the Millsburg business establishments.

The next issue of the Press gave details of the Corn Roasting Festival in Millsburg along with pictures. Olivia wrote an article encouraging Rexford kids to write letters and find pen pals in Millsburg. The next week, she posted some of the letters and within days there were dozens of replies. Of course, these children and their families now planned to meet at the festival, bringing more people to the small town.

Millie received many applicants to deliver the paper. She selected one to start and explained to the others, as more people subscribed, additional carriers would be added.

"Olivia, there's a Miss Beckford on the line. Can you take the call?" Millie asked.

"Olivia McDougle," she said into the phone.

"This is Kristen Beckford. I teach English at Millsburg High and would like to volunteer to write local news for the Press."

"Great. We're glad to have your contribution. I'll send you an outline for the information we want to use."

After a long conversation, they decided to get together in Millsburg for lunch the next day. It would give Olivia the opportunity to meet Kristen in person, and patronize the local restaurant.

The Millsburg project promised success. Millie adapted to Olivia's way of doing business and the Press flourished. For the first time in months, Olivia felt a sense of accomplishment.

EIGHT

The weeks flashed by. Olivia became more adept at composing the weekly editorial, the only part of the job that had caused her concern. When she realized editorials were like writing letters, it put the task in prospective. Once Millie complimented her effort, Olivia felt she had finally earned a passing grade.

After working past six o'clock every night the previous week, she made a point to leave early on Tuesday evening. She looked forward to a quiet, relaxing evening as she entered the front door of the Anderson house.

"I'm glad you're home, I have a surprise for you," Etta said when she met Olivia at the door.

Mitch James appeared from the entry way. "Etta invited me to sample some of her famous stew."

Olivia didn't know quite how to react. Dr. James was the last person she expected or wanted to see. She quickly collected herself, "How nice to see you." Then she turned her attention to her aunt, "You know you shouldn't be in the kitchen all day."

"Nonsense. You'll appreciate my effort when you taste the stew."

"I'll attest to that," Mitch added.

Olivia excused herself to freshen up before dinner, determined to make the most of what she perceived as a bad situation. When she returned, Aunt Etta and Dr. James were enjoying a glass of wine and engaged in a humorous conversation. His laughter echoed through the house. Olivia stood back and watched them. Incredibly handsome, and well over six feet tall, Mitch obviously worked out to keep in shape. His piercing blue eyes astounded her but his brash behavior gave her pause.

He stood when Olivia entered the room. "I brought white and red." He held the bottles up for her to choose. "Do you have a preference?"

"Should Aunt Etta be drinking wine?"

"Livie, dear. Don't talk about me as if I'm not here. A glass of wine before dinner never hurt anyone."

The doctor agreed as he handed Olivia a glass. She chose the white, joined the two of them, and made every attempt to hide her discomfort.

"Etta tells me you're making changes at the Press." Mitch flashed a smile that made Olivia catch her breath.

"Nothing too radical. We're developing a plan to provide service to some of the neighboring communities."

"Good idea. Some of the smaller towns are left out of the loop. Where are you going first?"

In spite of herself, enthusiasm crept into Olivia's voice when she told him about the Millsburg campaign. Mitch seemed to ask the right questions, and had valid comments and suggestions. They were so involved in the conversation, they didn't notice when Etta left the room to check on dinner.

"Stew's ready," Etta announced as she lead Mitch and Livie to the dining room.

"It smells wonderful." Mitch held the chairs for the ladies. "Let me serve, Etta."

Mitch ladled the stew into hand-painted china bowls, passed around Etta's special buttermilk biscuits and placed bowls of crisp salad at each place. Homemade apricot jam and whipped butter completed the meal. Mitch refilled Olivia's and his wine glasses and poured herb tea for Etta.

"Etta, I swear your stew gets better every time I taste it. What's your secret?" Mitch asked.

"Humph, if I told you it wouldn't be a secret."

"You got me there," he laughed.

Olivia listened to their easy banter. Aunt Etta's eyes glistened and she had quick come-backs for Mitch as he baited her.

"Livie?"

"Sorry, Aunt Etta. What did you say?"

"I asked if you would get the apple pie—and put a dollop of ice cream on top."

Mitch gathered the dishes and followed her to the kitchen. "Are you okay? You seem distracted."

Olivia swung around. "What are you doing here?"

"Do you mean enjoying Etta's wonderful meal or bringing the dishes to the kitchen?"

"I mean what are you really doing here?"

"I came to see you."

His blatant honestly shocked her. She expected, well, she didn't expect his dazzling smile and those deep blue eyes that locked onto hers.

"I'm not ready to see anyone."

Mitch sat the dishes on the sink and took her in his arms.

"I'm going to make it my mission to change your mind." He ran his fingers through her hair and pulled her closer to him. His kiss made her head spin. Her first impulse was to run.

"I need to bring the pie..."

"I don't believe Etta is waiting for dessert. I heard her go to her room."

"But..."

"Come here. You're beautiful, Olivia." He brushed his thumb across her lips. "I knew kissing you would feel like this." He took her in his arms, this time he kissed her deeply. His tongue searched hers. He couldn't get enough.

Olivia could feel the warmth of his body as he pressed against her. She responded with a passion from deep within.

"My God, you're sweeter than I imagined," he said as he cupped her face and kissed her mouth, then her neck and nibbled on her ear.

He stopped suddenly and reached for his beeper and pulled it from his pocket to check the number. "Gotta go." Without further explanation, he rushed out the door.

Confused by her emotion and the rash Dr. James, Olivia finished cleaning the kitchen, checked on Aunt Etta and then went to her room. After tossing and turning most of the night, she finally fell into a fitful sleep. She woke the next morning with mixed feelings. Months after the humiliation Brian Mercer caused, it still left a bitter taste in her mouth. She vowed she would never again allow herself to become vulnerable again. Then the abrupt, rude Mitch James came into her life. She was prepared to dislike him, did dislike him until he kissed her. Oh God, did he kiss her. Her face flushed as she recalled her reaction. She swayed in his arms. "Lord, I swooned."

Good thing he had to leave on an emergency. It gave her time to catch her balance.

Aunt Etta tapped on the door. "Livie, coffee's ready."

Olivia smiled. Her delightful aunt was chomping at the bit to find out what happened between Mitch and her.

"Coming," she called and grabbed her robe.

"Do you want pancakes?"

"Coffee and toast will be fine. I'll get it."

Aunt Etta buzzed around her, bringing jam and cream to the table. "I snipped some flowers for you to take to the office."

Olivia didn't offer any information. She sat quietly sipping coffee.

"Are you going to tell me what happened last night or must I call Mitch James and ask him?"

"I can't imagine what you're talking about. Look at the time. I have to shower." She looked over her shoulder as she left the room. "He kissed me. I didn't expect it and didn't want it."

"But?"

"But nothing. It was an innocent kiss, that's all."

When Olivia closed the bathroom door, she heard a muffled, "Yes."

Olivia almost skipped to the office, reminding herself that she was a grown woman, not a teen-ager. The radiant smile hadn't yet left her face when Millie met her at the office door.

"You won't believe the letters and phone calls we've received about our Millsburg promotion." She spread out the messages on the desk.

"Good or bad?"

"Our merchants are begging for advertising space and I've sold eighty subscriptions and three merchant ads in Millsburg. Harvey's has offered a valuable prize for the drawing and wants to talk to you about a full page ad for the event."

"That's great news. I didn't think it would take off this quickly. Can we handle it?" Olivia smiled at Millie's enthusiasm. Maybe she had finally won her over.

"It will take a few extra pages but the advertising income will more than cover the cost. Plus, the reception kicking off the ballet season in Lima, was held last week. We have pictures of Victoria Gillette and her escort, Dr. James, to put on our society page." She shoved the prints across the desk for Olivia to see. "You need to select the one you think we should run. Victoria sent notes and I've written the story."

Olivia pursed her lips to keep from revealing shock as she looked at the pictures, shuffling from one to the other. Victoria in a skin-tight gown clinging to Mitch. Victoria kissing his cheek. Mitch dressed in a tux, beaming as he had his arm around Victoria's waist with Judge and Mrs. Gillette positioned like book-ends on either side of the couple. Everyone appeared smug, sophisticated and comfortable. They seemed like a happy, comfortable family. Olivia wanted to scream. Instead she said, "They all look fine. Use whatever one you think is suitable. I trust your judgment. Anything else?"

"Do you want to take care of these advertising calls?"

"I'll get on the phone now," Olivia said, thankful that she had something to occupy her mind.

At lunch time, Millie rapped on Olivia's office door. "Dr. James is on line one."

"Would you take a message? I've lined up appointments to meet with advertisers." She grabbed her purse, dashed out the door and found herself on the street before she realized she didn't have a car. She walked home to get Aunt Etta's. It provided her the opportunity to regain control.

Unfortunately, it also gave her time to think about Mitch and the way he kissed her—and the way she melted in his arms. She admonished herself and quickened her pace. He's the worst kind of cad, coming on to me when he's obviously involved with Victoria Gillette. I can't believe I've been so stupid. I must have a sign pasted on my back that says, "Kick Me."

By the time she reached the front porch, she made a decision. She would take charge of her life and not allow some two-timing doctor to play lightly with her heart.

NINE

Are you okay?" Etta asked as Olivia came in the front door. "I didn't expect you home so early."

"I'm fine. I'll need to borrow the car, if you don't mind. I made appointments to talk with some prospective clients."

"Humph, Mitch forbids me to drive. Consider it yours. Are you sure you're not coming down with something? You look flushed."

"I rushed home. I wanted to grab a quick lunch before my first appointment."

Aunt Etta insisted on fixing sandwiches, while Olivia told her how successful the Millsburg project had become.

"I can't believe it. All these years, we've never attempted to support the neighboring communities. Livie, I think you've done a great service for Millsburg."

"And to the Press."

"That goes without saying."

"I plan to go to Newton City next. Didn't you take me there as a child to buy pumpkins for Halloween?"

"I'd forgotten about that. Remember how you and your friends would pile in the car and I'd drive you to the field to choose your own pumpkin. Then we'd come back here to carve them. I never heard such giggling."

"Then we'd enlist the neighbors to choose the best one," Olivia added.

"And I would fix some hot mulled cider."

"Everyone loved to come here." Olivia said.

"Because I let you girls make a mess."

Olivia smiled at the memory. "Maybe the Press will sponsor a Jack-o-Lantern carving contest this year and if things go well at Newton City, I could incorporate it with my campaign. It might be fun. I'm going to make a trip there to talk to the mayor and see if they're interested in a fall celebration. If not there, I'll try Harlen Grove. Either town is close enough to plan the same kind of advertising event."

"Olivia, you're certainly motivated."

"When you drove us home from the airport, I immediately noticed how all of the small towns were connected to one another. I want to make that connection personal. I believe the newspaper can help accomplish that goal."

Etta shook her head. "Livie, I knew you could handle the editor's job but I didn't realize how insightful you are. Good for you."

"I've got to run. Don't forget, this is the night I meet with Robyn for dinner. I invited Kristen Beckford from Millsburg to join us. She's a person I'd like to know better. Don't wait up." Olivia escaped before Aunt Etta could question her again about Mitch James, although she fully expected the third degree in the morning.

Olivia drove to 421 Maple Street to meet Jade Kendall, owner of J.K. Art Company, a small arts and craft store. Ms. Kendall had not previously advertised in the Press but had depended on word of mouth and flyers to publicize her business and announce her ongoing classes.

Before Olivia entered the building, she stopped to admire an elaborate mural depicting angels, painted on the side of the two-story brick structure. Multi-colored ceramic pots filled with flowers and ivy framed the doorway. The front window showcased beautiful paintings and a myriad of hand-crafted items.

A serenade of bells attached to the door heralded Olivia's arrival into the shop. The sweet aroma of vanilla permeated the air.

"May I help you?"

"Hi, I'm Olivia McDougle from the Rexford Press. What smells so good?"

"Scented candles. I made a batch this morning."

"They're wonderful."

"Thanks. They're my favorite. I'm Jade Kendall," she said. She set her paint brush in a container of turpentine and wiped her hands on a well-soiled canvas apron.

"What an interesting shop."

"It's my life's dream. I paint, create all kinds of ceramics, decorate and give private and group art classes. I'm planning a second adult craft class."

Olivia fingered a small beaded purse. "I love this."

"That's my latest project. I find working with beads very relaxing. I'm going to give beading and jewelry making classes this fall."

"I'm impressed. I received your message regarding advertising. What do you have in mind?"

"I'm interested in Millsburg. I've researched the town and found they don't have a store for crafts or supplies there. I'd like to get their business. I can offer competitive prices on supplies and I hope I'll be able to enroll some of their residents in my classes."

"The Press can handle that. Would you consider offering a free lesson to first timers? Once you get them in your shop, you have the possibility of signing them up for ongoing classes."

"That makes sense. Everyone likes something free." Jade glanced at her watch, "Let's take a break. Come up to my apartment and we can work out the ad over coffee." Jade put the CLOSED sign on the door and Olivia followed her around to the back and up the stairs to the second floor. Once inside, Jade directed her to the kitchen. Olivia sat at the table while Jade filled two mugs with the already prepared brew.

"I can't believe how large your living space is. It's deceiving from the outside," Olivia said as she looked around Jade's apartment.

"I have the entire top floor. There are extra rooms up here I don't use. It's quite comfortable.

"My grandfather owns the building and rents the two downstairs offices in back of my shop to an insurance agent and a CPA. They're very quiet neighbors." Jade said.

Olivia made a mental note to contact them for her Millsburg campaign.

Jade, tall and shapely, wore a colorful long caftan. Her mass of dark brown curls were gathered on top of her head and fastened with a gray pearl encrusted clip. Her infectious laugh make Olivia feel warm and welcome and after a few minutes of conversation, they fell into an instant friendship. With Olivia's expertise and Jade's suggestions, they completed the ad for the J.K. Art Company.

"Are you free for dinner tonight? My friend Robyn and I meet every Wednesday night at the Steak Grill. A new friend from Millsburg is also joining us."

"Just the girls?"

"Girls night out," Olivia said as they walked back to the shop.

"That sounds like fun. I could use some girl-talk with people my age."

"Great, I'll meet you in front of the restaurant at six." Olivia couldn't resist buying the beaded purse before she left Jade's shop.

Olivia spent the rest of the day visiting clients and revamping their ads to coincide with the Millsburg Corn Roasting Festival. It also gave Olivia the opportunity to introduce herself to more of Rexford's merchants.

Millie had a handful of messages for Olivia when she returned to the office. "Dr. James called again. Is Etta feeling okay?"

"She's fine. Perhaps he wants to make sure we run the picture of him with the Gillette's. I'll call him later."

Millie shook her head. "I don't imagine he'd care. The Gillette's are social climbers. The judge retired and joined a law firm here in town that specializes in divorce and personal injury cases. Olivia, he has clout with the town council. Nothing is done in this town unless Judge Gillette gives his stamp of approval. The mayor wouldn't have his position without the judge's say-so."

"That's interesting. I can't imagine residents putting up with that kind of thinking."

"You'd be surprised what people put up with. I almost forgot, Victoria Gillette called and asked if we'd use the picture that included her family. She said she might want to save one of the others for her engagement. I told her whatever she decided would be fine. We need to stay politically correct."

Olivia looked puzzled.

"We don't want to lock horns with Judge Gillette. His entire life revolves around Victoria. I'm sure he'll be delighted that we're running that particular picture."

Olivia shook her head in disbelief. "I'll close up, go on home, Millie. See you in the morning."

After Millie left, Olivia allowed the recorder to answer the phones while she sorted the new ads. She attempted to put thoughts of Mitch James behind her. She didn't need the aggravation.

A little before five, Olivia closed the office and left to meet Robyn and now two new girls for dinner. She looked forward to spending the evening with them.

Robyn met Olivia at the door of the Steak Grill, looking her usual neat self. Barely 5'4", Robyn weighed less than 100 lbs and wore her short, honey blonde hair brushed to a dazzling shine. She appeared the same as she had in high school.

"There are two others joining us tonight." Olivia told Robyn. "I can't wait for you to meet Kristen Beckford, a teacher from Millsburg and Jade Kendall, owner the J.K. Art Company on Maple Street."

"I've driven by her shop, but haven't been inside."

"It's worth the visit. She has an assortment of hand-crafted specialty items. I bought this purse there today." She held it up for Robyn to admire.

As if on cue Jade arrived, attracting attention in a long, and very colorful, caftan. Jade's long curly tresses were tamed with a large gold clip. Her olive skin glowed and her dark almond shaped eyes flashed when she laughed. An essence of Jasmine surrounded her.

"Robyn, this is Jade Kendall."

"So glad you could join us," Robyn said. "Your necklace is striking. Is this a piece from your shop?"

"Yes, thank you. Jewelry design is one of my favorite pastimes. Stop by the shop one day and I'll show you around," Jade said.

Within a few minutes, Kristen joined the group. She provided an obvious contrast to the effervescent Jade. Kristen wore black slacks, a gray silk shirt and styled her brunette hair swept back in a smooth twist. Sophisticated would be the proper word to describe her. Their distinct appearance and unique style attracted attention as they walked through the restaurant.

The girls quickly found they had a great deal in common. All were under thirty and single except Robyn, whose husband was stationed overseas, and they all craved female companionship. During dinner they conversed as if they had been friends for years.

Robyn's hazel eyes sparkled and with animated gestured, recounted her day at the bank. Jade's infectious laughter rang out through the room. The quieter Kristen blushed with mirth when Robyn narrated a saga about how one of the older citizens brought money to the bank tied in a sock.

"He couldn't decide how much he wanted to deposit. He unknotted the sock and brought out a wad of bills. Then he peeled off a few twenties, stuffed the rest back in the sock and knotted it again." Robyn mimed the action sending Jade into hysterics.

"Then," Robyn continued, "he decided to add to the amount and repeated the drill. The line at my station grew longer and impatient customers began to mumble complaints. The bank manager came to see if I had a problem.

"I tried to keep a straight face as I told him about the sock. The old man became indignant when the manager suggested he get out of line and fill out a deposit slip. Finally, we convinced him to follow the manager to his office and they would make the deposit slip together. By that time the customers waiting in line had forgotten the delay and were attempting to muffle their laughter."

"And they say working in a bank is dull," Olivia said.

By the time they finished eating Kristen and Jade decided they would like to join Robyn and Olivia every Wednesday for dinner.

"I don't know when I've had so much fun," Jade said. "I needed this outlet."

"This is my second year teaching in Millsburg and I haven't met any girls my age. I've really enjoyed myself." Kristen said.

"I'm so glad. We'll see you next Wednesday," Olivia said. They said their good-byes and went their separate ways. Olivia smiled as she drove home and parked the car in the driveway. She felt the four of them would become great friends. A voice startled her as she walked onto the porch.

"I called you three times today, Olivia."

TEN

"Dr. James, you startled me. You have a habit of doing that."

"It's Mitch, Olivia. You ignored my calls. Have I done something to offend you?"

"I told you I'm not ready for a relationship. I don't know how I can make that more clear."

Mitch took hold of Olivia's wrist and pulled her close to him. "I know you felt the same spark I did when I kissed you last night."

"I felt surprised, nothing more."

Before she could protest, he kissed her with unexpected passion. She struggled to keep her knees from buckling.

"You can't deny it, Olivia McDougle. We share a mutual attraction."

"We share nothing," Olivia said as she distanced herself from his grasp. "You might be better served to seek out company with Victoria Gillette. I saw the pictures. You two make a lovely couple."

"So that's what this is about."

"That is exactly what this is about. I have no intention of becoming involved with someone with your lack of principles. Miss Gillette can have you."

"Wait a minute, lady. I'm not a commodity that can be traded like stock. I have a mind of my own. I know what I want."

"And I know what I don't want and I don't want to have anything to do with you."

"You are the most aggravating female I've ever met." He put his hands on her shoulders. "I don't know whether to kiss you or shake you." He knew he would like to carry her off to bed. He had never been so attracted to anyone.

"Believe me if you try to kiss me again, I'll kick you in the shins."

"Damn, you would. Your hot temper matches your red hair, Miss McDougle. At least give me the opportunity to explain."

"Not necessary. Goodnight, Dr. James." She rushed into the house and closed the door with a snap. She couldn't help but remember the look of shock on his face when he started to protest. She shut him out, wouldn't listen. Olivia didn't believe she could tolerate his lame excuses.

His taste still lingered on her lips. A sudden chill ran down her spine. How she wanted him. It pained her to make that acknowledgement. She still reeled from the trauma Brian caused her. She would never put herself through that torment again. Better to concentrate on her work.

Aunt Etta came out of her room. "I thought I heard voices."

"Just me." Olivia inhaled quickly, pushing the events on the porch from her mind.

"How was your dinner?"

"Great. There were four of us and I think we'll become good friends." She told her aunt about the girls. "Kristen and Jade plan to join us every week. I'm looking forward to getting to know them better."

"I wanted to ask you about Mitch."

"I've had a busy day and I'm really exhausted. Let's talk tomorrow. Goodnight." Olivia left Etta standing in the bedroom doorway.

Olivia, more confused than tired, attempted to sort out her feelings. Why did Mitch wait for her on the porch if he was interested in Victoria Gillette? Her fingers brushed her lips. His kiss still lingered and the heat of his body remained an uncomfortable presence. She longed to feel his arms around her again. His touch excited her. He brought to surface feelings that she had never imagined existed.

She visualized the pictures of Mitch and Victoria. Victoria Gillette, with her long blonde hair and sexy figure made Olivia seem boyish in comparison.

Obviously, Judge and Mrs. Gillette approved of the couple. Their faces beamed...smiles all around. It made Olivia sick. Or did she bear the sting of jealousy?

What did Millie allude to when she mentioned Judge Gillette? Why would he have a firm grip on the community?

And Victoria. Was she referring to her upcoming engagement to Mitch James?

She considered those questions as she prepared for bed. Many answers came in her dreams. Most were not what she wanted to know.

ELEVEN

Mitch couldn't believe Olivia closed the door in his face. Damn, she irritated him. He had female patients propositioning him on a regular basis. Some extended dinner invitations and made more than casual suggestions as to what else they would do, if given the opportunity. He could have his choice if he was so inclined. But this red-haired, stubborn, head-strong woman dismissed him as if he were a child.

Mitch couldn't explain why her actions bothered him so much. He did perfectly well on his own. Maybe those few freckles that dotted her face, or the way she shook her long hair back from her shoulders got to him. And her eyes. Dear God, those green-blue eyes mesmerized him. It didn't help that he kissed her. That sealed his fate. He knew. He was obsessed by the stunning Olivia McDougle.

Olivia made her position clear. She had no intension of fawning over him. He'd change his approach; make it his business to win her over. Mitch decided to court the lady, the good old-fashioned way.

He didn't have the luxury of agonizing about his relationship with Olivia McDougle. An emergency call from Lima General resulted in an all-night vigil with a critical patient. By the time he returned to Rexford, he had little time to shower and grab a quick breakfast before office hours began.

God, he loved his practice. He loved the patients, even the cranky ones. He liked to tease them out of their sour moods and offer comfort along with good medicine.

Maxine commanded the office like a military base, bless her. He couldn't survive without her organization. She had an expert sense for basic diagnosis and by the time the patient reached the examining room, she had Mitch completely prepared for their needs. She was quick to offer practical guidance, which included instructions on hygiene, that some of the less affluent patients neglected. She made sure he took a break, no matter how many people crowded the waiting room. And for his protection, she never left him alone in a room with a female patient.

His usual schedule included rounds at the hospital, then house calls in the mornings followed by office hours from one until at least six. Wednesday evenings he scheduled late office hours, convenient for his working patients.

Etta mentioned that Olivia and Robyn met for dinner every Wednesday night and Olivia usually didn't return home until ten, which accounted for his appearance the Anderson porch.

After his last patient left, his thoughts turned back to Olivia. He could still taste her kiss, smell her perfume. Her long silky hair fell in soft waves as it framed her face and glistened in the moonlight as they stood on Etta's porch the night before. Olivia's 5'6" frame, fit perfectly in his arms, barely reaching his chin. His body warmed thinking about her.

Olivia harbored anger from a previous relationship. Etta mentioned a broken engagement but she didn't elaborate. Whatever happened in her past made her cautious and guarded. She seemed to have built a protective wall around her emotions.

The thought crossed his mind that perhaps he came on too strong, but he couldn't resist her. Her beauty, self-confidence and spunky personality mesmerized him. He had to find a way to convince her to spend time with him.

He reached for the phone.

"How are you doing, Etta?" he asked when she answered.

"I'm fine, Mitch."

"Is Olivia there?"

"You're so fickle. I thought you were devoted to me."

His laughter rang in her ear. "You'll always be my first love."

"Livie, the phone's for you," Etta called.

"I didn't mean to startle you last night," he said when Olivia answered.

"Dr. James?"

"Mitch. I'm not sure what you know about the Gillette's, but I had an obligation to attend that party. I want you to give me a chance to explain."

"That's not necessary."

"It is. Have you had dinner?"

"No, Aunt Etta ate early and I…"

"I'll be by to pick you up in ten minutes."

Before she could protest, the phone went dead.

In spite of her resolve not to become involved with him, she checked the mirror and repaired her lipstick. Before she had a chance to run the comb through her hair, she heard Mitch's infectious laughter ring through the hallway as he teased Aunt Etta.

"Did you call from your car?" Olivia asked Mitch when she entered the foyer.

"I did get here in a hurry. I had to leave the office before another walk-in patient came in. They'd saunter in all evening if I left the lights on and the door open.

73

"There's a place on Route 65 that makes the most wonderful chicken fried steak you've ever tasted. You'll be glad you haven't eaten." He held the door for her and called to Etta on the way out. "Don't wait up."

Mitch displayed more confidence than he felt as he took Olivia's arm. He couldn't be sure how she would react. He made sure she was comfortably inside his Jeep before he slid into the driver's seat beside her. After a few moments of awkward silence Olivia asked, "Did you have a busy day?"

"Non-stop. Fortunately, nothing serious. The usual run of summer colds, follow-up visits, and a case of hives. Maxine keeps things moving. I'd be lost without her."

"You said you wanted to talk. It's not necessary to go out to eat."

"Yes it is. I'm starved."

Olivia didn't attempt to contain her laugh. "You know what I mean."

Mitch reached over and touched her arm. "I know, Olivia. I'm afraid we got off on the wrong foot from the day you arrived at your aunt's porch. I want to set it straight. Will you give me the chance?"

"There isn't anything..."

"There you go. You jump at the opportunity to dismiss me." He pulled onto the highway. "I'm the good guy here. When we get to Jolt's Tavern, I'll explain."

Olivia listened as Mitch gave her general information about his practice. A few miles out of Rexford, he pulled into the parking lot of a roadside bar, illuminated with bright clashing colored neon lights advertising everything from beer to peanuts. Posters in the window told of upcoming events, including an arm-wrestling contest, pool tournaments, and an unknown country, western singer appearing on Saturday night.

"Don't let the outside fool you. You're in for a treat." He opened the car door for her, extended his hand, and led her inside.

Olivia scanned the surroundings. The furnishings consisted of worn wooden tables and chairs with patched plastic cushions. The wide plank floor was littered with peanut shells and western memorabilia splashed the walls. Used and abused saddles straddled bales of hay stacked at different locations along the walls. An antique juke box, next to the doorway, blasted loud country music. The place reeked stale beer and kitchen grease. Olivia couldn't imagine eating anything in that atmosphere.

Before she could protest to Mitch, a waitress directed them to a table near the window, away from the small dance floor and the blare of the juke box.

"Haven't seen you for a while, Dr. James. What will you have?"

"The usual Helen, and bring a pitcher."

Olivia started to protest but Mitch's upraised hand silenced her.

"Trust me. You'll enjoy this."

In place of a salad, they served a dish of raw vegetables, hard boiled eggs, pickles and olives. Helen set frosted mugs and a pitcher of beer in front of them along with the tavern's trademark basket of peanuts in the shell.

"You must come here often. The waitress knows you," Olivia said.

"As often as I think my cholesterol will allow."

Olivia laughed in spite of herself. She picked at the veggies and sipped the beer. The meal arrived on Ironstone platters that overflowed with chicken-fried steak, mashed potatoes, white gravy and corn on the cob.

"Good Lord, I'll never eat all of this."

"Once you taste it, you'll be surprised how much you can eat. It melts in your mouth. We'll take a break half way through and dance it off." Mitch grinned and added, "I do a mean two-step."

"I bet you do." Olivia began to relax. The beer tasted good on the warm June night and the food, fabulous.

"You're staring at me. Do I have something on my face?" Olivia took the napkin and wiped it over her chin.

"Caught in the act of watching a beautiful woman eat. I'm guilty as charged," he laughed. "I didn't mean to make you blush, but I'll have to say, it becomes you." He refilled her glass.

"The food is incredible. I didn't expect..."

"You couldn't imagine a dive like this could serve something so good. I know what you're saying. Are you ready to take that break?"

"You're serious."

"You bet I am," he said as he stood beside her chair and offered his arm.

Mitch could feel Olivia shiver when he placed his hand in the small of her back and guided her to the dance floor. That made him smile, especially when she tried so hard to hide her emotions.

It wasn't the two-step, but a slow dance. He pulled her close, aware that he had a captive audience and she would have to hear him out. He whispered in her ear. "Olivia, there are things I need to explain. I want to get to know you better. I know it's difficult to date a doctor. My life's not my own. You need to know how attracted I am to you."

"I told you, I'm not..."

"Shh, just listen. Judge Gillette led a committee from Rexford to find and bring a doctor to town. When they approached me, the financial agreement they presented said I must practice medicine in Rexford for at least five years. I jumped at the chance and believe I received the best part of the deal. It's the type of practice I've dreamed of. I never plan to leave.

"The pictures you saw were from a fundraiser. A portion of the income was set aside to fund the clinics I run in areas that don't have access to a doctor. I'm obligated to attend these events and the judge volunteered his daughter, Victoria, to be my escort. There are some things I can't change and because I'm single, I didn't object to accompanying Victoria to these kinds of events. She's the daughter of a very influential man. I want you to know, Victoria Gillette means nothing to me. She's rich, spoiled and very immature. The fact that she has a crush on me doesn't help. I hope you'll change that."

"What do you mean?"

"I want to get to know you better. I want us to spend time together, be a couple."

"I told you, I'm not ready."

He flashed a smile and pulled her closer. "I intend to convince you I'm worth the effort."

Olivia pushed back and looked Mitch in the eye. "Victoria called our office and suggested we keep one of the pictures for her engagement. You need to understand that I have no intention of coming between the two of you."

Mitch threw back his head and roared with laughter, causing others on the dance floor to stare. "That's not even worth a comment, but I'm glad you're concerned."

"I'm not concerned. I want you to understand how I feel."

"It's duly noted. Are you ready to finish the meal?"

"I couldn't eat another thing. You were right. It was heavenly."

He brushed his lips against hers. "Those were my sentiments about you."

"I told you, I'm not ready for..."

"I know what you said. I intend to make every effort to change your mind. Give me a chance, Olivia."

"It's getting late."

Mitch sighed. "It is. I have early rounds at the hospital." He paid the tab and took Olivia home. He didn't want to leave but he also didn't want to make the same mistake as before. He kissed her lightly after he walked her to the door.

"I'll call you. Olivia, don't shut me out. I want a second chance to get to know you."

***

As Olivia lay in bed that night, confusion surrounded her. She couldn't deny the attraction she felt for Mitch. His arms were strong and protective. His closeness caused her to catch her breath. She found herself wondering what it would be like to be his completely. She attempted to push those thoughts from her mind. They didn't escape her dreams.

TWELVE

Determined to formally date Olivia, Mitch called her Friday morning before she left for the Press to inform her of his intention to take her dancing. "Dress casual and wear flat shoes."

"Don't take for granted I'm available. Maybe I have other plans."

"Miss McDougle, will you please do me the honor of escorting you Friday evening?"

Olivia suppressed the laugh that threatened to erupt. "Where might that be, Dr. James?"

"I take that to mean you agree. I'll pick you up before dinner, around seven."

Mitch appeared at the door that evening wearing Levi's and a plaid shirt. Unsure of what he meant by casual clothes, Olivia dressed in a cotton skirt and blouse and wore flats as he suggested.

"You look terrific," he said as he led her to his car.

"Are you going to tell me where we're going?"

"Worthville."

"Worthville is little more than a crossroads. Why on earth are we going there?"

Mitch grinned. "We're not exactly going into town. There's a place called, The Country Pub, about a mile outside the city limits. You're in for a great time."

Olivia waited for Mitch to tell her more, but he shook his head when she questioned him further.

"Just wait and see," he told her.

She sat back in the leather seat of Mitch's Jeep and watched as the miles passed by. At last, Mitch turned onto a gravel lane and followed the twisting road to a parking lot. He jumped out of the driver's side and opened the door for her.

The Country Pub was little more than a barn with lights. Music saturated the night air.

"We had to arrive early in order to find an empty table. The joint starts bouncing around nine. From experience, I suggest the fried fish."

"After Jolts, I'll take your word for it."

Mitch ordered two fish baskets and a pitcher of beer. Before they finished eating, the crowd began to arrive. The owner silenced the juke box and a blue grass band took the stage.

"I lived in this county from my early childhood until I graduated high school. I've never heard of this place. How did you find it?"

"I donate my time to a free clinic in Worthville. Some of my patients told me about it."

The fiddle gave a flourish and couples began to gather in squares. Someone called out, "Dr. James, over here." Mitch took Olivia by the hand and led her to the group and introduced everyone.

"I don't remember how to square dance," she protested.

"It'll come back."

They danced until they were both ready to drop. Olivia never remembered having so much fun. Mitch was soaked with sweat and Olivia's hair began to stick to the nape of her neck.

"We have to take a break," she pleaded. "Now I know how you keep in shape."

Mitch wrapped his arm around her and gave her a light kiss on the cheek. "Okay, we'll sit the next one out. Are you having fun?"

"I am. I can't believe you know how to square dance. Aren't you a city guy?"

"Well you know, when in the country. Besides, I love the small towns. Each one is unique."

"I realized that when I returned to Rexford. I've found my home again."

"I'm glad to hear you say that, Olivia. I hope you'll include me in your long range plans."

At midnight they left the tavern and headed back to Rexford. They sat on Etta's front porch swing and talked. Mitch put his arm comfortably around Olivia's shoulders, glad she didn't resist.

"A daughter of one of my patients is getting married in Findlay next Saturday. I can't attend the wedding because of the clinic I hold in the morning, but I'd like you to come to reception with me?"

"I don't know."

"Olivia, give me a chance. I'm serious about you. I want to spend time with you and convince you how much we have in common. A doctor's life in a small town isn't easy. I have terrible hours. I'm called out on emergencies at the most inopportune times. Some days I don't sleep at all. I'm not complaining, just explaining. When I have the chance to have some fun, I want to include you."

"We hardly know each other."

"Exactly my point." He pulled her closer to him. "I have to go. I have an early start tomorrow morning. The reception is at five. I'll call you during the week." Before she could say anything, he kissed her. "God, I don't want to leave."

***

As she watched Mitch drive off, Olivia knew she didn't want him to leave either. All of her dark thoughts of the doctor vanished. He seemed as comfortable with his patients from the free clinic as he did with everyone else.

She thought of the selfish, lying, status-seeking Brian Mercer and couldn't help but compare the two men. Opposites couldn't begin to describe them. Although they were both handsome, Brian, about 5'11', had blonde hair and light blue eyes and always dressed as if he stepped out of GQ magazine. He wouldn't accept anything but the best and constantly sent food back at restaurants if he felt it was less than perfect. She snickered as she pictured Brian at Jolt's or the Country Pub. The only beer Brian ever drank had to be imported. He did, on occasion, wear jeans...five hundred dollar designer jeans. He wouldn't be caught dead rubbing elbows with farm workers, or anyone else with a menial job.

Then there was Dr. Mitchell James. At 6'2", his jet black hair fell into easy waves. Dark blue eyes seemed to look through to her soul. He had a habit of rubbing his hand over his square chin when something puzzled or worried him. But most of all, Olivia loved his laugh and his sense of humor that put everyone at ease. Olivia couldn't picture Mitch putting on airs. He was honest and down to earth.

Olivia went into the house and turned off the lights. She thought about how passionate he felt about his practice, and reminded herself what an important presence he had become in her life.

THIRTEEN

Monday morning, Victoria slept late. After a long week-end in Lima with a college friend, she was exhausted. The two girls reminisced about their time at Ohio State University, old boyfriends and what they planned to do with the rest of their lives. Neither girl had permanent employment, but Victoria spent time in her father's office. Judge Gillette referred to her as his executive assistant, although she did little more than shuffle papers.

The two girls had shopped, and then partied too much and too long. Victoria waited until late Sunday night to return home so she wouldn't have to answer her parent's questions. Better to do that with a clear head. Besides, the judge always left early for work on Monday mornings and Victoria's mother had a standing nine o'clock hair appointment. Carla, the part-time housekeeper and cook, would be the only one in the house.

Late in the morning, Victoria made her way to the kitchen.

"Hello sleepyhead. Can I fix your breakfast?"

"Thanks, Carla. Guess I'll have coffee and maybe an English muffin."

"That's not enough to keep a person going. How about I make French toast or scrambled eggs?"

"Mmm, French toast sounds good. You don't mind?"

"Not for you, kiddo. It'll take a few minutes. Meanwhile, I'll pour you a glass of orange juice while you wait."

Victoria took the juice and plopped down in a kitchen chair.

"Carla, you spoil me. How was your week-end?"

"Great. Rex and I drove over to Worthville."

"What's at Worthville?"

"The Saturday night square dance at The Country Pub. Rex and I go at least once a month."

"No kidding. I never figured you guys as square dancers. Did they have a good crowd?"

"The place was packed. We saw Dr. James with that new editor of the Press."

"Mitch was there with Olivia McDougle? Are you sure?"

"Couldn't miss them. They were quite close, if you know what I mean." Carla set a plate of French toast in front of Victoria. "Dr. James didn't let that lady out of his sight. They were still dancing when we left at eleven."

Victoria could barely choke down the breakfast Carla served. The mere thought of Mitch and Olivia McDougle together infuriated her.

"Are you feeling okay? You look a little pale."

"I'm fine. I remembered I have an appointment this morning. Gotta get going. Thanks for breakfast." Victoria refilled her coffee cup, took it along to her room and closed the door. "I believe Miss McDougle and I need to have a little talk."

After a quick shower, Victoria searched the closet to find the perfect outfit. Had to have a killer look for the face-off with Olivia McDougle. She wanted to put together something knock-out chic, like she saw the rock stars wear in magazines. The bed became piled with clothes before she chose a white military-type jacket with gold buttons, purchased on a trip to Europe last year and paired it with a hip-hugging pleated mini skirt. Then she rummaged through the dresser drawers until she found a stretch blue top to enhance the color of her eyes.

Victoria took extra time to apply make-up, with emphasis on the eye shadow. She pulled her long blonde hair into a loose knot and fastened it with a blue scunchy. A pair of strappy heels, gold jewelry and a white purse finished the ensemble.

Victoria scrutinized her image in the mirror. "I need more bling." She exchanged the handbag for a gold glitzy one with dangling bangles, added another necklace and gave another admiring look. "Perfect," she said aloud. Satisfied, Victoria left the house and headed for the Press in her bubble-gum pink convertible, a birthday present from daddy.

During the five minute drive to the Press, Victoria became determined to give Olivia McDougle a lesson in respect. You simply didn't date someone else's guy, editor of a newspaper or not. That newcomer didn't know who she was messing with when she crossed Victoria Gillette.

The best way to handle any problem was face to face. That's what daddy always said. Well, Miss Editor would get the whole picture by the time Victoria was done with her. Full of self-confidence, she parked the car and sashayed into the newspaper office.

"Miss Gillette, what brings you to the Press this morning?" Millie asked.

"I'm here to speak with the editor." Victoria's voice held enough frost to cool the room.

"Is there something I can help you with?"

"No, it's, like, personal."

Millie tapped on the door of Olivia's office. "Victoria Gillette is here to see you."

"Send her in." Olivia rose to greet her visitor. "Please sit down and tell me how I may help you."

Victoria bristled and shoved her sun glasses to the top of her head. "I'm going to help you. I'm going to keep you from embarrassing yourself."

"I see." Olivia walked behind her desk and sat down.

"I don't think you do. I've heard you've been seeing Mitch James. I mean, like, he's taken, just so you know. Like, we're practically engaged. Don't even think about getting involved with him. He's strictly off-limits."

"Miss Gillette, I…"

"Don't try to talk your way out of it. I know what you're up to. Like you think you can sneak off out of town to spend time with him. You can't get away with it. My spies tell me everything, so there's no point in lying."

Olivia sat quietly and listened to the attractive, but childish, Victoria Gillette spout utter nonsense.

Victoria put her hands on her hips and stared at Olivia.

"Well, don't you have anything to say? I guess not. Like, even you know when you're outclassed."

"It's obvious you've put some thought into this. I certainly will take your comments under advisement."

"Good, I'm glad we understand each other. Mitch James is not available." Victoria stressed every word. She didn't speak to Millie as she swept through the reception area, pulled her sunglasses down to cover her eyes, and went out the front door. Victoria felt satisfied she'd gotten her point across.

"Do I want to know what that's about?" Millie asked after Victoria left the office.

"Miss Gillette had a personal problem. I'm not sure I helped her solve it. We'll see."

"Someone should solve her clothing problem. I couldn't

believe that outfit she had on. She looked as if she were dressing for a costume party."

Olivia failed in the attempt to hold back a laugh, "It did demonstrate her own personal statement."

FOURTEEN

Mitch stopped by after office hours, or called Olivia every spare moment he had. They went to movies, out for a quick dinner or simply sat on the Anderson porch and talked. He made sure she understood he intended to become a permanent presence in her life.

When Olivia questioned his involvement with Victoria, Mitch assured her the relationship existed only in Victoria's head, a young girl's fantasy.

"She's spoiled, self-centered, and the only reason I've ever tolerated her was because of Judge Gillette's on-going fundraising efforts on behalf of the free clinic. The entire operation depends on contributions."

Olivia hoped that proved to be true. Still, Victoria seemed quite adamant about the future she had planned with the doctor. Olivia tried to escape the veil of doubt and the nagging feeling that hid in the corner of her mind.

***

The annual Fourth of July celebration had always been a big event in Rexford. This year, sponsorship from the Press made the event more spectacular than ever. Flags hung proudly from light poles in the business district. The exploding of fire crackers could be heard echoing across town. The parade began at the high school, wound through town and ended at the cemetery where military graves were decorated with red, white and blue carnations. After dark, fireworks were set off at the park, lighting the sky with a brilliant display. Mitch found Etta and Olivia in the crowd.

"I hoped you two would be here. What a show," he said.

"It gets better every year. Olivia solicited the merchants to obtain funds and then printed a list of donor's names in the paper," Etta told him.

"Publicity helps," Olivia agreed. "Next year I'm thinking of a children's parade in the afternoon and maybe provide hot dogs and ice cream at the swimming pool afterward. I didn't have time to organize anything this year. The Press will sponsor the activities."

"I'm impressed. Sounds like you are keeping the town involved with its citizens. Did you and Etta walk here?"

"We did. We both needed the exercise."

"That's good," he laughed, "because I parked my Jeep in your driveway. I'll walk you home."

"Mitch James, that's a sneaky way of coming in for a piece of my pecan pie," Etta said.

"My very favorite."

As they made their way through the crowd and headed toward the sidewalk, a voice called out.

"Mitch, Mitch darling. I've been looking for you. Weren't the fireworks incredible?"

As he turned, Victoria Gillette wrapped her arms around his neck and brashly kissed him on the lips. She caught Mitch off guard but he managed to gently push her away.

"Quite impressive," he said.

Victoria wore a cropped tank top and low-riding shorts that clung to her shapely body. A red, white and blue scarf tied her long blonde hair into a pony-tail. Too much make-up masked her pretty face.

"I'm having an 'after fireworks' party," she cooed. "You simply have to come."

"Victoria, you know Mrs. Anderson and this is her niece, Olivia," Mitch said.

"We've met," she directed her comments to Olivia. "You're both welcome, of course." A definite chill punctuated the invitation.

"Thank you, child, but I'm afraid I'm not feeling well. Dr. James has agreed to escort me home. Maybe another time," Etta said.

"Ooh, sorry, Mrs. Anderson. Mitch, I'll call you later," Victoria planted a kiss on his cheek before she left.

"Aunt Etta, that was outrageous," Olivia reprimanded.

"I thought it was one of her better performances," Mitch laughed. "Good save, Etta."

"You're both hopeless."

Etta and Mitch carried on the banter, much to Olivia's amusement. By the time they reached the house, the three of them were near hysterics.

"Etta, I'm ready for that pie. Hope you have some whipped cream."

"I'll make some, not that store bought-stuff either," Etta replied.

Olivia poured freshly brewed coffee in a frosted, ice-filled glasses, dished out the pie and served everything on the porch.

Etta finished eating. "It's been a long day and I'm tired. You two have a nice evening." She went inside before Olivia could respond.

Mitch set his plate on the wicker end table and joined Olivia on the porch swing. "I'm crazy about you. I hope you understand how I feel. You're on my mind day and night."

"You don't know me."

"It's not my fault. I'm trying."

"I believe you have too many irons in the fire."

"What do you mean?"

"Victoria Gillette." Olivia didn't mention Victoria's visit to the Press, but she couldn't keep their conversation from crowding her mind.

"Ahh," he rubbed his palm over his jaw. "There's not much I can do about her for now. However, if we were to be seen together on a regular basis, she'd get the message."

Olivia glared at him. "I'll not be your excuse. If you don't want to see her, tell her."

"I wish it were that simple. Victoria is infatuated with me. She shows up at the office with home-cooked meals, and brings cookies for the children to the Saturday clinics. I don't want to be rude to her."

"But you'd rather be rude to me."

"Whoa, you're not making this easy."

"I'm not."

"We could elope and put an end to her crush once and for all."

"Be serious."

"You could move in with me and then Victoria could bring dinner for three."

Olivia picked up the cushion from the swing and jammed it in his face. "I should tell you that I'm not going to see you again until you get this sorted out."

"But?"

"I don't know. Maybe I'm afraid you won't take me back to Jolt's or to The Country Pub."

"What a letdown. It's not me that holds your interest, it's the food." His beeper interrupted their conversation. He took it from his pocket and stood under the porch light to read the caller's number. He didn't want to tell Olivia the call came from the Gillette house. He wrestled with the idea of not answering, but what if the judge had a medical emergency? Mitch treated Judge Gillette for high blood pressure. He pondered his decision when Olivia interrupted.

"Want to use the phone?"

"No, I'd better go." He kissed her quickly. "Umm you taste good." He grinned and then took her in his arms and kissed her again, this time with added passion. "I'll call you tomorrow."

FIFTEEN

Mitch maneuvered his Jeep into the only available parking space near the Gillette residence, grabbed his medical bag and squeezed his way between the cars in the driveway. Lights blazed from every window of the house, and the front door stood ajar. Loud music drowned out the sound of his knocking and he impatiently rang the doorbell. When no one answered, he walked inside and called for the judge.

"Oh there you are," Victoria purred. "You're just in time. The party's in full swing."

"Where's the judge? Is he okay?"

"Dad's fine," her words slurred. "He and mom are out of town for the week-end."

"Victoria, you're drunk."

"Not really," she giggled. "Just relaxed." She draped her arms around his neck. "I've been waiting all evening for you."

Mitch removed her arms and stepped back. "You called my beeper. I gave that number to the judge to use in case of an emergency."

"It is an emergency. Like, I knew you needed an excuse to escape the stuffy Andersons. Come on, you'll have much more fun here."

Mitch's eyes blazed. "I have no intention of staying. We need to talk and you, young lady, need some coffee."

"Of course, sweetie. Come on out to the patio."

"You're not listening, Victoria. You cannot call me on my beeper."

She grabbed his arm and dragged him outside where a group of young people gathered at the patio area. Some danced, a few were in the swimming pool, while others sat in lounge chairs.

"At least have one drink to celebrate the Fourth." Victoria handed him a flute of champagne from a tray on the outside bar.

Mitch sat the glass down and turned to leave when he noticed a young girl sitting in a large wicker chair, her head tilted at an awkward angle.

"Who's that?" he asked. "I don't recognize her."

"Billy Zelman's cousin. She's visiting from Detroit."

Mitch walked over and touched the girl's shoulder. She slumped to the side.

"My God, Victoria, how long has she been sitting here?"

"I don't know. I guess I didn't notice."

"Do you know her name?" Mitch asked as he shook the girl. He could not get a response.

"Sally or Sandy, I think. I'm not sure."

Mitch, aware of her noisy breathing, grabbed the stethoscope from his bag. Her heart beat was steady but slow. He wrapped the BP cuff around the girl's arm. Her pulse was low and the respiration rate, slow and labored. Her skin felt cool and clammy. He pinched her earlobe between his thumb nail and index finger. She squirmed and pulled away. The young girl presented serious symptoms of alcohol poisoning.

"She's in trouble. Call the Rexford Fire Department and ask for emergency services."

Victoria stared at him.

"Move, Victoria. Call them now and tell them to send an ambulance. Then turn off the music and get Billy over here."

Victoria paled, snapped off the stereo and picked up the phone.

Mitch shouted over the noise, "The party's over, everyone out."

The crowd grumbled and murmured but the look on Mitch's face let them know he was dead serious.

He lifted the limp girl from the chair and turned her on her side on the floor. An empty vodka bottle dislodged from the cushion and rattled across the patio tiles.

Billy Zelman came up to Victoria and put his hand on her shoulder, "What's going on?"

She began to explain when sirens announced the arrival of the EMT unit. One of the departing guests directed them to the patio.

"What do you have here, Doc?" One of the EMT's asked.

"It looks like alcohol poisoning."

The EMT's checked the girl's vitals, hooked her to an IV and loaded her onto a gurney.

"Take her to Lima General," Mitch ordered. "Use the respirator if necessary, but watch that vomit doesn't block her airway. I'll call Lima General ER to alert them, and then follow you there." Then he turned to Victoria. "Young lady, you make sure everyone leaves this house. I know how upset your family will be when they hear about this incident."

Victoria lowered her head and put her hands over her ears. "You can't tell mom and dad what happened here."

"You can be damn certain I will if you don't. You're responsible for what goes on in the house when your parents are away." The angry tone of Mitch's voice left no doubt that he meant business.

Victoria sobered immediately. "Please, I'll take care of things. This has been a terrible accident."

Mitch shook his head as he left the house and headed for his Jeep. He sped to the hospital followed closely by Billy Zelman.

SIXTEEN

When Mitch questioned Billy at the hospital, the young man admitted it had been a mistake to take Sandra to Victoria's party, adding that he told his cousin not to drink anything but soda.

Mitch was in no mood for Billy's lame excuse. "You take a teen-age girl to a party where alcoholic drinks are available and you honestly believe she'll abstain? What were you thinking? It's a good thing drugs weren't passed around."

Billy looked toward the floor, his face flushed.

"Wait a minute, did Sandra use drugs too? I need to know."

"I, ah, I don't think so. No, I'm sure she didn't hang around the group that—well, you know, smoked dope."

"Damn, don't you realize how dangerous it is to combine alcohol and dope?" Mitch started to give Billy a lecture on responsibility but decided it wouldn't do any good. He'd rather let the families sort it out. Furious didn't begin to describe his feeling for Victoria for allowing Sandra Zelman to get in that condition. The girl would recover, but remained at the hospital for observation.

Now Mitch could concentrate on his relationship with Olivia. He realized this no-nonsense lady meant what she said, when she told him to get his affairs in order. He had to make sure he told her about the fiasco at the Gillette house before she found out from anyone else.

By the time Mitch returned to Rexford, it was too late to call Olivia. First thing in the morning, he'd make rounds at the hospital and check on the Zelman girl. As soon as he had the opportunity, he'd phone Olivia and explain what had happened. That thought weighed on his mind as he collapsed into sleep.

Millie contacted Olivia first, catching her before she left for the office. "We had a scandal in town last night," she said when Olivia answered the phone.

Olivia grabbed a pencil and paper. "What happened?"

Millie filled her in on the events that took place at the Gillette residence. "My source told me the judge and his wife went out of town for the week-end and Victoria had twenty to thirty guests at her party. It's a good thing Victoria's date, Dr. James, was there. He saved the Zelman girl."

Olivia dropped her pencil. "Did you say last night?"

"After the fourth of July fireworks display."

"I see. Is your source reliable?"

"My brother-in-law called first thing this morning to give me a report. He rode with the EMT's over the holiday. How do you want to handle it?"

"Let me give it some thought."

"We should try to get pictures—maybe of the girl or at least Billy Zelman. Billy played on the Rexford High School basketball team several years ago. I'm sure we have his photo on file. I could send Julius to interview Dr. James."

"Let's hold off on that for now."

"This is big, Olivia. When Judge Gillette served on the bench, he came down hard on underage drinking. To have this type of incident occur at his home is unbelievable."

"If he wasn't home, I don't see how we can hold him responsible."

"But he's a judge. That's all the more reason to make an example. I don't think we should handle it any differently than we would for any other citizen. I can put a feeler out and see who else attended the party. I'm certain someone would like to get their name in print. We'll get the facts straight and avoid criticism. Take my word for it, this will rock the town." Millie's exuberance spilled into the phone.

"I'll be at the office in thirty minutes. We'll discuss it then."

"Who called so early?" Etta asked.

Olivia gave her aunt a quick recap of the call, leaving out the part about Mitch being Victoria's date. She couldn't bring herself to repeat that aloud.

"What do you plan to do?"

"Millie wants me to print the facts, complete with pictures."

Lines deepened on Etta forehead. "Be careful you don't bite off more than you can chew."

"Are you suggesting I ignore the story?"

"I'm saying that Judge Gillette is a powerful man in the community. He could cause trouble."

"That may be, but I can't play favorites. If Joe Blow, who lived on the other side of the tracks, had a party that ended with the same results, I'd run the story—unless you don't want me to. It's your call. Grandpa Anderson started the paper and Uncle Fritz made it what it is today."

"And Fritz never backed away from a challenge. My only advice is to verify the facts. It won't hurt to get written confirmations."

By the time Olivia arrived the office, Millie had made calls to people her brother-in-law had recognized at the party. It only took a few conversations to find someone eager to make a statement. Millie was on the phone when Olivia arrived and stood beside her desk. Millie held her finger to her lips as she listened and made notes.

"Thanks, I appreciate your information," Millie said into the phone.

"That call came in from one of the party-goers," she explained to Olivia. "She thought it shameful that Victoria Gillette served alcohol to the Zelman girl. She claims Victoria knew Billy's cousin was underage, but Victoria said, and I quote, "It's the Fourth of July. You should celebrate.""

"Are you kidding? We'll need someone else to confirm that statement. Do you have the names of any other attendees who can verify it?"

"My source gave me a list of twelve other names she could remember. I'll contact them."

While Millie continued to make phone calls, Olivia paced the office and carefully weighed her options. She finally came to a conclusion and walked to the front of her assistant's desk. "Millie, this is how I believe we should handle the situation. If we sensationalize the story, our readers will think we're taking sides. I suggest we put a brief account of what happened on the second page under emergency services where we list speeding tickets, fires, and court cases. We'll simply state the facts. 'Minor treated for alcohol poisoning. The EMT's were called to 1241 Mulberry Street Thursday night to transport a young girl to Lima General Hospital for treatment.'"

"But..."

"Think about it. Everyone knows where Judge Gillette lives. As soon as our customers read the address, we'll receive calls and letters. Then we can print those letters on the editorial page. We'll make our point without being put in the position of defending any bias."

Millie's look indicated she wasn't convinced, but she nodded in agreement. She called Frank and asked him to make a space for the blurb in that afternoon's paper.

Olivia couldn't concentrate. Thoughts of Mitch invaded every part of her mind. It would be impossible to stay at the Press office and face the possibility that he might stop by. She couldn't trust her emotions and definitely didn't want Millie to overhear a conversation she and Mitch might have. She straightened her desk and made a decision. She picked up her purse, closed the office door and walked to the reception area. "Millie, the paper has gone to print, and I'm leaving early. If it's an emergency you can contact me, but I won't be available to answer any other calls." She stopped and turned, "Millie, I'm serious, do not give my cell phone number to anyone no matter what. I'll check in with you later today."

Olivia walked home to get the car. She told Etta about the item they put in the paper. "I won't be home until late. I'd appreciate if you tell no one where I am. I need to do some soul searching."

"That would be difficult since you're not telling me."

"I don't mean to be mysterious but if you don't know, you won't have to lie. I'll call you later."

Olivia had decided to go to Jade's or Robyn's house. Either of them would welcome her without question. Then she realized it would be more discreet to get out of town, where Etta's car wouldn't be recognized. She hugged her aunt. "Don't worry about me. I need some time to think." Olivia took the car and drove to Millsburg, hoping to find Kristen at home.

SEVENTEEN

Kristen Beckford's small brick and stone residence, located in an older section of Millburg, sat back from the street on an oversized lot filled with shade and fruit trees. It didn't surprise Olivia to find window boxes filled with herbs and beds of flowers rimmed by natural round stones placed on the manicured grounds. She gave a light tap on the door and Kristen met her with a warm smile.

"Olivia. This is a pleasant surprise."

"Sorry for not calling first, but I had to get away. I hope I'm not disturbing you."

"Of course not. Come on in. You're so pale. Are you ill?"

"Sick at heart, would be a better description."

"Let's go to the kitchen, I'll brew a pot of tea. On second thought, maybe you could use something a little stronger." Kristen led the way and pulled a chair from the table for Olivia. She filled large glasses with orange juice and laced them with a healthy shot of vodka.

"That's exactly what I need."

"Want to talk about it?"

"No...yes. I guess I do." Olivia told Kristen about Mitch and Victoria. "He told me he wanted to date me. He said we should be a couple and all the time he planned to slip off and go to a party at the Gillette's."

Olivia told her story while Kristen spread crackers with brie and arranged a plate with fresh fruit, set it on the table and refilled the wine glasses.

"Have you given him an opportunity to explain?"

"What could he possibly say?"

"You won't know unless you give him the chance. There could be a logical explanation."

Olivia couldn't contain the tears. "I don't think I can stand the lies." She told the short story of her experience in New York, "I seem to have the ability to attract that kind of man."

"I don't know Dr. James, but I'm sure there's another side to the story."

"You're such an optimist. May I ask you a personal question?"

"Of course."

"I noticed a slight drawl in your voice. I suspect you're not from around here. What brought you to a small town in Ohio?"

"Much the same as you, a broken engagement."

"But you don't have family here, do you?"

"No one."

Olivia started to inquire further, but not wanting to pry, changed the subject. "I love your house. The colors are warm and inviting. Did you decorate it?"

"I did. It was my first attempt at tackling this kind of project. I had plenty of time, limited funds, and I wanted a quiet and comfortable place to live.

"I fell in love with the house the moment I saw it at an estate sale. It's one of the original homes in Millsburg. It's built well structurally, but the interior needed major repair. The rooms were small and dark. To allow more light inside the house, I removed the wall between the kitchen and dining room, creating a bar and eating nook. It opened the space and made a better traffic pattern. I've learned to be a painter, carpenter and plumber. I couldn't afford to hire the work done on the salary I earn as a teacher, but the owners of the local hardware store have been a great help."

"Even your furniture is unique."

"Some of it was left with the house and the rest were garage sale finds. It's amazing what you can do with elbow grease, a little imagination and a sewing machine."

They talked the rest of the afternoon. Finally, Kristen suggested they prepare dinner. "Why don't you stay the night? Things might look better in the morning."

"You wouldn't mind?"

"I insist. I'd love the company. Call your aunt and let her know where you are. I'll prepare pasta and a salad."

Kristen's easy manner calmed Olivia. She called Aunt Etta and told her she was spending the night with a friend and would see her in the morning.

"Why don't you switch the phone to the recorder, I don't want you to be bothered by calls regarding the item in the newspaper."

"I've already done that. I picked up when I heard your voice. If you're okay, I believe I'll turn the ringer off for the night," Etta told her.

"That's a good idea. I'm fine. I simply needed to get away. See you tomorrow."

The Press would be closed for the week-end. Olivia didn't need to hurry back to Rexford. Relieved that her aunt didn't ask questions, she placed the second call to Millie's private line.

"I hoped I'd catch you before you left the office. How are things going?"

"A few hours ago I let the answering machine handle the phones and I locked the front door. We've been inundated with calls. You were right. We received the reaction you predicted."

"I see."

"The consensus is that we should have named names. I suggested that they put their thoughts in writing and mail them to the editor or put them in our mail slot at the office. Some wanted their names withheld and others said they would be happy to sign.

"Secondly, Dr. James called three times. He became quite upset when I wouldn't tell him where you were. Am I missing something here, Olivia?"

"I'm sure he didn't want to see his name in print. Don't worry about him. Did you hear from the Gillette's?"

"Victoria hasn't phoned, but she probably doesn't read the Press. Judge and Mrs. Gillette are still out of town, according to my sources. I don't expect the judge will contact us until Monday morning."

"I can hardly wait. Go on home and have a good weekend, Millie. I'll see you Monday."

Olivia returned to the kitchen to help Kristen with dinner. Kristen had the table set with fine china and lit scented candles. She filled crystal goblets with red wine. Olivia couldn't help but notice the disparity in Kristen's lifestyle. Her friend lived in the smallest of towns, worked as a teacher in a community where the pay had to be minimal and bought an old and probably inexpensive home. She had excellent taste and exhibited an air of class that seemed to come naturally. It became obvious that at some point in time, Kristen Beckford had been exposed to the finer things in life.

After dinner, they carried their wine out to the back patio. Kristen lit citronella candles and they sat in wicker chairs overlooking a small lily pond. And talked.

"I'm supposed to be in charge of the Press and I can't even control my life," Olivia said.

"We all feel that way at times. I'm so afraid I'll do or say something dumb in my classroom. High school students pick up on everything. I must watch every word or I'll hear from the parents or worse, the school board."

"How is it teaching teen-agers?"

"Scary. They're so smart and perceptive. Some of them have an uncanny ability to pick up on my moods and make the most of it if I'm having a difficult day.

"The gossip in school is terrible. When an older male teacher took a newly widowed lady for coffee it became the topic of conversation for months. I felt sorry for both of them. I know they still see each other, but now they meet in another community."

"I find gossip and innuendoes in all small towns. Everyone knows someone who knows something, true or not. We must check everything we print in the Press. We hear immediately if we make a mistake."

"Look at the time. Olivia, you must be exhausted." Kristen led her to the guest bedroom. "There's a nightgown in the top dresser drawer. If you need anything, call me. I'll see you in the morning. Sleep well, Olivia. Tomorrow may give you a new prospective."

EIGHTEEN

Victoria Gillette woke fully clothed, sprawled sideways across the bed. She squinted and tried to focus on the clock. The red numbers showed three-fifteen. She lifted her head and quickly closed her eyes as the room seemed to spin in a sickening motion. Again, she attempted to peer around the room to determine if it was morning or afternoon. Slits of light invaded the space around the edge of the drapes and pierced her eyes like razor blades. Afternoon, she had been out for over twelve hours.

When she moved, an empty champagne bottle fell from the bed and clattered to the floor. Another lay on its side near the edge of the nightstand. "I must have finished the rest of the opened bottles. I can't believe how horrendous I feel." The words slammed loudly in her head.

With great care, she moved to the side of the bed and tried to sit up. The floor rolled like waves in the ocean. Victoria felt sure she would barf. It took all of her effort to walk to the bathroom.

"Where are the damn aspirins?" Brushing aside the cosmetics and creams from the medicine cabinet shelves, she grabbed the bottle, and ignored anything that fell into the sink or bounced down to the floor.

As Victoria filled a glass with water, she caught her likeness in the mirror. Dark circles hung under reddened eyes and matted blonde hair pressed close to the side of her head reflected back an image of a lopsided cartoon character. She held a cold, wet washcloth to her face and fought the bile that bubbled in her throat.

"God, I'm sick, sweaty and my shirt reeks of cigarette smoke or worse." She stripped off her clothes, kicked them into a corner and stepped into the shower only to have the throbbing pain in her head magnified by hot pulsating water.

She stepped out of the shower, wrapped her hair in a towel and grabbed her bathrobe. Gingerly, she walked to the kitchen.

"What a hangover. My mouth feels like sandpaper, my eyes burn and I feel like shit. What the hell do we have in the fridge? Tomato juice, maybe eggs?" The thought of food made her nausea surface again. She settled for ginger ale in an ice filled glass and grabbed a handful of crackers to nibble on. It didn't settle her stomach.

She carried the drink into the living room, picked up a magazine from the coffee table and eased herself down into a chair. She tried to forget the piercing pain on the side of her head—and Mitch. Damn him. She'd never forgive him for the way he yelled and embarrassed her in front of everyone, and then had the nerve to make her friends leave the party...her Fourth of July party. She felt totally pissed at the way he ordered her around like a child, all because that little twit, Sally or Sandy or whatever the hell her name, couldn't hold her liquor.

She'd get even with Billy too. He didn't need to bring his snippy little cousin along. Like, couldn't he get a date? Maybe he should place an ad in the Press.

Oh God, the Press. She forgot the pain for a moment and rushed to get the paper from the front porch.

The delivery boy missed again. She swore and went to retrieve the paper from the driveway, hoping no one had their eyes turned toward the Gillette house. Once back inside, she tossed the rubber band on the table and opened the Friday afternoon edition. She expected to see the events of her party splashed across the front page. Satisfied that the Press didn't bother to print anything about the small incident, she gave a sigh of relief and stuffed the paper in the magazine rack. By the time next week's edition came out, her party would be old news.

At least Daddy wouldn't find out right away. She'd mention it to him in passing, saying something like, "A couple of the guests drank to excess before they arrived. Outraged by their lack of manners, I told them to leave. What else could I do?" She'd pout and then snuggle up to Daddy and he would agree she behaved properly.

She couldn't help but smirk. "If Daddy knew about the other things that went on around the house, I'd really have something to worry about." She remembered how Brittney stripped and jumped into the pool and one of the gang passed pot around, and Lord only knew what Mark and Sherrie were up to in the bathhouse.

Victoria rubbed her temples and walked to the patio to look around. Everything looked neat and orderly. *Yeah, Carla had been there, thank God. It's a good thing she came this morning. I'm sure as hell not up to cleaning the mess.*

She saw no point in suffering any longer. She turned the ringer off on the telephone, found her mother's codeine capsules and escaped to the comfort of her bed. *If anything unpleasant comes out of this, I'm sure Daddy will handle it.* Victoria relaxed as the pills began to work. *He always does.*

NINETEEN

When the sun beamed through the window early Saturday morning, it took Olivia a few minutes to realize she had stayed with Kristen Friday night. Olivia had today and tomorrow before she had to address whatever wrath Judge Gillette and some of the Rexford's residents planned to vent on the Press and its editor.

And Mitch. Sooner or later she'd have to face him and address their situation. The thought of it made her ill. How could she have allowed herself to believe him and his lies? She had stayed away long enough. It was time to return to Rexford and check on Aunt Etta. Olivia dressed, thanked Kristen for her hospitality, and drove back home.

Etta sat on the porch holding a coffee cup when Olivia drove onto the driveway.

"You missed Mitch," she told her niece. "He came by bright and early asking for you."

"I spent the night with Kristen. She owns a lovely old house in Millsburg, and has completely redecorated it herself."

"You're avoiding the subject. What did Mitch have to do with the party at the Gillette's and your heading out of town?"

"I might as well tell you." Olivia sighed as she sat next to her aunt. "You'll not be satisfied until I do. Mitch received a so-called emergency call while we were sitting on the porch after the Fourth of July fireworks. It was simply a ploy to go to the

Gillette house for a late night date with Victoria. Remember, she invited him to a party and said she would call him later."

"Livie, that's only hear-say. You should listen to his side of the story."

"Don't try to stand up for him. I don't trust him any more than Brian."

"Well, I'm sure he'll be back tonight. He seemed honestly distressed."

Olivia's immediate reaction was to find someplace else to go, maybe leave town for the rest of the weekend. No, she wouldn't hide from Mitch. Better to get it out in the open and deal with it once and for all.

"If you make a list, I'll get groceries."

"I'm betting you won't want to go to the store today. Everyone you meet will question you about the statement in the Press and Victoria's party."

Olivia shook her head. "You're right. I'd rather put that off until later. Would you like to go for a drive? We could pack a picnic."

"Some other time, Livie. I didn't sleep well last night. I believe I'll lie down for a while." Aunt Etta set her cup down and went into the house. She seemed unsteady as she walked down the hallway toward the master bedroom. Olivia started to say something but thought better of it. She took Etta's cup to the kitchen and noticed the telephone recorder light blinking furiously. *Might as well get this over with.* She sat at the table with a pad and pencil and listened to the messages.

1. "Olivia, It's Mitch. Please call me."

2. "The newspaper is responsible for reporting all the news. The Gillette's had a drunken party and an underage girl landed in the hospital. You shouldn't cover up the truth because he's a judge."

3. "Olivia, Where are you? I need to talk to you. Call me on my cell phone." Mitch's voice shook her reserve.

4. Again Mitch, "Olivia, please call me as soon as you get this message. It's noon on Friday."

5. "It's irresponsible for your newspaper to publish that trash about the Gillette's. It's just like the Press to take pot-shots at one of our leading citizens."

7. Another message from Mitch, "Olivia, I've just read the paper. It's five o'clock Friday. Please, please call me."

8. "Like you didn't know the address the EMT's were called to was Judge Gillette's residence. You should have printed all the facts, not reduce them to a blurb on the back page."

9. "Olivia, where are you? It's important that I talk to you," Mitch's voice rang of panic.

Olivia erased the rest of the messages and went to her room. She decided to keep busy and catch up on the laundry. At noon, she peeked in on Aunt Etta. "Want some lunch?"

"I don't think so, Livie. I'm feeling a bit queasy."

Olivia walked over toward the bed. "Maybe a cup of soup and toast or I could soft boil an egg."

"I think you better call Mitch."

A sickening feeling clogged Olivia's throat. She put any personal feelings she harbored about Dr. James aside and rushed to the phone. Aunt Etta didn't complain. For her to ask for Mitch meant she had a serious problem. Mitch might still be at the free clinic. She didn't have that number. She dialed his cell phone number.

"Dr. James."

"Mitch, it's Olivia. Aunt Etta's ill. She asked me to call."

"Where is she?"

"In her room, in bed."

"No point in calling the ambulance, she won't go on her own. I'm finished here and should be there in a few minutes. Remember the pills for her heart I gave her when you first came to town?"

"Yes."

"Give her one of them and try to get her to drink a full glass of water with it. I'm on my way." He hung up before she had a chance to say thanks.

Olivia found the pill bottle in the medicine cabinet and brought one of them in to her aunt. "Mitch said to take this. He'll be here shortly."

Mitch James burst in the front door when he arrived at the Anderson house, went directly to Etta's room and sat down on the side of the bed. "Feeling a little puny?" he asked as he sat down on the side of the bed to examine her.

"Dizzy—short of breath," she gasped.

He listened to her heart and took her pulse. "We can't ignore it this time," he told her. "You're going to the hospital."

Olivia expected an argument but her aunt sunk deeper into the pillow. Mitch went to the kitchen and phoned for an ambulance, then called the heart specialist, Dr. Henry Walters, to meet them at Lima General. Like a newsreel running too fast, the EMT's arrived, attached oxygen and an IV to Etta and loaded her into the ambulance. Mitch raced to his Jeep and followed behind. Olivia grabbed her purse, closed the house and took the car. Worry caused her heart to ache. Olivia felt responsible. Tear flooded her eyes as she sped to the hospital.

By the time Olivia arrived, Etta had been admitted into the hospital's intensive care unit. Hours passed before Olivia could see her. She paced the floor in the waiting room until Mitch finally found her.

"Etta had a heart attack. She's weak and the next few hours will tell us how much damage she suffered."

Olivia collapsed in his arms. "It's my fault. I shouldn't have stayed with Kristen last night. I should have been home with her."

"That's nonsense. Etta has been living with this for years. There's nothing you could have done. You can see her for a few minutes but she probably won't know you're here. Dr. Walters has her sedated."

Olivia was hesitant as she entered the room. Aunt Etta appeared small and vulnerable, hooked to lines, tangled wires and beeping equipment. Mitch crossed his arms, leaned on the doorframe and waited until Olivia looked up.

"I have to return to Rexford to check on a patient. Are you going to be okay?" he asked.

"I'll be fine."

"I have to talk to you."

"Not now. I can't think about anything but Aunt Etta." Distress covered her face.

Mitch sucked in his breath. There was so much he wanted to tell her, so much to explain. He nodded and checked his watch. "I have to go."

Olivia didn't acknowledge him. She felt overcome with guilt. She stayed a few minutes longer before she left the room and stopped at the nurse's station. "I'm going for coffee. I'll be back in a few minutes."

"Miss McDougle, please take as much time as you want. Mrs. Anderson is under heavy sedation. There is nothing you can do for her.

"But…"

"Don't worry. We'll keep a close eye on her."

TWENTY

Olivia remained at the hospital all day Saturday and whatever time the floor nurse would allow, she spent in ICU, sitting quietly next to Etta's bed. Anxiety became Olivia's companion, exhaustion her adversary.

By the time the night shift nurse came on duty, Olivia felt the raw edge of nerves. "Try to get some rest, Miss McDougle." The nurse placed a pillow and blanket on the couch in the waiting room.

Olivia attempted to stretch out on the sofa, trying to find a comfortable position on the small space; sure she would never be able to fall asleep.

Mitch found her there when he arrived late Sunday morning. He observed Olivia for a long time before he sat on the edge of the couch and took her hand.

Olivia blinked her eyes and looked up at him. "Don't you get enough of hospitals and patients six days a week?"

"Etta's my friend as well as a patient. Besides, I had to make sure you were taking care of yourself."

"Me?" She sat up and rolled her shoulders to relieve the stiffness.

"From what people were saying at the Rexford diner this morning, your paper caused a firestorm."

"I completely forgot about that. I must go to the office tomorrow. Millie will be swamped."

"About that incident, I need to explain."

"Not necessary." Olivia turned away.

"There you go again, dismissing me." He grabbed hold of her shoulders and made direct eye contact. "I'm not leaving until you hear me out. Victoria beeped me when you and I were sitting on the porch. When I saw the number, I hesitated, not sure what I should do. But then I remembered Judge Gillette's medical problems and decided I needed to see him. Of course, he wasn't home. The call was a ploy of Victoria's to get me to her party. As it turned out, it was a good thing I went. Sandra Zelman might have died if she hadn't been treated immediately."

"But you didn't tell me."

Mitch released his hold. When Olivia didn't pull away, a look of relief swept over his face. "And what would you have done? You're reaction would have been the same." Mitch could see the hurt in Olivia's eyes and soften his words. "Sweetheart, I made a mistake in judgment. I should have made the call from your house, but I felt we were beginning to connect with each other and I didn't want to spoil things. But if I wouldn't have gone, and the judge had serious medical problems, then what?"

Olivia felt her spine stiffen. "Don't put this back on me."

"Olivia, I don't want to put anything on you but my lips."

"You always take the easy way out. If you can't be honest with me, we have nothing."

Mitch grimaced and rubbed his hand across his chin. "Honey, I know I'm making light of the situation, but I didn't mean to hurt you. I'm sorry. I don't know what else I can say except I'm crazy about you."

"This isn't the place."

"It is when you're here. I want you to know that I'm serious about you and our relationship."

"We have no…"

"We will have a relationship, a long and loving one. Now, go see your aunt and then I'll take you to lunch."

Olivia shook her head. Mitch had a way of turning things around. "I need to splash some water on my face." As she walked to the ladies room she realized how much she needed him. He gave her strength. But that nagging question nettled her. Could she trust him?

When Olivia returned to the ICU, she found Mitch sitting next to Etta's bed. They changed places and the movement caused Etta to blink open her eyes, only to close them again. Mitch stood behind Olivia for a few moments before he left the room to allow Olivia have time alone with her aunt.

Olivia held Etta's hand, dismayed at how fragile her aunt appeared. Olivia prayed she would recover. After a time, she kissed her aunt on the cheek and went to the waiting room to meet Mitch.

"Do you think it's safe to leave?" she asked.

"I think it's mandatory. There's a place a few blocks from the hospital that has excellent food. If there's an emergency, the nurse will beep me. I can get the car."

Olivia stretched her shoulders. "That couch was a killer, let's walk."

"I hoped you'd say that." He took her hand as they made their way out of the hospital and down the street. Mitch led them to a side alley.

"This isn't another one of your chicken fried steak places, is it?"

"No, but they have the best Chinese food in Lima."

"That sounds good," she said.

They entered a small restaurant that offered only three tables.

"Dr. James. Good to see you and with a pretty lady. Come sit." An ageless oriental man held the chair for Olivia.

"Are there menus?" she whispered when the owner went to the kitchen.

"No," Mitch laughed. "Mr. Wong will bring us what he feels we'll like."

Olivia gave Mitch a suspicious look. "Do you know every quirky eatery in Ohio?"

"Aah, a bachelor's life. What can I say?"

Olivia had to admit the food tasted delicious. It amused her to see the way Mitch teased Mr. Wong, and how the two of them kept the banter going throughout the meal. The restaurant owner beamed with the attention. After the meal, Mitch left a generous tip and he and Olivia returned to the hospital.

Dr. Walters stood at the nurse's station, going over Etta's charts when Mitch and Olivia stepped off the elevator. "Dr. James, Miss McDougle, I'm happy to tell you Mrs. Anderson has improved. I expect her to recover." Dr. Walters gave Mitch the latest test results. "She still has a long way to go, but we're going to give her excellent care."

"Thank God. I've been so worried," Olivia said.

"You can sit with her, but don't wear her out. It's better if she gets as much rest as possible."

Olivia went into Etta's room while the two doctors conferred.

TWENTY-ONE

Mitch talked Olivia into leaving the hospital early Sunday evening. "Etta's in good hands. There is nothing you can do here but watch her sleep," he explained.

"What if she calls for me?"

"I left word with the ICU nurse to beep me if there's any change in her condition and I'll phone you immediately." He led her to the parking lot and waited until she started the car before he got into his Jeep and followed her back to Rexford.

Olivia pulled into the garage, stepped out of her car and found Mitch had parked in the driveway. He stood at her side before she could push the button that closed the garage door. His closeness prompted a smile to cross her worried face.

"I'm over twenty-one. I don't need a babysitter."

"Baby, I'll sit with you anytime."

"You might as well come in and have a nightcap. I believe we have a decent bottle of brandy in the cabinet."

"Make mine coffee. I should go over some medical records later."

"Coffee's good." Olivia set two mugs on the kitchen table and started the coffee maker. She dropped to a chair while she waited for the brown liquid to fill the glass container.

Mitch stood behind her and massaged her shoulders. "You're exhausted. I should go and let you get some sleep."

"You should, but I wish you wouldn't. I don't want to be

alone. I'm so worried about Aunt Etta. She's been a mother to me. My parents were in their forty's when I was born. Etta was my mother's older sister. She'll be seventy-six this year. She and Uncle Fritz took me in when my parents were killed in an automobile accident. It couldn't have been easy for them to raise a young child, but they were completely dedicated to me."

Mitch walked in front of her chair and pulled her up into his arms. "I'm completely dedicated to you, Olivia. Thoughts of you wrap around my heart and keep me awake at night." He kissed her greedily and plunged his tongue into her inviting mouth. "My God, I love you. Olivia, I love you. Don't you feel the connection?"

Olivia pushed closer, feeling his warm taut body warm against hers. The heat seared her soul. She wanted to bury herself inside him. She returned his kiss with an ardor that came from deep within.

"Stay with me, hold me," her soft voice words caused an explosion in his heart. He lifted her into his arms and effortlessly carried her to her room. Before he set her on the bed he said, "I need to know you're sure. This has to be for both of us."

She unbuttoned her blouse and reached for his shirt to do the same for him. Delight danced in his eyes as he finished undressing. Their clothes dropped in a rumpled heap beside the bed.

Mitch lay beside her, caressing her breasts, kissing her neck. "You're amazing, Oliva. I love you." He brushed her hair back from her face, and kissed her lightly, softly. "I want to spend the rest of my life with you. I want a house and a family."

"Mmmm." Olivia's pressed her body close to him, lost in the thought of new love, perfect love.

"I can't get enough of you." He buried his face in her hair and whispered, "I was sick with worry when you left Friday before I had the chance to tell you about the fiasco at Victoria Gillette's party. When you didn't answer your phone, I didn't know where to look, where to go. Olivia, I love you. I'm so sorry I caused you a moment of pain." He could feel her tremble as he embraced her. "We're so right for each other. I knew it from the first day I saw you on Etta's porch."

Slowly, he ran his hand along her inner thigh. Her body arched as he parted her legs and softly aroused her until she moaned with pleasure and obvious desire. He took his time until he felt her body tense. Olivia responded to his touch, and so filled with desire, pulled him to her calling out his name when they came together.

"Sweetheart, you should have told me. I had no idea. I mean I didn't consider—I'm not saying this right, am I? I didn't know I was your first lover. Are you okay?"

"I never imagined—I thought, well never mind. I love you, Mitch James." Olivia laid her head on his chest, listening to the thump of his heart. "There aren't words to express how I feel. It was everything I expected and more."

They lay in each other's arms, each lost in their own thoughts and absolute contentment. Mitch ran his fingers through her hair, reluctant to disturb their happiness.

"Sweetheart, I have to leave. This is a small town and people will talk if they see my Jeep parked in your driveway so late."

She knew that was true but didn't want to let him go. "We'll have to make better plans next time."

"And the next and the next." He sat on the side of the bed and kissed her again before he reached for his clothes. "I'll turn off the coffee and the lights on my way out." He lingered a moment. "You're absolutely fantastic. I'll call you when I get home."

TWENTY-TWO

Early Monday morning the sound of a ringing telephone shook Olivia into consciousness.

"I wanted to tell you how very much I love you," Mitch said when she answered.

"What an amazing way to start the day."

"I can't wait to take you in my arms again. I can't wait to make love to you."

"Me too."

"I talked to the ICU nurse on duty at Lima General this morning. Etta had a restful night. I'm on my way there now. If there's any change, I'll let you know."

"Thank goodness. Tell her I love her and I'll be there this afternoon."

"I'll do that and call you later. Gotta go."

Olivia sang every love song she could remember as she got ready to go to work. Her face took on a radiant glow. She danced around the kitchen while making breakfast, and felt sure nothing could possibly ruin the love she shared with Mitch. Her feet didn't seem to touch ground as she walked to work and she hummed all the way to the office.

"You're in a good mood today," Millie said. "A few of these phone calls will change that, and wait until you read the mass of letters shoved through the mail slot over the weekend."

"I'll get to that in a minute. I wanted to tell you Aunt Etta had a heart attack Saturday morning. She's at Lima General and is in stable condition. Dr. Walters told me yesterday she's doing better and he expects her to recover. I'm so relieved."

"I'm so sorry to hear that. Can Etta have visitors?"

"Not until she's moved to a regular room. She's still in ICU."

"I couldn't imagine you would be happy about facing this hullabaloo. Just as you predicted, our readers are in an uproar."

"What's the general feeling, pro or con?"

"They're divided. The majority believe Victoria Gillette should be arrested for serving alcohol to a minor. A few have alleged we are picking on her because her father is a judge."

"I feel it's imperative that I address this in my editorial this week. The Press should take a stand."

"I was afraid you'd say that." Millie followed Olivia into her office and set a cup of coffee in front of her along with the bundle of letters.

"How do you have them sorted?"

"I made a list of the phone calls taken from the answering machine and noted those I thought deserved a call back. I pulled out the letters that had something unique to say. The other stack is either obscene or uninteresting. Maybe you should pick out four or five to run in Friday's paper along with your editorial."

"I agree. Let me look over the lot and decide. I'll include the total number of calls and letters in my comments." After a few minutes she called out to Millie. "Some of these are vicious."

"Tell me about it. You should have listened to the calls."

Olivia picked four letters to print in full and took excerpts from several others. Then she started on her column.

"Disasters come in many forms. The tragic, almost fatal incident, at the Gillette house caused us pause.

"Underage drinking has always been a problem. Our young people have no fear of the sad results of overindulging in alcohol. Their youthful minds don't know when to say, "I've had enough." But to have an adult provide liquor to a minor, is against the law and should be addressed. The Press has received over twenty-five phone calls and as many letters. The following is a cross section of letters put in our mail slot over the weekend from concerned citizens." Olivia McDougle.

Then she wrote an article about Etta Anderson.

Millie looked over the editorial. "I think you've been fair. You've included both sides of the issue with the letters. It will be interesting to see the feedback when the paper comes out Friday. You know, Olivia, this could divide the town."

"What are you telling me? Do you think I should back off?"

Millie closed her eyes a moment before speaking. "No. I'm saying definite lines will be drawn across Rexford before this is over. You're bound to make enemies."

"We made our stand and let's hope that's the end of it," Olivia said. "What else do we have to deal with?"

Millie gave her a draft of the news section to read. Olivia made minor changes and announced it was ready for print unless something of significance came in before press time.

After lunch, Olivia prepared to go to Lima to see her aunt. "Call my cell phone if you need me," she said as she left the office. The walk home gave her the opportunity to digest what Millie told her. She shook her head. It couldn't be as bad as her assistant alleged. The whole Gillette incident would be forgotten by the next edition of the Press.

Etta was sitting up in bed when Olivia arrived at the hospital. The lunch tray they served her remained untouched.

"How are you feeling?"

"I'd feel better if they gave me something decent to eat."

Olivia burst out laughing. "That's the Aunt Etta I love. Regardless of how bad it is, the sooner you eat and build up your strength, the sooner you'll be out of here." She sat on the side of the bed and brought spoonfuls of broth to Etta's mouth. Despite protests, Olivia continued until it was finished.

"Want to try the gelatin?"

"No thanks. It looks like rubber, probably tastes like it too."

"I can't say as I blame you on the gelatin. At least drink the juice. Even hospitals can't manage to ruin that."

"Dr. Walters said I'll be moved to a regular room this afternoon. I guess that means I'm going to live after all."

"I never had a doubt, but you gave me a scare."

"You stayed with me. Mitch told me you were in the waiting room."

"Mitch?"

"Every time I opened my eyes, he was sitting in the chair next to my bed. He whispered to me early in the morning that he was going back to Rexford to check his calls and get breakfast."

"I thought he went home Saturday night. He must have slipped in while I was sleeping. I didn't see him until Sunday morning."

"The way he was grinning this morning, I expect you saw him Sunday night too."

"Aunt Etta."

"Now Livie, I may be old, but I'm not dead...yet. I could see Mitch fell in love with you the moment he saw you." She leaned back against the pillow.

"Let's talk about you. Would you like me to bring anything from home, slippers or a robe? Aunt Etta?"

She had fallen asleep. Olivia tucked the sheet around her and quietly left the room.

TWENTY-THREE

Early Monday morning, the ringing phone jarred Henry Gillette out of a deep sleep. Within the hour, the mayor and members of the city council, among others, had contacted him and wanted to know what went on at his house over the holiday weekend. Of course, Judge Gillette wasn't aware of any events that had happened in his absence until he talked to Victoria. He digested bits and pieces of information as news of the party spread like a bad case of poison ivy.

He decided not to leave for the office until he questioned Carla. He met her at the door when she arrived at nine.

"What do you know about this infamous Fourth of July party?"

"Not too much, Judge. When I arrived the next morning, I noticed Victoria had entertained out on the patio. I did my usual cleaning and then left at noon. Victoria hadn't come out of her room so I didn't have a chance to talk to her." Carla didn't mention the empty liquor bottles and some of the other suspicious things she found stuffed in waste cans on the patio.

The judge excused Carla to go on with the housework while he paced the floor, his lanky body rigid with anger. He had no intention of leaving for the office until he heard the full story. Any attempt his wife made to pacify him managed to intensify his agitation.

"Quit fluttering around me. Don't you have an appointment at the beauty salon?"

"I cancelled. I didn't want to leave while you're so upset. I'll have Carla make breakfast."

"I don't need anything to eat, Dorothy. We have a crisis here."

"I'm sure it's not as bad as it seems."

"Not as bad? Have you buried your head in the sand? Certainly even you can see the disaster here. Victoria threw a party and the police were called. God only knows what else happened."

Dorothy ignored his criticism. "Now Henry, don't jump to conclusions. Remember your blood pressure."

"Conclusions? Damn it woman, as soon as I heard about this so called party, I went through the garbage. Plastic bags are stuffed full of empty liquor bottles and beer cans. Carla thought she hid them. I've a good mind to fire her."

"You can't do that. She's been with us for years. Besides, you wouldn't expect her to leave them out in the open for the neighbors to see. Be glad she had the good sense to keep them out of sight."

"Don't tell me what I can or can't do. I'll decide who works for us." He started to say more, but decided it was time to hear what Victoria had to say. He burst into his daughter's room to confront her.

"Daddy," she shrieked. "Like, shouldn't you knock or something?"

"What the hell went on here while your mother and I were away?"

Victoria sat up in her bed and pulled the sheet tight around her neck. "I planned to tell you that I had a few of my friends over. It was nothing, really." She went over the story as she had practiced, trying to keep it low keyed. "Obviously, someone has blown this out of proportion."

"Out of proportion," he roared. "The phone has been ringing all morning. The story is all over town. What's the matter with you?"

"I'm sure Dr. James can clear it up. He was here." She hoped if she mentioned Mitch's name, daddy would compose himself.

"We'll talk about this later." He slammed the door on his way out of Victoria's room.

"Henry, you're going to have a heart attack if you don't calm down." Dorothy tried to quell her husband's temper. While Victoria had a way of finding her father's softer side, Dorothy took the brunt of his anger. "Do you want me to bring you a cup of coffee?"

He brushed her aside and sat down in his favorite chair.

"Where's the paper?"

"The Lima news?"

"No, damn it. Friday's Rexford Press."

Dorothy reached into the magazine rack but before she had the opportunity to give it to him, he snatched it from her hand.

He searched page by page for any reports in the newspaper and finally found the small item regarding the incident. Although he had seldom voiced his anger to Victoria, his face turned scarlet and he lost all control. "Victoria, get the hell out here, now."

Victoria grabbed her robe and stumbled out to the living room. She had never heard her father use that tone to her before. Completely awake now, she tried to think of the proper answers to appease her father.

"This doesn't look like it was blown out of proportion," the judge said as he slapped his hand on the newspaper. "The police and EMT's were called. They took an inebriated girl to the hospital. Damn it, Victoria, did you ever take a minute to think about the consequences of having a teenager at a party where you served liquor?"

"Daddy, this is all a mistake. I didn't invite that girl. She tagged along with her cousin and had been drinking before they arrived. I had no idea she took a bottle from your liquor cabinet. Like, I couldn't watch her every minute." Victoria sat on the judge's lap and ran her fingers through his graying dark blonde hair and squeezed out a few tears to impress him.

"Daddy, this is, like, horrible. I invited a few friends over, and others crashed in. I did my best to keep order, but how do you handle a situation like that. I'm so sorry." She inhaled sharply and faked a sob. As Victoria expected, Henry Gillette backed down.

"Humph. Let's hope we hear no more about this. Surely no one will blame you for the accident, but Victoria, don't ever allow this to happen again. I, ah, we have a reputation to uphold."

Victoria nodded and returned to her room. She smiled, assured that daddy would handle everything.

TWENTY-FOUR

Customers, who didn't frequent the bars or coffee shops, lingered in the bank lobby Monday morning and exchanged views about the incident at the Gillette house. The gossip ran hot and heavy. Everyone had their own version about what happened, and those who hardly knew the Gillette's, became an authority on the events of Victoria's Fourth of July party.

Robyn Martin hadn't taken a break, hadn't wanted one. She inhaled every word with curious humor.

"It was a wild party. Everybody got drunk," the first one in line told all who would listen. "Can you believe it? This younger generation is going to hell in a hand basket."

"I heard they smoked dope," someone announced.

"Wouldn't surprise me," another agreed.

"And they were all swimming in the nude," an elderly lady added. "Imagine parading around like that."

"That's called skinny-dipping," a customer said with confidence. "Lord only knows what else went on."

Robyn didn't offer any comments as she took a deposit from the next person in line. She listened and shook her head. Not much escaped the rumor-mill of a small town. What they didn't know, they made up. She hoped Olivia had prepared herself for the aftermath. Robyn decided to stop at the Anderson house after work.

"I heard Dr. James attended the party?" someone in the crowd said loudly.

"I wouldn't have believed that of him," said another voice.

"You know, he's young and single. Stands to reason he'd want to be seen at the Gillette's. That doctor is ambitious," came another comment.

"I heard he couldn't make it in Philadelphia. Had to come to a small town to set up his practice. You know that wife of his left him. Yes sir, she probably knew more than we ever will about the doctor's past," someone added.

"That's nothing, I saw his Jeep parked in front of the Anderson house in the wee hours of the morning while Etta Anderson lay sick in the hospital. That perky niece of hers was home. Doesn't take much to put two and two together. She's a big city girl. I'll tell you she doesn't fit in here. She's not our kind."

Robyn felt her face redden. That comment brought back terrible memories. The words, 'doesn't fit in, not our kind,' parroted in her mind. She remembered hearing those statements as a child when she attended family events at school. She struggled to keep her voice steady as she spoke.

"I'm sure Dr. James must have driven Miss McDougle home from the hospital. She probably rode in the ambulance with her aunt and didn't have transportation."

"That makes sense," a customer agreed.

And so it went. Everyone had their take on the events that occurred at Victoria's party. It seemed as if they all stood on the Gillette patio and observed the action. The more people talked, the wilder the party became. They didn't confine their comments to the party. Once the ball started rolling, nobody's reputation remained sacred.

As soon as the bank closed, Robyn drove over to see Olivia.

"I hoped you'd be home. How's Etta?"

"Doing so much better. She insisted I leave the hospital and not return until tomorrow."

"Olivia, I don't know how to say this."

"What is it?"

"Gossip. Nasty, vicious gossip."

"About?"

"First, the party at Victoria Gillette's house and later about you and Dr. James."

"Oh dear God."

"A customer at the bank this morning said she saw his Jeep parked in front of your house early in the morning."

"He..."

Robyn held up her hand, "You don't have to explain to me, but I wanted to let you know what people are saying."

"Are you in a hurry to get home? Stay for dinner, I don't want to eat alone."

"Let me give Mom a call," Robyn walked to the phone and after a few minutes said, "All set."

"Soup and salad okay?"

"Perfect. Let me help."

Olivia opened the refrigerator and gathered ingredients for the salad while Robyn found a jar of Etta's home made soup in the pantry.

"This seemed like old times in your kitchen, elbow to elbow." Olivia said.

"Remember when Etta tried to teach us how to cook?" Robyn asked. "Lord, did we make a mess. I don't know how she could stand it."

"If I remember correctly, she made us clean up."

"She probably had to redo the kitchen after we left."

"Olivia, Etta influenced in my life in such a positive way. While Mom worked, Etta looked after me in the summer. I loved spending time here. I'm so glad she's doing better."

Over dinner, Robyn told Olivia about all the remarks she heard at the bank.

"Did someone really say people were swimming nude at Victoria Gillette's party? Where do they come up with this stuff?" Olivia asked.

"While that wouldn't surprise me, I believe if I hadn't interrupted them, they would have decided Victoria held an orgy. And the one with the most authority on the rumors was Estelle Johnson."

"Does she still signal Bill Meyers by hanging her husband's overalls on the line when he's away on a trip?"

"Like clockwork. After all these years her poor husband still hasn't caught on."

"Or maybe he doesn't care. Maybe he has an affair going on somewhere along his truck route."

"We're as bad as the customers at the bank," Olivia snickered.

"Look at the time. I should go home. Mom's been acting strange lately."

"Is she feeling well?"

"She hasn't complained. It's almost as if she's keeping something from me. Sometimes she doesn't come home until late, especially Friday night after her bowling league. And one day last week, she told me she and Beatrice Miller were going shopping, and later Beatrice called to talk to her."

Olivia couldn't contain her amusement. "Sorry, but think of all the times she worried about you. Robyn, I'm sure your mom doesn't feel required to tell you everything that goes on in her life."

"Of course, you're right. This role reversal stuff is for the birds. I guess it's payback time. Thanks for inviting me. I'm so glad you're back in Rexford."

As if on cue, the phone rang. Robyn waved at Olivia and whispered, "See you later." She let herself out the front door.

***

"Hi beautiful. I miss you," a voice rang out when Olivia answered.

"Mitch. I miss you too."

"I want to see you. I'm coming over."

"You can't."

"What are you talking about?"

Olivia told him of the conversation Robyn overheard at the bank. "Someone noticed your Jeep in front of our house early in the morning."

"There would be more gossip if they knew what went on inside."

"Dr. James, have you no shame?"

"Baby, I'm sorry you were the topic of rumors, but shame...no. What we had was amazing. Meet me at the curb. I'll pick you up in ten minutes." He disconnected the phone before she could reply.

"Where are we going?" Olivia asked when she got into Mitch's Jeep.

"There's a coffee shop in Ottoville that serves excellent homemade pie." Mitch drove until he passed the city limits and then he pulled over to the side of the road. "I can't stay away from you any longer. Come here." He took her his arms and kissed her. "I love you, Olivia."

"It's been a long time since I've made out in a car, doctor. What would your patients say?"

"That I have exceptional taste." He kissed her again before he restarted the car and drove to the coffee shop. Two hours later he dropped her at the curb in front of the Anderson house. "We have to make better arrangements. I need to be with you."

"The gossip will die down after Aunt Etta comes home from the hospital. Meanwhile, we have to be discreet."

"I'd much rather be indiscreet."

"You're absolutely incorrigible"

"I'm absolutely in love with you. I'll call you in the morning. Do you have plans for your Wednesday dinner with the girls?"

"We'll probably postpone it."

"Save some time for me this week. I want to spend time with you."

"I'll pencil you in."

"Indelible ink, lady." He kissed her again and sped off.

Olivia hummed to contain the love she felt inside her heart. She wanted to shout, dance, and laugh all at once as she walked to the house. She couldn't hide the joy of being unquestionably loved.

TWENTY-FIVE

The Rexford Press ran a front page update on the Millsburg Corn Festival, complete with pictures of large barbecue grills, and carpenters erecting a temporary stage on the main street of town. An announcement reminded parents to get their children vaccinated early in preparation for kindergarten to avoid the last minute rush. The high school football coach posted a schedule for the squad to start pre-season practice. There were the usual birth and death notices. Most of the items were ignored by the readers of the Press. They turned directly to the editorial page to see if Olivia McDougle would dare say anything about the Gillette's. She didn't disappoint them.

And if the judge thought his anger had reached its peak when he returned from his weekend to find his daughter had thrown a party that ended in a disaster, it paled in comparison to the wrath that surged through his wiry body when he read Friday's Press.

"How dare her." He slammed the paper on the table. "My family made this town. I brought in a doctor when the city council couldn't get a visiting nurse to come. I developed the industrial park before Olivia McDougle graduated from high school. I'm a judge, for God's sake." He got up from his chair and paced across the room. "Miss McDougle will find it isn't smart to take potshots at the Gillette family."

"What is going on? I could hear you all the way from the kitchen." Dorothy said.

"This." He handed her the paper folded over to reveal the editorial page. "This is what's going on. That bitch is out to ruin us."

"It's just an editorial. No one reads..."

His blow hit the side of her face and knocked her to the chair. Her mouth flew open and tears sprang from her eyes.

"We read it. Everyone will read it. Think of our reputation. Just think, for once in your life," he raged.

Dorothy edged out of the chair and took solace in her room where she would stay until Henry came in to apologize, as she knew he would. He always did.

The judge ignored Dorothy's tearful departure. He needed to regain control. He had to devise a way to put a better spin on the situation. Victoria mentioned the girl had been drinking before she arrived at the party. He nodded his head as a plan formed. 'Victoria, noting the condition of the young girl, called Dr. James. Her quick thinking saved Sandra Zelman's life.' He went to his desk to write a letter to counteract the bad press. It took three drafts before he felt satisfied with the content. He called the mayor and members of the city council and gave them his version of the situation. He dictated line by line, what they should write to the Press. His bloodshot eyes brightened and his sneer turned into an evil grin. By the time Rexford residents read next Friday's edition, the opinion would be swayed back to his point of view. Olivia McDougle and the Rexford Press would come off looking foolish and unreliable.

"What are you smiling about, daddy?" Victoria asked when she walked into the room.

"Power, my dear. Control is all encompassing."

"What do you mean?"

"I mean you don't have to worry about the Rexford Free Press or whatever else Olivia McDougle has to say."

"Thank God. It's beginning to be a real downer the way everyone is carrying on about it. Like, I can hardly talk to my friends without someone asking stupid questions."

"Don't let your guard down, Victoria. Don't add anything or change the story. Gossip has an ugly way of bouncing back to bite you. Maybe you'd like to visit your friend in Lima for a few days. You always have a good time with Jenny." The judge whipped out his wallet and peeled off a couple hundred dollar bills. "You could go shopping, eat out...do whatever you girls do."

"Thanks daddy. I'll call her now. You're the best." Victoria kissed her dad on the cheek and then phoned her friend. When the plans were made, she packed a few things and drove to Lima.

Henry looked toward the bedroom and rubbed his hand on the back of his neck. He inhaled and then let his breath whistle between his teeth before he knocked on his wife's door.

"Dorothy, let's go to that restaurant you like in Findlay. I believe we need a night out. All of this aggravation has placed a horrendous toll on our family. We mustn't let Olivia McDougle and her two-bit newspaper get us down."

The door edged opened and a timid Dorothy Gillette faced her smiling husband.

"Grab your purse, my dear. We'll have an enjoyable evening out. Just the two of us."

TWENTY-SIX

"Ham, what are you doing here?"

"Gal, how did you know it was me? The lights are out and I parked myself in the rocking chair in the corner."

Jade's easy laugh rippled through the darkness. "I smelled the leather of your gun holster and your shoe polish. Besides, you're the only other person who has my key."

"I certainly hope so." Ham stood and walked toward her, ducking under the archway that separated the living room from the entry way. He wrapped his arms around her. "What took you so long to close the shop tonight?"

"Some of the ladies in my art class were extra chatty. I couldn't seem to get them to finish up and go home."

"I missed you."

"You shouldn't be here. Did anyone see you come up?"

"No."

"Where's your car? Everyone will know if they see the patrol vehicle outside."

"Honey, I ain't a cop for nothing. I left it parked beside the Quik-Stop and walked through the back alley. I needed to see you." He nuzzled her ear and nipped at her neck. "You sure smell good."

Jade relaxed. "So do you."

Ham took the clip out of Jade's hair, ran his fingers through the cascade of curls, and spread them around her shoulders.

"Gal, I had a terrible day. That friend of yours at the Rexford Press opened a can of worms. Half the population demands I arrest Victoria Gillette, while the mayor and the judge insist I take Billy Zelman into custody. I had calls from every member of the city council. One of those hot-shots told me if I didn't do as he said, he'd have my job."

"Good Lord, Ham, what did you say?"

"I told him to go for it, but remember I have a ten-year contract they'd have to buy out. That shut him up real fast." He brought Jade's face up to his and kissed her intensely.

Jade melted in his arms. She couldn't resist Hamilton Bowers. The Rexford Chief of Police released her, took off his gun belt, and laid it on the table. While he unbuttoned his shirt, Jade walked to the kitchen and lit one of the new jasmine scented candles she made earlier that week. They moved to the bedroom where she slipped out of her caftan and underclothes. A flickering of light seeped into the room through the open door.

"My God, you're beautiful." He quickly took off the rest of his clothes and tossed them over a chair.

Jade started toward the bed but he stopped her.

"Stand close to me. I want to feel your body."

Jade draped her arms around his neck as he caressed her. He placed his hands under her buttocks and lifted her to him. She wrapped her legs around his waist and they came together in a spasm of love.

"Gal, you are fantastic." He kept her in his arms and carried her over to the bed and laid her down gently, and then dropped his muscular body down beside her.

"You're not so bad yourself, cowboy."

He covered her face with kisses as he caressed her soft

body. "Jade, I don't know how much longer I can stand being away from you. I miss you."

"Me too. How's Janie?"

A sigh came from deep within as Ham rolled over on his back. "She hasn't recognized me the last few times I've been to the nursing home. The doctor told me she's refusing to eat. She's literally wasting away. They don't seem to think she'll last too much longer."

"I'm so sorry, Ham." The number twenty-six flashed across Jade's mind. She knew it would be over in a few weeks.

"She's been restless the past few days as if she's in pain. I insisted they up the morphine dose."

"That's good. She can't tell anyone how she feels. No one in her position deserves to be uncomfortable. She's lucky you're so attentive."

Ham propped himself up on his elbow and traced his finger across the side of Jade's face. "Janie was a vibrant lady. She wouldn't want to live this way. Before we were married, she signed a living will requesting no extraordinary means be taken if she was unable to care of herself or make rational decisions. That means no feeding tubes or ventilators."

"I have the same in my safe deposit box. I wouldn't want to live as a vegetable."

Ham grunted in agreement. Tall, wide shoulders and tough talking, the former Marine worked for the Ohio State Patrol before his wife became terminally ill. He took the position in Rexford to be closer to the nursing home in case of an emergency. The job proved easy to manage as the small town had little crime, aside from the usual drunk and disorderly, shoplifting and an occasional Saturday night brawl at one of the bars. Ham had five officers working under his supervision.

Jade loved the gentler side of this outwardly rough and

ready man. She pressed his body back down on the bed and positioned herself on top of him. She kissed her lover again and again, his chest, his shoulders, his soft lips.

"Ah, baby," Ham whispered as they made love again. He groaned in appreciation as she fell beside him, damp with perspiration.

"Lord, you wear me out," Ham laughed as he pulled her close.

Jade snuggled in his arms. "It's a good tired, I hope."

"It's a damn good tired."

"Have you had dinner? I could make an omelet."

"I ate at the diner, but I'd better move the patrol car. I'm sure by now there's a traffic jam of rubber-neckers wondering if I have my radar gun pointed at the intersection."

"I think you should let them worry. Let's shower and then spend the rest of the night in each other's arms."

A grin hugged his face and he held her close. "That sounds like a hell of an idea, but lay here with me for awhile. I don't want to let go of you yet. Jade, I..." He didn't finish. Hamilton Bowers felt torn. He loved his wife, but he was in love with his mistress, although he never allowed himself to say those words to her.

TWENTY-SEVEN

Mitch James brought a copy of the Rexford Press to the hospital for Etta to read. He couldn't conceal his amusement when she let out a hoot. "Olivia has the backbone of her Uncle Fritz. You can bet the judge is in a stew about now. What really happened, Mitch?"

He told her about the events that took place at the party and explained the misunderstanding he had with Olivia.

"Unfortunately, she found out before I had the opportunity to tell her."

Etta nodded her head. "So that's why she spent the night with Kristen. I imagine Livie wasn't too excited to learn you went to the Gillette's house without telling her. I saw how Victoria came on to you while we were at the park. That girl was on a mission."

"That's an understatement. Victoria had unrealistic plans for the two of us. Etta, I've never given her a minute of encouragement. It took a bit of convincing to get Olivia to understand."

"Can I give you a piece of advice?"

"As if I could stop you."

"Livie is a straight forward girl. You need to be upfront with her."

"Or she'll dismiss me. I'm well aware of that. I should tell you, I'm in love with your niece."

"How does she feel?"

Mitch grimaced and rubbed his temple. "Wary, but I think she's coming around."

"What's going on here?" Olivia stood at the door glaring at the two of them."

"We were just talking about you, Livie. Mitch brought the paper."

Olivia looked from one to the other, "What do you think?" she asked Etta.

"I believe you have your work cut out for you. Don't think for a minute that Judge Gillette is going to let this die. He's planning something as we speak, I'd bank on it."

"Millie told me the same thing this morning. We made our stand, let the chips fall where they may. Meanwhile, how are you feeling?"

"Much better now that Mitch has made arrangements for me to come home. I can't wait to get in my own bed and have some decent food."

Olivia's smile lit the room. "Is that true?" she asked Mitch.

"Dr. Walters signed the release papers this morning. It should happen within the hour. Etta will probably be more comfortable in your car than my Jeep, but I'll follow you and help get her settled. I called Sarah this morning and she agreed to spend the next month with you."

"Humph, I don't need anyone to tend to me."

"If you want to go home, Sarah will stay at least a month. Is that clear?" Mitch's expression left little room for discussion.

"I guess I have no choice. It seems like you've made the decision for me." Etta said. It was a bitter pill to swallow. She had always been independent, but in her heart, she knew it was for the best. The fact that she genuinely liked Sarah made Mitch's arrangement easier.

"Sarah is a great lady. I hope to hire her permanently. With the hours I work and the care you'll need, it would be convenient to have her live with us," Olivia added.

A nurse entered the room and told Mitch and Olivia if they would step outside, she could get Etta ready to leave. Once in the hallway, Mitch wrapped his arms around Olivia. "I've missed you. Between your job, my impossible hours and the gossip mongers, we don't see nearly enough of each other. We should make a permanent statement. We should become engaged."

"I think you're rushing things. A better approach would be to plan more carefully."

"I intend to marry you, Olivia McDougle. I want to spend the rest of my life with you. Get used to the idea."

The nurse interrupted, "Mrs. Anderson is ready to go." She brought Etta out in a wheelchair.

"We'll finish this conversation later," Mitch said as he turned his attention to his favorite patient.

Mitch had arranged in advance for Sarah Edison to meet them at the Anderson house. Sarah prepared a light meal, changed the linen on the beds and waited at the door for their arrival.

"Let's get Miss Etta into bed. I know the trip home was tiring," she told Olivia when they entered the house. "I'll get her settled."

Mitch pulled Olivia out to the foyer. "I love you. I don't want to leave, but I have to get to the office." He kissed her quickly and turned toward the door. "I'll call you later."

"Miss Etta's all set. She wanted to sleep so I'll bring her something to eat a little later. Can I get anything for you?" Sarah asked Olivia.

"Let's have coffee. There's something I want to discuss with you."

"Have I done something wrong?" Sarah pursed her lips. "Tell me. I'll fix it."

"No, nothing like that. I want to offer you a full-time position." Olivia sat at the kitchen table and asked Sarah if she'd consider room and board plus a small salary.

Sarah jumped at the chance. As a widow, she had a difficult time making ends meet and couldn't always depend on sporadic Home Assistant assignments to support her. Etta Anderson always treated her as an equal, not a paid employee. Olivia did the same.

"Miss Olivia, you've saved my life. My car is almost beyond repair and my landlord is raising the rent on my apartment next month. After this assignment, I didn't know what I was going to do."

"Then it's settled. You can move into the bedroom next to Aunt Etta. There's a small sun-room at the end of the hall. Consider that your space also. If you need anymore room, let me know. I believe this will work out for all of us."

***

Mitch called twice during the day and couldn't wait to pick up Olivia after his office hours were over.

"Let's go out to eat. I want some private time with you."

"I shouldn't leave Aunt Etta alone."

He swept her in his arms. "You're not. Sarah's here, remember. Besides, Etta will probably sleep through the night. I'll check on her and then we'll go."

"Where are we going?" Olivia asked when Mitch backed the Jeep out of the driveway.

"There's a mom and pop bar and grill called Billie's Place, on the outskirts of Ottawa. They serve excellent food." He reached for her hand and brought it to his lips. "It's quiet and secluded."

"That sounds good." Olivia placed her hand on his leg as they drove out of town. The affection she felt for Mitch almost erupted from her heart.

In less than twenty minutes Mitch parked his Jeep beside the small bar.

"Was that Robyn's mother?" Olivia asked as a car passed them as it left the parking lot.

"Probably not. This is a quiet, out of the way place. Not too many folks from Rexford come here. That's why I picked it. I wanted to be alone with you."

Once inside, they ordered and then held hands across the table while they waited for the food to be served.

"You want a glass of wine?"

"Not tonight. Coffee's good," Olivia said. "You look beat."

"I had a busy day." Mitch stretched his shoulders. "It was non-stop. Thank goodness for Maxine. I couldn't manage without her."

The waitress set the plates on their table and reluctantly, Mitch released Olivia's hands, but not before kissing each finger.

That gesture didn't go unnoticed by a figure sitting in the shadows at the end of the bar. Earlier in the day, Judge Henry Gillette represented a client at the Putnam County Courthouse. By the time he had finished working out a deal at the opposing lawyer's office in Ottawa, he was more than ready for a cocktail and some companionship. Before he went home, he met an old friend for drinks. Thank goodness she left before Dr. James and Olivia McDougle came into Billie's Place, not that they had eyes for anyone but each other. The judge ordered a second drink and sat quietly, not wanting to be seen by the happy couple. They couldn't seem to keep their hands off each other. When Olivia fed Mitch a forkful of food from her plate, the judge smirked. Love in bloom, he thought. This answered a lot of questions he had about Dr. James. Now the judge knew Mitch's weakness, a vivacious young Olivia McDougle. That might be his ace in the hole if push came to shove.

TWENTY-EIGHT

The letters began to arrive at the Rexford Press on Tuesday. One came from the mayor, a few from the city council members and of course, a two page re-enactment from Judge Gillette. They all gave similar accounts, praising Victoria for her quick thinking in saving the Zelman girl's life.

Wednesday night, Mitch received a call from the judge encouraging him to comply.

"Judge Gillette, you don't want to hear what I have to say." Mitch told him how he happened to be called to the party. "It wasn't an emergency. Victoria used my beeper under false pretenses. I happened to notice the Zelman girl on my way out."

"Now listen, Mitch. I'm the one who is responsible for your job. I..."

"Hold on, judge. Don't go there. This isn't about me. I treated the girl and made sure she was transported to the hospital. I couldn't say when or where she began to drink but I did see an empty vodka bottle fall from her chair."

"If Victoria is arrested, you will verify her story if you know what's good for you. I brought you here and I can move you out." Judge Gillette slammed down the phone. He'd deal with Mitch later. In the mean time, he'd talk to some of the Rexford Press advertisers. He'd hit Miss McDougle where it hurt.

***

"Something is going on," Millie said when Olivia arrived at the office Wednesday morning. We've received five cancellations for ads this month." She spread the phone messages on the desk.

Olivia looked at the names. "Did anyone give you an explanation?"

"No. They simply said pull it until further notice. Are you going to phone them?"

"I believe a personal call is in order." Olivia took Millie's notes and went out the door. She would walk to the businesses that were closest. Larson Law Offices, located a block away on Main Street would be her first stop.

A soft tone at the door announced her entrance.

"May I help you?" the receptionist inquired.

"I'd like to speak with Mark Larson."

"Your name please?"

"Olivia McDougle."

The receptionist rapped on an ornate oak door before entering. A few minutes later she returned to say Mr. Larson was unable to see her.

"I'll wait," Olivia said as she sat on a couch and picked up a magazine. After fifteen minutes, the girl mentioned again that Mr. Larson was busy.

"Tell Mr. Larson I plan to remain here until he's free."

The receptionist again rapped at the door. She returned and said, "Mr. Larson will see you now. He's expecting a client and can't give you more than a few minutes."

Olivia followed her into the office and introduced herself to the attorney.

"What can I do for you, Miss McDougle?"

"You withdrew your ad. May I inquire why?"

"It's strictly a budget item," he said.

"I see. You know Millsburg doesn't have general law offices. Your ad reaches them. I'm sure you'll pick up clients for wills and estates as well as general law. I'm told most of their business goes to Lima. One client a year will pay for your ad and I feel confident you could garner many more."

Mark Larson squirmed ever so slightly in his seat.

"You're a businessman as well as a lawyer," Olivia continued. "I gave you first shot at the Millsburg page because you're a loyal subscriber. I can throw that business to the new law firm that opened on Brentwood Street."

"Wait. You don't understand."

"Judge Gillette?"

Olivia noticed a tinge of pink appear above Mark Larson's collar. He sank a little deeper in his chair.

"It's your call. I can only say that you're not responsible for Victoria Gillette's bad judgment. When this blows over, and it will, someone will get the business from Millsburg. I might add the Press hopes to make the same arrangement with Harlan Grove and Newton City in the future." Olivia turned to leave.

"Miss McDougle." Mark rose from his chair. "Run the ad and put us down for the other city pages if you get them signed up."

"Thanks Mr. Larson. I'll bring some new advertising copy for you to look over. I'm sure we can improve your ad and give you a professional, as well as a friendly message."

When Olivia left the law office, she looked at the next two cancellations. One came from O'Brady's, a tavern owned by one of the councilmen. No point in talking to him. Instead she went to Bar None, a new establishment that opened a few months before. Olivia ran their grand opening announcement but they hadn't opted for further publicity. She had meant to get back to them. This gave her a good opportunity.

She ran over in her mind how she would approach them and finally decided to be direct. She would tell them O'Brady's hadn't renewed their advertising and this would be the ideal time for them to take advantage of the opening. By the time she walked to the bar, she had mentally worked out the entire campaign. Thirty minutes later, she had their check in her hand for a six month option.

That was enough for one day. She returned to the Press with the information.

"Go on home, Millie," Olivia said when she entered the office. "I want to work up the ad copy before I leave. I'll close up. See you tomorrow."

Jade had invited the girls to her apartment for dinner that evening. She promised an exciting meal and some fun besides. Olivia couldn't imagine what Jade had in store for them, but she looked forward to spending time with her friends.

TWENTY-NINE

"Come in. You're the first to arrive," Jade told Kristen. "Let's have a glass of wine while we wait for Robyn and Olivia. Would you prefer red or white?"

"White, thank you. Your apartment is charming, much larger than it looks from the outside."

"We're here," Robyn said as she knocked and then she and Olivia entered. "What is that heavenly aroma?"

"Stir-fry. I hope you like it." Jade handed Robyn and Olivia each a glass of wine and set a plate of homemade egg rolls on the coffee table in the living room. "Be careful girls, the dipping sauce is spicy."

While the girls chatted, Jade placed dishes of food on the kitchen table. "Bring your wine and let's eat while it's hot."

"This is incredible. You've outdone yourself," Robyn said as she filled her plate.

"Everything tastes so authentic. Wherever did you learn to cook like this?" Olivia asked.

"My paternal grandmother came from the Orient. Grandfather met and married her while he was stationed overseas. She taught me how to make her family recipes."

The girls sampled everything, questioning the ingredients in each dish. Kristen asked if Jade would share the recipes.

"Come over some afternoon, I'll show you."

"Cook and eat? I'm in," Robyn said.

"Me too, but I couldn't eat another thing tonight," Kristen said.

"I have a surprise for all of you," Jade said as she cleared the table and set delicate china tea cups and saucers in front of each of her friends. She filled an exquisite porcelain tea pot with boiling water and loose tea. She made a ceremony of pouring tea into each cup. "Enjoy the tea, but leave a little in the bottom of your cup. When you're finished I'll read the tea leaves."

"You're kidding. Can you do that?" Kristen asked.

"Only if you want me to."

"Me first." Robyn set her cup in front of Jade.

Jade performed an elaborate ritual by turning Robyn's cup three times counter clockwise before causally placing her hand on her friend's shoulder. Jade could easily read the leaves but she received more information by touching her subject. "Robyn, concentrate on a wish." Jade looked into the cup. "Ah Robyn, the men are missing from your life. I see some turmoil in your immediate future. It's imperative that you take charge of your finances. Don't worry. Just when the events in your life seem to become the most difficult, things will work out for the best."

Olivia pushed her cup in front of Jade.

"Clear your mind and make a wish," Jade said as she repeated the ritual. "You lost a cheating lover and found a true soul-mate. Whatever friction is in your life now will settle. After a few road blocks, better times will prevail." Jade unconsciously said, "Oh."

"What? What else do you see?" Olivia asked.

"An older woman in the shadow. She's pointing at you."

"Probably Aunt Etta. She's always keeping me in line. I'd be lost without her," Olivia said.

Jade didn't comment further. What she saw and felt around Olivia filled her with concerned.

"A soul-mate," Robyn said. "I knew it. You and Dr. James."

"Is that true?" Kristen asked. "Are you two serious?"

"Yes, I'm seeing Mitch, but that's between the four of us. I'm not in a position to let that news become public yet. You know how the rumor mill works in Rexford."

Jade nodded and added, "Watch out for an older man. He wants to cause trouble."

"This is fun," Robyn said.

"Kristen, are you game?" Jade asked.

Kristen hesitated before allowing Jade to look into her cup.

Jade's eyes darkened when she touched Kristen's shoulder. She carefully hid her emotions as she read the leaves. "There's a wall between the old and the new. See this trail of leaves?" Jade pointed to a dividing line in the cup. "Put the pain of the past behind you because someone will enter your life and make positive changes."

"I don't think I need to find anyone. I'm perfectly content with my life."

Jade's eyes twinkled. "You can't change fate. The leaves don't lie."

"Jade, we can't read tea leaves. You have to tell us something about yourself that we don't know," Robyn said.

Jade stood and led the girls to the living room. "I am blessed or cursed with a gift. I read tea leaves and tarot cards." She didn't tell them about sensing auras and that she also had visions. She knew about Olivia and Mitch. She was aware of the terrible secret Kristen kept hidden and she knew Robyn's father lived in Rexford, and that her marriage to Greg was in jeopardy. She wouldn't reveal these things unless asked. She could only make suggestions.

"When did you find out you had this talent?" Robyn asked.

"My grandmother on my mother's side of the family recognized it in me when I was very young. It's a Kentucky family trait.

"I didn't know you were from Kentucky," Olivia said.

"I guess I never mentioned it. Grandfather Kendall bought this property years ago and opened a plumbing business here. When he retired, he moved back to Covington. When I approached him about my arts and craft business, he agreed to allow me to live here rent free. I only have to pay for the utilities. That dear man trusted that I'd make a success of the J. K. Art Company. He gave me a chance of a lifetime."

The girls spent the rest of the evening talking and laughing. Jade felt troubled when they left. She wished she didn't know the next hurdle Olivia had to overcome. She hoped Kristen would come to grips with her past and prayed that Robyn would listen to her advice and stay strong.

Jade's gift came at a price.

THIRTY

I have to tell you babe, I'm jealous."

"Mitch, you have a terrible habit of hiding on my porch."

"Come here, I've missed you." He took Olivia in his arms and kissed her. "We have to make this a permanent arrangement. I can't stand being away from you. Come home with me. I promise I'll have you back before Etta wakes in the morning."

"What if she needs something in the middle of the night?"

"That's why you hired Sarah."

"I'm tempted."

"But?"

"You know I can't, especially after all the gossip. You have to think of your reputation as well as mine."

"Aah, I know. But at least, come with me for a drink."

Olivia looked at her watch. "One hour."

Mitch grabbed her hand and pulled her toward his Jeep, knowing full well it would be more than an hour. He drove down the quiet street to the private entrance to his apartment behind the office.

"This is comfortable," Olivia said as she scanned the living area.

"It is now that you're here. Coffee?"

"I don't think..." before she could finish, Mitch had her in his arms.

"I love you Olivia. Marry me. I don't want to put you in an awkward position here, but I want to be with you. I don't like sneaking around. I want to tell everyone about us."

She pushed away. "It's too soon. You don't know me."

"I know the sparkle in your eyes and your smile that drives me crazy. I know how you brush non-existing hair from your face when you're tense. I know you love your aunt and you're fiercely independent and driven. Is that enough?"

"Mitch James, you've been spying on me." Olivia put her hands on her hips in mock anger.

"I've been observing you because I want you so badly, I can hardly stand it. I know you want me too."

Olivia dissolved in his open arms. It was true. She wanted him. She needed him.

His kisses turned into caresses. "Oh baby, let me prove how much I love you."

She followed him to the bedroom and within minutes they were undressed. A slight breeze from an open window moved the curtains as he lay beside her on his bed. He kissed her neck and ran his fingers along her inner thigh. Olivia shuddered with desire.

"My God, I love you. I can't think of words to describe my emotion," he told her between kisses.

Their lovemaking felt comfortable and satisfying as they brought each other to ecstasy.

"You're amazing. I can't get enough of you. Do you realize how very much I love you, Olivia McDougle?" Mitch gathered her in his arms. "I think about you constantly. I find myself humming as I examine patients. Maxine questioned my behavior. She couldn't imagine anyone being so cheerful around all the sick people in the office."

"I walk around in a fog. I want to touch you, feel your body next to mine." Olivia pressed closer to him.

The urgency aroused them. Olivia couldn't believe how much she wanted him again. She became the aggressor as the need overwhelmed her. Mitch moaned in appreciation as she found his erotic zones. She flicked her tongue over his nipples and bit him lightly on his lower stomach. He lifted her on top of him and when they came together the second time, an explosion erupted between them. Olivia lay across his chest, their bodies' slick with perspiration.

"I never thought it would be like this. I can't put my feelings into words."

"I believe we exceeded the hour. I don't want you to go, but I promised," Mitch said.

"You did. I'll get dressed." She leaned over to kiss him again.

"You're making this difficult. I never want you to leave," he pulled her to him again. Stay with me. Marry me, Olivia. I promise to make you happy."

"You already do. I've never felt so content. I can't stay tonight but we need to make a commitment."

"Do you mean it?"

"I do. We'll make definite plans. I love you Mitch James." She sat on the side of the bed and touched his face. "I have to go home." She dressed and reluctantly, Mitch put on his clothes

When the apartment door opened, a figure ducked into the shadow of the tree-lined street and watched as Miss Olivia McDougle and Dr. James embraced before they got into his Jeep and drove off.

THIRTY-ONE

Kristen's hands trembled as she drove home from Jade's dinner party. Visibly shaken, she fought to regain control as she tried to make sense of Jade's entertainment. Surely Jade couldn't really read tea leaves. It had to be a party trick. Frown lines deepened on her forehead as she thought about Jade's remarks regarding Olivia and Mitch. Maybe Olivia told her ahead of time. And the bit about Robyn's finances, how did she come up with that?

Oh my gosh, she can't possibly know about my past. I used every precaution. Fear gripped Kristen as she rehashed the extreme measures she took to escape the dreadful truth.

Kristen pulled over to the side of the road and stopped the car. She had to talk to Jade. She needed to find out exactly what her friend knew, and more importantly, how she came across the information.

Kristen made a u-turn and drove back to Jade's apartment. Still shaking, she parked the car and walked to the back of the J.K Art Company. She hurried up to the second floor, taking the steps two at a time, and inhaled sharply before she willed herself to knock.

"Come in, Kristen," Jade said before she opened the door.

"How could you know it was me?"

"I knew you'd come back. You have some serious unresolved issues."

"Jade?"

"Don't worry, Kristen. I'm not about to reveal your secrets. Didn't you notice, I never went into detail about anything that I read in your tea leaves to either Robyn or Olivia?"

"Just how much do you know?" Kristen hugged her arms and began to pace. Her usual calm demeanor, rattled.

"Enough to realize you've faced serious trauma, were betrayed by the people you loved the most and everyone suffered as a result."

"But how could you?" Kristen faced Jade and looked directly into her eyes. "Did you have someone check on me?"

"Sit down, Kristen."

Kristen's body stiffened as she sat on the sofa, unsure of what to expect.

"Do you want to tell me about him?" Jade asked.

"No, I can't."

"Kristen, there is no way you could have known he was your half-brother."

"You know. You know about Blaine." Kristen's voice came as a whisper.

"I didn't know his name, but yes, what I didn't read in your tea leaves, surfaced in your aura the minute I touched your shoulder."

Kristen shifted uncomfortably. "This is so difficult. I don't know..."

"Believe me, I understand. You need to talk it through. That's the only way you'll free yourself from the past."

Kristen fought to regain control before she spoke. "I met him in my junior year at college. Blaine and I were both from Tennessee, although I lived outside of Nashville and he and his family came from Memphis. We talked for hours and found we had so much in common, our religion, strong family background, even our taste in books and movies. We began to date steadily and soon fell in love.

"I wrote home to tell my mother and father about Blaine. They seemed thrilled when I said we would become engaged after graduation. They wanted to know everything about him and insisted I bring him home to meet the family.

"My father managed a horse farm for his widowed mother who owned the operation, the house, all the stock and the land. He bred, raised and trained her prize-winning Tennessee Walkers.

"Grandmother, a cold, calculating woman made no secret of her hatred for my mother and she barely tolerated me. But my father, her only child, could do no wrong. I'll amend that. In Grandmother's eyes, the one terrible wrong occurred when he and Mother married.

"We all lived in the big house. In spite of my mother's pleading to get a small place of our own, my father acquiesced to grandmother's wishes. He had no choice, grandmother held the purse-strings."

Jade nodded in agreement. She got that part, almost by osmosis.

"Don't get me wrong, we never wanted for anything. We had the best clothes, new cars, went on expensive trips, and whatever else we needed. Grandmother simply liked to be in control. Her staff took care of the house and did the cooking. She spared us nothing as long as we obeyed the rules, her rules." Kristen stood and started to pace as she continued her story.

"The main stable housed the business office. The horse buyers or horse owners seeking stud service for their mares, and those who brought their horses to be trained, always hung around the stables. Before my birth, mother ran the office, set appointments and kept the books. She also did some training and gave riding lessons. She earned many prizes for her expert horsemanship and father kept her ribbons and trophies in glass cabinets that lined the office walls. That's where she met Black Jack McCready.

"Dad told me that before I came along, Mother went to a spa in Nashville every Tuesday for relaxation and to have time away from the ranch and probably, Grandmother. Often she stayed overnight to shop before returning home. I mention this so you'll understand that she stayed in the city for another reason as well.

"When she became pregnant, father was very protective of her and insisted she not be around the stables. When I was old enough to understand, mother would tell me of the extraordinary care he provided. Father hired workers to take her place and she never worked around the horses or at the office again. Mother said it was the only time in her married life that Grandmother showed her any respect. Looking back, it must have been a trying time for my parents. They tried to live together, with as much peace as possible, while Grandmother second guessed everything either of them did."

Jade walked to the kitchen and returned with two glasses of wine. "I know this isn't easy, Kristen, but the sooner you get this over with, the sooner you can put it behind you."

Kristen graciously accepted the wine and the advice. She sat back on the sofa and took herself back to that time in Nashville.

"Blaine McCready was incredibly handsome. Dark eyes and hair, tall and muscular, he looked like he belonged on the cover of GQ magazine. I was absolutely crazy about him and he professed his love for me. We couldn't wait to be married.

"Blaine and I made the decision not to have sex before marriage because of my Southern Baptist background. The longer we dated, the more difficult it became to abstain. We made plans to go to Nashville at spring break to meet my parents, and officially announce our engagement. We spoke of eloping and moving in together for our final year of college. But of course, that never happened.

"Mother phoned me at college to ask for Blaine's father's name and his occupation. I thought it odd but Blaine laughed and said my parents had every right to look into the background of their future son-in-law. He said his father's name was John and he owned a car dealership in Memphis. That information seemed to satisfy mother.

"I didn't keep my car on campus so when we finalized our plans; Blaine drove me home to Nashville.

"Grandmother surprised everyone by getting into the mood of celebration. She had the best champagne brought up from the cellar and various appetizers were served before we sat down to dine. The staff prepared an exceptional meal for the occasion and everyone welcomed Blaine.

"The dinner conversation went well until my father asked if Blaine had a relative in Nashville called Black Jack. Father said he had done some horse trading with a Black Jack McCready many years ago.

"Blaine's natural laugh erupted. He said he recalled being told that in his younger days, his father was called Black Jack but he didn't know if his dad had ever bought and sold horses. Blaine told us his father dabbled in many things before he bought the car dealership.

"My mother gasped and her face turned sickly pale. Her hands trembled as she excused herself from the table. She could hardly keep her balance as she made her way upstairs.

"Father started to follow her, but grandmother told me to see about mother. She said it would give them the opportunity to learn more about Blaine and his family.

"Once upstairs, I found mother sitting on the bed in her room crying hysterically. I remember our conversation as if it were yesterday."

"You tell that young man to leave our home immediately," mother said.

"You can't mean that. He's the man I plan to marry."

"Christina, you'll not marry him. I forbid it. Now do as I say."

"I don't understand what's wrong with you. Blaine and I are going to be married. If you don't agree, we'll elope."

"You can't," mother said dropping to the bed. *You can't."*

"Why? Give me a reason. Don't you like him? Did he say something to offend you? If he did, I'm sure it was unintentional. He's a perfect gentleman—and mother, I love him."

I turned and started to leave the room. Mother jumped off the bed, grabbed my arm and spun me around to face her. She slapped me hard. It was the first time in my life she had ever laid a hand on me. I reeled back in shock.

"Listen to me. You can't marry Blaine McCready. You can't marry him because he's your half-brother."

"What? Oh my God, what are you telling me?"

Her voice trembled. "I had an affair with Jack McCready. I know for a fact, he's your father."

"An unearthly roar came from the doorway. I turned to find my father standing there, his face scarlet with rage. He had come upstairs to check on us and overheard the last part of the conversation. The look on his face terrified me. He said nothing, but turned and left the room. Mother put her face in her hands and sobbed. I shook uncontrollably as I tried to digest the terrible truth.

"I learned later that father told Blaine he would have to leave. He explained that we had a personal emergency and I would call him later. Blaine had no choice but to drive off.

"I could hear grandmother talking to father and for the first time ever, yelling at him. They argued violently. Doors slammed and then she came upstairs and told me to get out of the house. When I hesitated, she grabbed my arm and literally dragged me down the stairs and through the kitchen. She screamed at the staff to leave immediately. The tone of her voice commanded everyone to do as she ordered. She herded all of us to the gardener's shed.

"What happened next remains a blur. We heard two blasts of a shotgun and then an explosion followed by another crack. Before we could react, flames burst from an upstairs window.

"One of the help ran to the office in the stables and called the police and fire department. I attempted to go back into the house, but grandmother kept a firm grasp on me. She knew it was too late. My father shot mother twice, started the fire with some kind of explosive device, and then killed himself."

"I'm so sorry, Kristen," Jade said as she put her arms around her friend and encouraged her to finish the story. "How did you end up in Millsburg?"

"I mentioned before that grandmother barely tolerated me. After this happened, she told me to leave the farm and never come back. I pleaded with her to reconsider as she was the only relative I had. Her voice grew cold when she reminded me, we were not related.

"I had no place to go. One of the employees took me to his house to stay with his family. In next few weeks, while I tried to come to terms with the total destruction of my life, he contacted the insurance company to see if there were any policies left by my parents naming me as beneficiary. Two policies were on record. One policy provided money to pay for my college education and the other afforded enough cash value for living expenses plus a small nest-egg.

"I phoned my college room-mate and had her send my belongings to my temporary residence. Then I packed everything in my car, withdrew all the money from my savings account and drove to Columbus, Ohio. I found a job, worked during the remaining of the semester and through the summer. I enrolled in courses at a community college until I established a work history and residency. Then I registered at OSU to complete my junior and senior years. I taught school in Columbus for two additional years while I earned a master's degree."

"You called yourself, Christina," Jade said.

"As soon as I could afford it, I changed my name, assumed a new identity and tried to erase my past. Grandmother blamed me for the entire tragedy."

"That may be true, but she did save your life."

"I'll never understand that. When I went back to the ranch to pick up my car, she had moved into the plush housing over the office at the stables. Father kept that apartment for people to stay in when they brought their horses for stud service. Two bedrooms, a living room and a fully equipped kitchen made up the suite.

"I stopped to talk to her before I left, but she had nothing to say to me. She made it clear that we would never have a relationship. I decided then to cut my ties with everything and everyone in Tennessee."

"Have you ever heard from Blaine?"

"Not directly. My college roommate wrote that Blaine had begged for my address, but we agreed before I left that she would not give it to anyone, ever. Blaine drove to Nashville to talk to grandmother and she evidently told him the story. My roommate told me after many confrontations with her, Blaine gave up the search. Once I changed my name, no one, not even my ex-roommate knew my location.

As the events played over in Kristen's mind, the reality overwhelmed her. The words, she had never allowed herself to vocalize, spewed from her mouth. "My God, I fell in love and almost slept with my brother."

"But you didn't," Jade said quietly. "You have to remember, none of this was his fault or yours. I'm sure Blaine felt as devastated as you."

"I'm sure he faced trauma when he confronted his family or at least his father. I want no more contact with him. It's better that we went our separate ways. I don't feel I could ever have a sibling relationship with him. This dark cloud would always hang over us.

"I knew if I wrote to Blaine, he would attempt to find me. I worried that he might hire a private detective. That was another reason I changed my name and took the teaching job in Millsburg. I reasoned no one would ever think to look for me in that small town."

"Kristen, you can't blame yourself. You were a victim of circumstance. As a young woman, your mother made a dreadful error in judgment. As a result, everyone paid the price."

"That doesn't alleviate my feelings of guilt. If I hadn't brought Blaine to Nashville, the tragedy would never have happened."

"But it would have been replaced by a far greater tragedy. It's over. Put it out of your mind and get on with your life. There will be someone in your future that will love you and take care of you."

Kristen shook her head.

"It's late, Kristen. Do you want to spend the night?"

"No. I need to go home. You were right, Jade. I do feel

better having told the story, but I'd appreciate it if you didn't repeat it."

Jade smiled. "There isn't any reason for anyone to know unless you decide to tell them."

THIRTY-TWO

Olivia had no choice but to print excerpts from the letters Judge Gillette and his cronies sent to the Press. In her editorial, Olivia wrote, "I find it curious that all of the letters read the same. It's as if they were carbon copies."

She made a point to mention that they were sent by the judge, the mayor and members of the city council, none of whom attended the alleged party. "We have not heard from Victoria Gillette. Perhaps she can shed some light on the alleged events of her Fourth of July celebration."

The editorial would appear in the following Friday's edition.

"I can't wait to see the reaction we get from this," Millie said as she read Olivia's copy. "I'll take it to the printing room and then let the recorder pick up the phone messages for the rest of the evening. Do you want me to wait and close shop?"

"I'll lock up. Go home and have a good week-end. I'll see you Monday morning." Olivia straightened her desk and turned off the lights after Millie left. She picked up her purse, reached for the front door knob and came face to face with Judge Gillette. He pushed his way into the office. Although shaken by the surprise encounter, Olivia casually walked behind Millie's desk, using it as a buffer between them.

"We need to talk, young lady."

Olivia watched the overpowering man carefully. His anger apparent, he seemed to struggle to control his voice. "What can I do for you," she said.

"It's what you're going to do. You will print a retraction and put it on the front page of your two-bit newspaper. You will state that you were in error and agree that Victoria did indeed save Sandra Zelman's life."

"I beg your pardon. Whatever would make you think I would print such a statement?"

The judge pulled pictures out of an envelope and thrust them at her. "I believe these might convince you of your misplaced opinion."

Olivia couldn't hide the shock from her face. She looked at the pictures that were spread before her. Shaken, she leaned against the desk for support. "Where did you get these?" She couldn't catch her breath. Her words came out hoarse and raspy.

"That's of no importance. I don't believe you'll want these circulated. The entire town will witness the tawdry behavior of you and Dr. James. What will his patients say when they see the two of you in this position." He sneered as he pointed to a photo of Mitch's nude body on top of hers.

Olivia sucked in her breath in an attempt to keep her voice as steady as possible before she spoke, although her knees shook violently. "I'm surprised you'd stoop to blackmail. Surely it isn't worth the risk."

"My daughter is my life. She's the only child Dorothy and I have. I will not have her name smeared."

"I'm sorry, Judge Gillette. Do what you have to do. I'm not about to be intimidated by you or anybody else."

He glared at her. "You have grit, I'll give you that, but I don't pick battles that I can't win. This is what will happen.

If you don't retract your statements, I'll make sure Dr. Mitch James is removed from his practice. I hold the purse strings, in case you forgot."

"This has nothing to do with Dr. James. You're complaint is with me."

"As I said, I don't pick battles I can't win. What do you think he'll do when he finds out you were the cause of his demise in this town? I'm sure he's told you over and over during your sordid affair, how much he loves his practice. It's your call, lady." He turned and went out the door, leaving Olivia holding pictures of her and Mitch making love. Their beautiful affair looked ugly in the black and white photos. Even the poor quality left no doubt of Mitch and Olivia's identity.

She studied the pictures and determined by the background, they were taken last night at Mitch's apartment. That was the only time Olivia had been there. How did the judge get them? Damn, the open window. Someone must have been watching—following them.

Olivia, too angry to cry, went back to her office and turned on the light. She paced while considering her options. What on earth could she do? She plopped down in the chair, grabbed a pencil and nervously tapped on the desk. What action would Howard Benson take? She couldn't ask him. He and his wife moved to Florida last month.

Howard, of course. She jumped out of her chair, took the painting down and leaned it against the wall. She removed the bricks, pulled out the huge black book Howard showed her and brought it back to the desk. She made a quick call to Sarah to explain she had planned on meeting Jade for a drink, and wouldn't be home until late. Then she spread the book on the desk and began to peruse its contents.

Two hours later she came upon pages and pages of facts about Judge Gillette. Olivia couldn't believe the information written in the book.

"Mary Margaret Taylor left town in November of 1979 only to return ten months later with a two month old baby she named Robyn Lee Gleason. In an envelope in the back of the journal are pictures of Henry Lee Gillette and Mary Margaret, and a copy of Robyn's birth certificate. Also included are copies of money orders made out to Mary Margaret along with a statement from Lloyd Hunt, Rexford's bank manager. Henry Lee is an up and coming lawyer, engaged to Dorothy Pruitt of Findlay."

Olivia flipped to the back of the book and found an expansion file taped to the inside cover. As she looked over the tabs she shuddered to think of what each contained. She found two files under Gillette. The first one had information subtitled, "Deals". Olivia spread the file on her desk. It went into detail about how the judge was forced to retire because of bribes he received. Judge Matheson, involved in removing Gillette from the bench, subsequently took his place.

The second file held pictures and the photo copy of a birth certificate, the father's name listed as Robert Gleason. Olivia set them aside and took out the folded paper.

"In November, 1979 Henry Gillette bought a money order in the amount of $500.00. He then purchased them monthly in the amount of $300.00, for the next year. Mary Margaret Gleason cashed these at our bank."

How on earth did Howard come across this information?

She sat back in her chair and digested what she had read. Robyn Gleason Martin is the daughter of Judge Henry Lee Gillette. She studied the photos: Henry and Mary Margaret, Mary Margaret very pregnant, and the clincher, Henry, Mary

Margaret and an infant. On the back of the picture was the date, September 1980. *He was still seeing her after she returned to Rexford.*

As Olivia studied the photos, she recognized the resemblance between a young, handsome Henry Gillette, with his thick dark blonde hair, and both Robyn and Victoria.

Olivia returned to the book. Henry Lee and Dorothy were married in January of 1980.

Now that I know this, how will it help Mitch without hurting Robyn?

THIRTY-THREE

"Hello Olivia," Mary Margaret said when she answered the phone. "Robyn isn't home. I could have her call you."

"Mrs. Gleason, I need to talk to you. Can you meet me somewhere?"

"Tonight?"

"I know this is short notice, but it's urgent. Do you know that new place, Bar None?"

"Yes."

"Meet me there. I'm leaving now."

Ten minutes later Mrs. Gleason arrived at the bar.

"Really, Olivia, I don't know what could be so important that we had to meet here." She pulled a chair from the table and sat down. A waitress took their order.

"I'm sorry, Mrs. Gleason. Where does Robyn think you are?"

"She takes a night class in Lima on Friday. I left her a note saying I went out with friends from the plant. Tell me what this is about."

Olivia didn't say anymore until after the waitress set drinks in front of them and left their table.

"I'm being blackmailed." She gave a short version of Judge Gillette's visit to the Press. Even in the darkened room, she could see Mrs. Gleason's face turn crimson.

"Why are you telling me this?"

"Because Judge Gillette informed me that if I don't print a retraction on the front page, he'll rescind Dr. James's contract and force him to leave town. If I do as he says, the Press will have no credibility. I can't allow the judge to manipulate the news. Somehow, he managed to have compromising pictures taken of Mitch and me together. No matter what I do, he'll use them against us."

"That bastard. I don't understand why you're telling me? I don't know what I can do to help you."

Olivia opened her purse and pulled out copies of the pictures of Mrs. Gleason. "I found these in my Uncle Fritz's private file. I don't want to embarrass you and I won't use them if you say no but I'd like to fight fire with fire."

Tears glistened in Mary Margaret Gleason's eyes as she fingered the photos. She took a few minutes to regain control of her emotions before she spoke. "My older sister Angela took these. I was seventeen when I discovered my pregnancy. When I told my father, he said I disgraced the family and put me out of the house. Angela came to the rescue. She drove me to Toledo and stayed there with me until I gave birth to Robyn. Angela found a job waiting tables at a diner and I clerked at a drug store for as long as I could. Henry drove up to Toledo on week-ends to see me. He did send money to help support me and the baby and continued to do so after I returned to Rexford.

"When Robyn was two months old, Angela, Robyn and I moved into the house where we live now. As soon as I could provide for myself, Angela returned to Toledo. Later, she married a young man she had met while she lived there.

"I was young, naïve and very much in love. Henry promised marriage as soon as he opened his own law office. You can't imagine the devastation I felt when he told me his father had arranged for him to marry Dorothy Pruitt. Henry claimed he had no choice in the matter. Lawrence Pruitt was a very influential man in Ohio politics. Henry's father, in order to further his own ambitions, needed that connection.

"Olivia, I loved him so much, I believed everything he said. Henry had a way of making me feel like the most important person in the world. We'd argue, I'd tell him to leave and never come back. A week later, he'd tap on my door and tell me how miserable his life had become and how much he loved me and Robyn. I'd welcome him back as if nothing had happened."

"But you finally brought it to an end," Olivia said.

"I don't feel comfortable telling you all of my past, but I want you to understand that I had never been with another man. I wanted to believe him. I had his child. In spite of all he did to me, a look, a glance or God forbid, a touch would bring me to my knees. He had a hold on me that I couldn't break. I dreamed about him for years after he left. To this day, I still have love-hate feelings..." Mary Margaret let the sentence hang.

Olivia didn't interrupt. She could see the turmoil in Mrs. Gleason's eyes as she spoke.

"Although I love Robyn with all my heart, I'm thankful I didn't become pregnant again. For more than a year after he married Dorothy, Henry continued to slip over at night to make love to me. It took me that long to face the reality that Robyn might soon recognize him. I had to protect my child and I told Henry he absolutely couldn't come anymore. He immediately stopped supporting Robyn.

"Angela hated Henry. She probably gave these pictures to your uncle."

"How would you feel if I used them?"

"Robyn is my only concern. I don't know how she'll handle this."

"I wanted to ask you about the birth certificate. The copy in the file lists the father's name as William Gleason. Were you ever married to him?"

Mary Margaret sighed. "Henry chose that name from an obituary column in a Toledo newspaper the month before Robyn was born. Henry had to be careful. He couldn't do anything that could be traced back to the Gillette family. Henry's father was a judge, and at that time, Henry had begun to make a name for himself as a lawyer. He had access to the proper forms and forged a marriage license and birth certificate with a phony name to protect Robyn and me. That saved Robyn from being listed as illegitimate and I would not be the subject of rumors and gossip. Henry knew that no one in our small town would bother to check the authenticity of the documents. Now that I look back, I realize he mainly wanted to protect the Gillette name."

"Do you have any contact with the judge now?"

Mary Margaret hesitated. "He blackmailed me just as he's trying to do to you. He said if I cause him any trouble, he'd make sure I'd lose my job. He told me no one in this town would hire me if he put out the word."

"Can he do that?"

"Not anymore. The ownership of the factory where I work has changed hands twice since Henry's involvement in it. He has no more influence there. I've worked there long enough to earn a good reputation. I'm sure Henry realizes he wouldn't dare say anything negative about me at this point. After all, Robyn is his child. He wouldn't want that information made public any more than I would."

Olivia watched as Mrs. Gleason weighed her options. They sat silently for more than a few minutes. Finally she said, "Let's go home and talk to Robyn. We can't let this man run rough-shod over us anymore."

"Thanks, Mrs. Gleason. I'll meet you back at your house." Olivia left money on the table to pay their tab.

***

Robyn sat quietly while Olivia told her of the evening events. She listened intently as her mother related the story of her birth.

"Don't you have anything to say?" Mrs. Gleason asked.

"Mom, I love you. Do you remember when I spent three weeks in Toledo with Aunt Angela and Uncle Bert the summer I turned sixteen?"

"Of course, you were excited because Bert promised to teach you to drive."

"He did, and Aunt Angela told me about you and Henry Gillette. She knew you'd never be able to tell me the story."

"But you never said anything."

"Henry Gillette isn't my father. You were both a mother and father to me. You were the one who gave me values and a happy life. When I look at Victoria, I feel nothing but pity. She's spoiled, immature and I imagine, very unhappy."

"Robyn, if I use these pictures, word might get out. I can't imagine the judge would want that to happen, but I can't guarantee it won't," Olivia said.

"It would be a bigger blot on his name than ours. I agree with mom. You have to put a stop to his dictatorial ways. Go for it. I wish I could be there when you face him."

"I'm sure he'll come to see me when I don't retract my statement in Friday's paper. I'll have a copy of these pictures available and tell him to back off. I'll let you know how it goes."

Robyn followed Olivia to her car. "Be careful of Henry Gillette. He's an evil man. I've heard of the dastardly things he pulled in this town. He's not above doing anything for his own gain."

"I realize that. I'll try not to face him when I'm alone."

"Are you going to tell Mitch about this?"

"No. I hope once I show the judge these pictures, it will be over. There's no need upsetting Mitch. I'm not sure how he'd react if he knew someone took compromising snapshots of us and the judge threatened to post them all over town. Mitch is an easy-going guy, but this might push him over the edge."

"I can understand that."

"He asked me to marry him."

"Olivia, I'm so happy for you. Does anyone else know?"

"Not yet. We haven't set the date so don't say anything."

"My lips are sealed."

"Robyn, I'm so in love. I want to be with him, touch him. He's kind and gentle. I can't wait to spend the rest of our time together."

"It's been written all over your face for weeks. You'll have a good life. You two were meant for each other."

"Thanks. I want to share the news with Jade and Kristen, but I'll wait until we set a definite date."

"Then we'll throw a big party. See you Wednesday," Robyn said. She waved as Olivia backed out of the driveway.

THIRTY-FOUR

I s this our standing date?" Olivia laughed as she met Mitch in the shadow of her porch Wednesday after the girl's night out.

"Come here, gorgeous." He took her in his arms. "Have you given anymore thought to a wedding date?"

"That's all I think about. What about June?"

"Way too far off." He kissed her nose, her eyes, teasing her until she forced his lips on hers. "Mmmm, you taste good. How about next week?" he countered.

"Be serious."

"Tomorrow?"

"Mitch. We need time to make plans."

"Baby, I have definite plans for us. Come home with me."

Olivia caught her breath. She couldn't go back to his apartment again, nor could she tell him why, but she didn't want to destroy the moment. "It looks like Aunt Etta and Sarah are in bed. Come inside with me."

"Are you serious?"

"You turning me down?"

"Not on your life, sweetheart. Lead the way."

Olivia opened the door and put her fingers to her lips. "You have to be quiet."

By the time they reached her bedroom door, Mitch had his shirt unbuttoned. When they were inside, he stepped out of his shoes and dropped his Levi's to the floor. He caught her in his arms and pulled her to the bed, undressing her in the process.

"Wait," she giggled. "I need to undo..."

"I got it." He slipped her bra off her shoulders and suckled her breast. "I can't believe how much I love you, Olivia. You're all I think about." He ran his hands over her body, exploring, caressing. Olivia trembled with anticipation but he wouldn't be hurried. He nibbled at her earlobe, ran his tongue down her neck and across her breasts.

"Oh my God, Mitch. I'm ready."

"Baby, you just think you are." Olivia squirmed as he kissed her inner thighs. "I want you to feel the passion." He slowly petted and teased her body until Olivia put her hand to her mouth to keep from crying out. Mitch waited until he could no longer keep control. Finally, as one, they collapsed in each other's arms and slept.

In the morning, Mitch blinked his eyes as daylight streamed in the window. He glanced at the clock—and Olivia lying beside him. "Good morning, sweetheart. I don't know when I've slept so well." He pulled her into his arms.

"Good Lord, Mitch, you're still here. Sarah is an early riser. You have to leave."

"That's a fine way to greet your lover." He stretched and put his arms behind his head. "I believe I'll sleep in this morning."

"This isn't funny. Get dressed. God, I feel like a teen-ager."

"Oh, did you do this when you were a teen?" He grinned as he pulled on his Levi's, stuffed his socks in his pocket and slipped his feet in his sneakers.

She pinched him. "You, of all people, know better."

"Ow."

"Quiet, you'll wake everyone."

"Baby, I want to shout to the world how much I love you."

"Some other time. Now wait until I make sure no one is up yet." Olivia opened the bedroom door a crack to check the hall and then motioned him to follow. They made their way to the front door and onto the porch.

He kissed her again. "I'll call you later. Did I remember to tell you how much I love you?"

"You did. Now get out of here."

Mitch blew her a kiss and jogged down the street to the Quik-Stop where he had parked his Jeep Wednesday night.

"You're up early," Sarah said as Olivia turned to go back to bed.

"You startled me. I thought I'd make coffee for a change, but it seems I can't manage to get going before you."

"I've always been an early-bird," Sarah laughed. "I thought I heard voices."

"Sorry, just me thinking out loud. I've so much to do today I needed to get a head-start."

"Miss Olivia, you go ahead and get your shower. I'll start breakfast."

All thoughts of getting more sleep were dashed. Olivia sang softly as she prepared for the rest of the day, and the rest of her life as Mrs. Mitchell James.

THIRTY-FIVE

The following Friday afternoon Judge Gillette suggested everyone leave early for the weekend. He remained at the downtown office and awaited the delivery of Rexford Free Press. He wanted to savor the headlines without interruptions and relish the pleasure of bringing the high and mighty Olivia McDougle to her knees.

He leisurely strolled to the front door to retrieve the paper, ripped the rubber band from the folded copy and returned to his desk. He sat back in the soft leather office chair and carefully spread out the front page. No retraction. He turned to the editorial page, nothing. She wouldn't dare hide the apology for the misinformation she reported on the inside of the paper. His directive clearly spelled out that he wanted nothing less than a complete retraction of the original story. Henry Gillette's face reddened as he searched the paper column by column. She didn't print it. That newcomer bitch ignored his orders. He couldn't believe Olivia McDougle had the nerve to defy him.

"If that's the way she wants to play the game, it's time to use my trump card." He unlocked his desk drawer and grabbed the sealed envelope that contained the negatives taken by the private detective he hired, along with the mock-up poster he made on his home computer and placed them in his briefcase. He stalked out of the building like a man on his way to witness an execution. The thought of Miss McDougle's face when she viewed the poster brought a sneer to his face. His brow furrowed with determination, he stepped into his car and drove to the newspaper office to confront the Rexford Press editor.

He burst in the front door, slamming it against the wall. Millie looked up from her desk. "Judge Gillette, you startled me. How may I help you?"

He didn't acknowledge the question or Millie, as he swept past her and headed straight into Olivia's office and closed the door with a snap. He stood quiet for a moment to make his presence known.

"Judge Gillette," Olivia said.

"Young lady, I don't make idle threats." His voice rose to a level of authority. He opened his briefcase and unrolled the obscene poster he made from copies of pictures taken from the window at Dr. James's apartment. "These will be all over town by this weekend. Then your reputation and that of the good doctor's will be ruined."

Olivia's face didn't reveal her inner turmoil. "I don't think you'll want to do that, Judge."

"Listen sister, you had your chance. No one will buy your paper. No one will make appointments to see Dr. James. It's all over, girlie."

Olivia could feel the heat of his breath as he leaned over the desk and literally spewed out the words. A look of contempt hung frozen on his angular face. Although her heart pounded as if it would burst from her chest and she reeled with fright, Olivia willed her hands not to tremble as she pulled an envelope from her desk drawer. "You might want to look at these." She spread the copies of the photos of Mary Margaret Gleason and Robyn in front of the judge.

His eyes grew wild. "What the hell—where did you get these?" He recoiled as if he had touched a live wire.

"That's immaterial. I also have records of your visits to Mary Margaret after you and Dorothy were married and the numbers and dates from money orders you sent for Robyn. I don't believe the amount of money you paid Mrs. Gleason comes close to the child support you owe, do you?"

"This is blackmail," he shouted and pounded his fist on her desk. The veins in his neck pulsated.

"You would know about that. I want the negatives of those pictures. If I see one copy of your poster, I will dedicate a full page of the Press to an expose of your sordid life, including the real reason you were removed from the bench."

Judge Gillette's face turned purple and then faded to deathly white. He threw the poster at Olivia and reached into his briefcase for the envelope of original pictures and the negatives. Choking on fury that bubbled in his throat, he could no longer speak. He stormed out of Olivia's office and collided into Millie. Before she could move, he pushed her aside and yanked the door open. He left it ajar as he made his way to his car.

"My God, Olivia, what on earth did you say to the judge?" Millie asked.

Olivia quickly shoved the poster and pictures into her desk drawer. "We reached an agreement. I don't believe Judge Gillette will give us anymore trouble."

By the time the judge arrived home, a deputy waited on the Gillette's front porch.

"I tried to call you," Dorothy said as she stood in the front doorway. "I didn't know what to do." She wrung her hands. Victoria sat on the couch and sobbed uncontrollably.

"What the hell's going on?" Judge Gillette addressed the deputy.

"I have an arrest warrant for Miss Victoria Gillette."

"Do you know who I am?"

"Yes sir."

"Let me see that." The judge snatched the paper from the deputy's hand and quickly read its contents. The warrant was issued by the Putnam County Attorney.

"Sir, if you'll please allow Miss Gillette to come with me," the deputy said.

"I'll do no such thing. You stand right where you are while I call our attorney."

Judge Gillette left the red faced deputy nervously shuffling from one foot to another.

"Henry, what are we going to do?" Dorothy asked. Tears streaked down her face.

The judge shoved her aside, went into his den and slammed the door. He could be heard screaming into the phone.

It took Gillette's attorney less than five minutes to arrive at the house. He looked over the warrant and informed the deputy that Miss Gillette would turn herself in at the Putman County Court house first thing Monday morning. He assured the deputy that he would personally accompany her.

After the deputy left, the attorney explained that Victoria would be processed and released. "I don't believe they can make the charges stick. It's that newly appointed Putman County attorney trying to make a name for himself. As soon as they realize who they're dealing with, they'll sing a different tune."

Monday morning, the lawyer picked up Judge Gillette, Dorothy and Victoria and drove them to the county seat. They entered the clerk's office and while the attorney completed the paperwork, Victoria cried, stamped her foot and blamed her father for not getting her out of the mess. Dorothy's attempt to placate her daughter did nothing but magnify Victoria's juvenile behavior.

The judge put his hand on her shoulder and tried to calm her. "It'll be okay, honey. This is simply a procedure we must follow." He had hoped to pay a fine and be done with it. That wasn't going to happen. The magistrate issued Victoria Gillette a date to appear in court.

Once they returned home, Victoria ran sobbing to her room and locked the door. While Dorothy went to the kitchen to make coffee, Judge Gillette escaped to the den to plan his next move. He paced. He couldn't use the pictures but he could make damn sure Mitch James knew about his lady friend. Although barely lunchtime, he opened the liquor cabinet, brought out a decanter of Jack Daniels and filled a silver rimmed glass. He whirled the contents, anticipating the smooth warmth, before downing it in one gulp and then poured a second.

Dorothy brought in a tray with sandwiches and fruit, but Henry didn't acknowledge the food or his wife. She left the den as quietly as she had entered.

Judge Gillette waited until Dr. James's office hours were over before he drove to Mitch's apartment. Contempt etched his face as he rapped on the door. Before Mitch answered, the judge produced a somber expression that clearly made him appear distraught. As much as he tried, he couldn't produce a tear, but years of hard drinking gave his red-rimmed eyes a watery effect.

"Judge Gillette. What brings you here? Are you feeling okay?"

"Victoria has been arrested. You must intercede and convince the court they've made an error."

Mitch raked his fingers through his hair. "I'm sorry. We went over this before. I can only say what I know as fact."

"This is Victoria. Surely after all this time, you can make an exception."

"Judge, I won't lie, not for you or anyone. Victoria will probably get a rap on the knuckles. I can't imagine they'll do anything more than that."

"But think of her reputation. You know how fragile she is. I don't believe she can survive the trauma. She was hysterical when I left the house."

"She'll be fine. Victoria is tougher than you think."

The judge changed his tactic. "You know this is a result of slander from the Anderson family newspaper."

Mitch shook his head. "The paper had nothing to do with it. This is a result of Victoria allowing an underage girl to drink at your residence."

"I see. You won't help the Gillette's but you have no problem hiding behind Olivia McDougle's skirts. I never figured you for that sort of man."

"I have no idea what you're talking about."

The judge raised his eyebrows. "I'm sure you do. It doesn't take much of a man to send his lady friend to beg for his job and bargain with me not to send him packing. She had the nerve to offer a bribe. Well, I'm a bigger man than that, but doctor, you disgust me." He paused a few moments to let his words sink in before he added, "You seem to be attracted to overbearing, assertive, manipulating women. It's as if you're unable to think for yourself. I find that interesting, for a man who is in charge of attending to the medical needs of the people in our town." The judge waited until he left the apartment before he dropped his control and allowed the smirk to grip his face. *Let Dr. James sort this one out.*

THIRTY-SIX

The entire world of Dr. Mitchell James crumbled. If Judge Gillette's remarks had not caught Mitch by surprise, he would have focused on everything that was said. But the words, bribe for his job, assertive, manipulating and overbearing were the ones engraved on his brain. Unforgettable shades of his ex-wife. The judge mentioned that also.

Do I choose women who take advantage of my good nature? Mitch grabbed a can of beer from the fridge and popped open the top. Before he had the opportunity to down the first cool gulp, another rap on the door interrupted him. He gazed in the direction and seriously considered not answering. The mere possibility that Judge Gillette forgot to tell him some other dastardly detail about Olivia or if he simply returned to gloat would prove to be more than Mitch could stomach.

The insistent rapping became fierce pounding, accompanied by a frantic voice that called out, "Dr. James. Please be home. Dr. James."

Mitch opened the door to find a man, white-faced and shaking as he held a young child in his arms.

"Come inside. What's going on?"

"Sorry to barge in on you like this, doc, but you weren't at your office. It's my daughter, Amy. Yesterday, we thought she had the flu. Now, she's feeling worse and complains about a nagging pain in her stomach."

"Vomiting? Diarrhea?"

"Yes, and fever too. She's become listless."

"Lay her on the couch," Dr. James directed. "Let me look her over." He spoke softly to the nine year old girl as he checked for the source of the pain. She pointed to her belly-button when Mitch asked where it hurt. He put a little pressure on her lower right side and she cried out.

"We need to get this young lady to the hospital. I can't be sure without a CT scan, but it looks like appendicitis. Are you okay to drive or do you want me to call an ambulance?"

"I can drive."

"Take her to the emergency entrance at Lima General. Don't speed or take any chances. I don't need to treat two patients when I arrive. I'll call ahead and let them know we're coming and then meet you there."

The man moved as if he were a robot as he picked up his daughter and carried her to his car. Mitch followed him outside and put his hand on the father's shoulder. "It'll be okay. I'll see you at the hospital." Then he added, "They'll take good care of her. Drive carefully."

The emergency kept Mitch from thinking about Olivia. He followed his patient to the hospital and remained with them until the surgeon arrived. After a quick consultation, and a series of tests, Mitch's diagnosis proved accurate. The CT scan showed appendicitis. Fortunately, there was no perforation.

Mitch observed the surgery and then took the opportunity to check on his other patients at the hospital before he returned home.

When he drove his car onto the driveway of his apartment, the conversation with Judge Gillette replayed in his mind. It felt as if someone turned up the volume to a deafening pitch. Mitch couldn't shut off the noise or the pain as the entire scenario crashed down on him again.

He sat in his Jeep and stared out the windshield. Anger fueled his disappointment. Frustrated, he slapped his hands on the steering wheel over and over until a burning pain spread across his palms and shot up his forearm. It didn't camouflage the hurt in his heart. Olivia went behind his back and offered a bribe to the judge. Henry Gillette said it was for his medical practice, but Mitch felt it was an attempt to manipulate his life. She didn't believe in him enough to realize he had the capability of handling problems the judge or anyone else threw at him. She had no regard for his feelings…his dignity.

Mitch couldn't think, couldn't see straight. Everything he hoped and planned for had vanished. She, like every other woman in his life, betrayed him. The strain of that exposure pierced his brain. He restarted the Jeep and drove to the Anderson house.

"Sweetheart, I didn't expect you tonight," Olivia said when she opened the door. Joy beamed on her face as she rushed to his arms.

Mitch stepped back and looked at her with disgust. "In my wildest dreams, I never imagined you would go behind my back and barter with my career. You were right, lady. I don't know you." He turned his back on her and walked toward the curb.

"Mitch, wait. I don't understand." It was too late. He sped off in his Jeep and left her standing on the porch. Olivia swayed and grabbed hold of the banister for support. Her hand shook as she covered her mouth to keep from screaming.

She closed the front door before Aunt Etta or Sarah heard her and slumped down on the porch swing. What had happened? What did he mean? The questions were overwhelming. She held her hands to her head as if it would surely explode. What had she done? Yo-yo emotions racked her mind. She loved him. There had to be a reasonable explanation. It was a misunderstanding, a mistake. She hated him. How could he leave without explaining? Olivia couldn't think what to do, where to go. Defeated, she sobbed as if her heart was broken.

Olivia had no idea how much time had passed before she felt able to pull herself together. Logic kicked in when she took stock of the situation. As a small child she faced the terrible grief and sorrow when her parents died. She survived. She survived Brian's betrayal and she'd survive Mitch James.

With new resolve, she walked into the house and to her room to pick up her purse. "Sarah, I'm going for a walk. Don't wait up." Then she slipped out quickly before anyone could reply and made her way to the J.K. Art Company on Maple Street.

THIRTY-SEVEN

Olivia arrived at Jade's shop and gave quiet thanks that the lights were off. That meant Jade hadn't scheduled evening classes. Olivia walked around to the back, climbed the stairs to her friend's apartment, and took a few moments to regain her composure before tapping on the door.

"Olivia, I've seen snow drifts with more color than you have. Come in and sit down." Jade put her hand on Olivia's shoulder and knew the difficulty had to do with Mitch. Jade hugged her friend and stroked her hair.

When confronted by the unconditional, sincere affection from her friend, Olivia found it difficult to form the words that raced through her mind.

"It's okay. It's okay. You don't have to say anything until you're ready. I'll get you something to drink." Jade pulled a bottle of brandy from a cabinet in the kitchen and filled two glasses, setting one on the kitchen table in front of Olivia.

Olivia finally found her voice. "He said terrible things to me, Jade."

"Olivia, Mitch didn't mean it. He can only act on the information he's been told."

"How did you know I was talking about Mitch?"

"My intuition, remember?"

"Why didn't you warn me?"

"I don't have the ability to predict precise events, but when you stood in the doorway, I knew something dreadful had happened. As soon as I touched your shoulder, I felt it had to do with Mitch."

Olivia took a large gulp of brandy waited a minute and then emptied the glass. "He appeared at the door, berated me and left." Olivia choked back a sob before she could continue. "The look he gave me shredded my heart. I don't understand any of it."

"Tell me everything. Start at the beginning and let's see if we can sort this out." Jade refilled Olivia's glass.

Olivia started slowly and soon emptied her heart and soul. She told Jade of her affair with Mitch and how much she loved him. "We planned to be married. I can't imagine what happened to make him attack me like that."

"Let me get the cards and see if I can shed some light on the cause of his anger."

"The Tarot cards?"

Jade's eyes twinkled. "I use them for show. I have my own special deck." She pulled a box of cards from the desk drawer and sat across from Olivia at the kitchen table. Jade shuffled the deck three times and laid four cards face up in front of her. She asked questions, adding cards as Olivia answered.

When the problem became apparent, Jade looked up at her friend. "You were visited by an older man and when he didn't get the satisfaction he sought, he spilled his venom on Dr. James. This older man will do anything to protect his younger daughter. Olivia, this man has no conscious or sense of morality. He will use his power to manipulate and destroy those that defy him."

Olivia gasped, "Judge Gillette."

"Mmmm. I see an older daughter. She'll intercede."

"You know, Jade. You know that Judge Gillette is Robyn's father."

Jade nodded. "I know. Have you told Robyn?"

"That's what started this." Olivia explained the entire situation including Judge Gillette's attempt to blackmail her and her plot to expose him. "But I don't want Robyn to face Judge Gillette. She doesn't deserve his spite."

"All I can tell you is, in some manner, Robyn will help."

"My life's such a mess. I should have never returned to Rexford."

"That's fate, my friend. I'm glad you're here." Jade refilled Olivia's glass again. "Meanwhile, I'm going to call your house and tell Sarah you're staying the night. That way your Aunt Etta won't worry and you and I will talk until neither of us has anything left to say."

Before the night ended, Jade told Olivia of her affair with Ham and about his wife's terminal illness. "I'm good at predicting the future of others, but I can't possibly imagine what will become of Ham and me."

"Let me give it a stab." Olivia giggled after too many glasses of brandy. "I'm going to dance at your wedding."

"We're getting entirely too silly. I'll find a nightshirt for you and get my robe. You take the bedroom and I'll pull out the sofa bed."

"Are you sure? I can sleep on the sofa," Olivia said.

"I insist. Olivia, I'm glad you're my friend. Most people are inhibited around me unless I'm giving art classes and if they knew I had visions, they wouldn't come near me."

"You didn't tell me about the visions. Now I'm intimidated."

"I think you're inebriated."

"You're right," Olivia giggled again. She took off her earrings and set them in a saucer on the kitchen counter. "I'll take that nightshirt now."

Jade sent Olivia to the bedroom, changed into her nightgown, and waited. Within the hour she heard the expected tap on her door.

"Ham?"

"Yeah sweetheart. It's over."

"I'm so sorry. Are you okay?"

"I feel sick. I couldn't do anything to help her."

"Ham, don't blame yourself, nothing could be done to save her. Come in. I'll put on coffee."

"Why's the sofa bed out? You expecting company?"

"It's Olivia. She's in the bedroom."

"Maybe I'd better go."

"Believe me when I tell you, she won't hear us."

"Jade, I need you."

Ham allowed Jade to unbutton his shirt and unbuckle his gun belt. He sat on the edge of sofa while she removed his shoes, pulled off his trousers.

"I'm here. I love you, Ham."

He stretched out on the sofa bed while Jade undressed and lay beside him. She caressed him gently.

"You have the touch of an angel," he said as he brought her close to him. He kissed her softly. His tongue explored her eager mouth. He ran his fingers through her hair and kissed her again, almost gruffly. "I, I care for you, Jade. I hope you know that." He covered her body with kisses.

Jade took over as she explored his body and found that special spot that brought him to rapture. He called out her name as they united as one and let the love flow from one to the other. Jade dissolved in his arms and sighed with complete contentment.

"Gal, you have mystical powers. You can't possibly imagine how much I wanted to be with you tonight."

Jade put her arms around him, not wanting to let go. "Can I do anything to help you with the arrangements?"

"It's taken care of. I called Janie's family this morning when she began to fail. Her mother preplanned everything last year when we found the doctors held no hope for her recovery." Then the reality of Janie's death hit him. Deep sobs racked his body.

Jade held him close and spoke softly. "You were a good husband, Ham. Don't ever forget that. You did everything you could."

"She'd been sick for years. Is it selfish of me to think she's finally at peace?"

"You know it isn't."

He kissed her again. "I'd better go before your friend comes in. I don't want to embarrass you."

"Let's have coffee first. You look like you could use a cup. I'll make a fresh pot." She put on a robe and went to the kitchen.

Ham dressed while Jade set the steaming mugs of coffee on the table. They held hands and talked until dawn. Ham slipped out the door a few minutes before Olivia came into the kitchen.

"Jade, you look as if you haven't slept. Are you okay?"

"A better question, how do you feel?"

"Like I've been hit by a truck."

"I have the remedy for that." Jade went to the cupboard and produced a small bottle. She uncorked it and poured a few drops in a glass of orange juice. "Drink this and lie down. You'll drop off to sleep and when you wake up, you'll feel great."

"What is it, a magic potion?"

"The usual. Eye of a newt, toe of frog."

"What?"

"Just kidding," Jade laughed. "Trust me, it'll do the trick."

Olivia wrinkled her nose, downed the liquid and went back to bed. Jade stretched out on the sofa-bed inhaling Ham's lingering scent. Both girls slept for hours.

THIRTY-EIGHT

Robyn Martin grabbed the mail from the box before she entered the front door of the house. She dropped her purse on the table and sorted through the ads and flyers until she came to the credit card statement. When she opened the envelope and read the balance, she allowed the rest of the mail to slide from her hand.

"What's this?" There were charges from a hotel in Seoul, along with expensive meals. "Look at these prices. What is going on with Greg?"

She remembered the e-mail she received from him last week saying he had to go on a covert mission. Greg had been assigned to protect the Korean border, for God's sake. He didn't go on covert missions. If he did, he certainly wouldn't charge a hotel room.

She didn't want to believe the thoughts that raced through her mind but she couldn't deny the outrageous hotel charge on the statement. Greg was having an affair. Her optimistic side argued with the obvious. What if she confronted him and it wasn't true? What kind of wife would she be then?

She went into her room and started the computer. *Think. Don't do or say anything rash.* Robyn deliberated a few minutes and then sent her husband a carefully worded e-mail.

"Hi Sweetie. Hope things are going well. We've been busy at the bank. There's been a rash of identity thefts here. Imagine, even in a small town like Rexford. I'm afraid someone has stolen our personal information and used our credit card. I had to put a hold on the account until this mess gets sorted out. I'll let you know as soon as I have an update.

The girls and I still get together on Wednesday night. Mom's same as always. Anything new there? Have you had time off to go sight-seeing?

I miss you and hope you get home soon. Love you, Robyn."

Her face colored with guilt when she clicked on the 'send' box, but that should take care of things for awhile. She turned off the computer and picked up the phone and gave the credit card company the same information. They said they would send her a new card and number. Robyn felt sneaky and deceitful, but for the time being, it was the best thing she could think of to do. If her suspicions were wrong, she'd send Greg the new card. Meanwhile, he couldn't max out their credit card or worse, take out a loan that she'd be responsible for paying. Instant remorse swept over her. She felt foolish for considering that her husband would take advantage of her. But yet, she had no explanation for the horrendous credit card bill.

Both frustrated and confused, Robyn pulled out the treadmill and worked out to relieve her anxiety. Exercise cleared her mind and working up a sweat loosened her muscles after standing at the bank all day.

Robyn tired of being Little Miss Happy Face. She wanted to scream and swear and kick things around the house, although that had never been her style. The mere thought of throwing a fit made her feel ridiculous.

Robyn's even disposition drew comments from Olivia. "Since first grade, you had a way of keeping everyone in good spirits," she would say.

That may have been true in grade-school. But when she entered junior high the bits of gossip about her parents, or more accurately, lack of a father caught her ear. Kids repeat what they hear at home. Apparently, the Gleason family had been the topic of more than one dinner conversation.

Olivia would have none of it. She defended Robyn to the end. She let everyone know that she and Robyn were best friends and if anyone picked on Robyn, they'd have to answer to Olivia. With her red hair and her determined temperament, everyone knew Olivia meant business. Robyn called her General Fearless. Olivia retorted, "If I'm General Fearless, you're Captain Obvious. You wear your heart on your sleeve." She spoke the truth. It went against Robyn's nature to be hurtful or deceitful.

Robyn and Olivia were constant companions until graduation, when Olivia went off to college and Robyn attended a business school in Lima. It seemed like yesterday. Once again, she looked forward to spending time with her friend. Their Wednesday night dinners became her salvation.

Robyn shook with anger as different scenarios ran across her mind. She envisioned Greg entering an expensive restaurant with a woman hanging on his arm, maybe an Oriental woman. Or it could be someone from the military. Oh my gosh, what if Greg and a woman from his outfit were involved? They'd be together constantly. Tears moistened her eyes as she pictured Greg flashing the credit card, their joint credit card, to pay the tab—and then the hotel room. Robyn allowed her imagination to run wild. She hated the suspicions feelings and her lack of trust.

She upped the pace on the treadmill, trying to run off her frustrations. What has happened to them? Greg mentioned a few months ago about his plans to come home for the

Christmas holidays. Maybe then they could sort everything out. She wouldn't ask too many questions over the internet. She'd rather face him and look into his eyes when they talked.

Greg loves you, Robyn's optimistic side reassured. The problems they faced were probably a case of separation and miscommunication. After all, he had been gone a long time— longer than they had been together. And what if he had the chance to get some R&R? Did she really begrudge him that small pleasure? Suddenly, Robyn questioned her doubts. Maybe she shouldn't have sent the e-mail.

Mary Margaret Gleason came home and interrupted Robyn's dark thoughts.

"You're home early, Mom. I thought you were going to help with inventory."

"I decided not too, all that lifting and stooping gets to me. You look like you've been crying. Are you all right?"

"It's perspiration from the treadmill. I guess I overdid it." Robyn grabbed her shirttail to wipe away the tears. No point in getting into a long, drawn-out explanation with her mom.

"Feel like going out to eat for a change. Maybe we could go to the Four Corners for pork tenderloin. We haven't been there in a long time."

"That sounds great." Robyn hid behind her happy face. "I'll put away the treadmill and take a shower. Then I'm good to go."

THIRTY-NINE

Y ou have no choice, Olivia. You must attend the Corn Roasting Festival. What would the people of Millsburg say if you were a no-show after all the promotion your paper did for the event?" Robyn's determined voice over the phone left no doubt. She would not let Olivia mope around the house. It had been two weeks since her break-up with Mitch and Olivia hadn't recovered from the shock.

"I don't feel very festive."

"Well, Kristen, Jade and I will take care of that. I'll pick you up at noon tomorrow. No excuses."

Olivia had no alternative but to agree. Her friends were on a mission to take her mind off Mitch and pull her out of her funk. Maybe for a few hours she could forget. Not likely. His face surrounded her night and day. She would awake and for a moment, forget and then reality would strike a blow to her heart.

The oppressive August temperature on Saturday morning convinced Sarah and Etta not to make the trip to the festival. Olivia wished she could stay home with them.

She studied her face in the mirror as she tied her hair back in a ponytail. Her eyes remained puffy from crying herself to sleep the night before. It seemed to be a pattern in her life now. She rummaged through her cosmetics to find make-up that would cover the dark circles. She had to get a grip. Her life and career would go on in spite of Mitch James.

She pulled on white slacks and a green and white stripped tee. Sandals and a baseball cap with an oversized visor completed the outfit.

Robyn, neat as usual, in tan cargo shorts, a white blouse tied at the waist and a safari hat. She came prepared to give Olivia a persuasive nudge if needed.

"Olivia, you look great," Robyn said.

"I feel…well never mind. Let's go."

Jade waited for them in front of her shop wearing a long, form fitting cotton print dress with straps knotted at the shoulder. Slits up both sides of the skirt revealed a glimpse of her shapely legs. She artfully wrapped a matching band of material around a very large floppy straw hat.

"I didn't know all those colors could be woven into one piece of material," Robyn teased as Jade climbed into the car.

"Girlfriends, when I get festive, I get festive," her infectious laughter lightened the mood. "Now let's get this show on the road."

When they arrived at Millsburg, Robyn drove to Kristen's house and parked the car. Kristen looked as if she stepped out of a fashion magazine wearing a mauve tunic trimmed in white, over white slacks and a matching white straw hat. The four of them presented a stunning contrast in style, and heads turned as they walked down Main Street to join the celebration.

"Friday's headlines in the Press read, SEE YOU ALL IN MILLSBURG TOMORROW. I believe my subscribers took it literally. Look at the size of this crowd," Olivia remarked.

Tables and chairs lined the block long street. Volunteers manned the barbecues and stands, selling every kind of food imaginable. Before the girls reached the far end, their plates were loaded.

"Miss Kristen."

"Hi Todd. Girls I'd like you to meet Todd Lowell, the man who taught me how to remodel my house. "This is Jade, Robyn and Olivia."

"It's my pleasure, ladies. Welcome to Millsburg."

"He's cute," Robyn said as they found a table and sat down to eat."

"He and his father own the local hardware and lumber store. I'd be lost without them."

Kristen was met with greetings everywhere they went.

"We should have worn name tags. It would have saved her a lot of introductions," Jade said.

"Small towns. Everyone knows the school teacher," Kristen explained.

"Do they know everything the school teacher does?" Jade teased.

"If they don't, they make something up," Kristen said.

"I couldn't eat another bite," Robyn said as she placed her paper plate in a garbage container. The others followed suit.

"I guess we should make an appearance at the bandstand," Olivia said without enthusiasm. "I'll need to write an article for the Press when I return to Rexford."

The Millsburg High School Band sat on a makeshift stage at the end of the street. The city council members gathered at a table in front of the bandstand. They applauded when Olivia approached.

The mayor spoke into a portable mike, "We want to thank you for helping make our festival a success. Your newspaper promotion brought three times the normal crowd to Millsburg." He pushed the mike at a surprised Olivia.

"Thank you. I believe all small towns have one thing in common, the need to stay connected. I hope the Rexford Press can continue to be that link."

Mark Henner, the Press photographer, recorded the event on film.

"Very nicely done," Jade said as they walked back toward Kristen's house.

"Are we ready to go home?" Olivia asked. Her voice fell flat and lifeless, exactly as she felt.

"We're ready to go to Kristen's. She invited us for a gabfest," Robyn said.

"I don't know," Olivia said.

"But we do," the girls insisted.

"I can see I'm outnumbered." A slight smile crept across Olivia's face and for the first time that day she exposed a glimmer of emotion.

They walked back to Kristen's house, sat on the patio and sipped iced tea.

"Olivia, you've been brooding long enough. What can we do to help?" Robyn asked.

"I don't know what you're talking about."

"You and Mitch. Are you ready to tell us what happened?"

"There's nothing more I can add. I have no idea what he meant. He verbally attacked me, and without any explanation, left me standing on the porch."

"What exactly did he say?" Kristen asked.

"Something about bribing someone and going behind his back to barter for his job. It made no sense."

They looked at Jade.

"I can only tell you the same thing I told Olivia when I read her cards. We determined the man who caused the problem is Judge Gillette, but I don't know what he did. I would have to talk to him to find out what he meant about Mitch's job, and that ain't gonna happen. I know he's protective of Victoria and he could be dangerous."

"It's over. There's no point discussing it further. I apparently made a huge mistake when it came to Mitch James," Olivia said.

"Well, I for one am not content with leaving it at that. You need to fight for what you want," Robyn said.

"I have no fight left in me. Let's drop it. I should have never left New York." Her expression confirmed the sadness in her voice.

"Don't ever say that. We would have never met if it hadn't been for you. You can't believe how lonely I have been here. I went from having no family at all, to finding three caring sisters," Kristen said.

"Kristen, you must tell us about Todd," Robyn said. "He's a hunk."

A slight color rose on Kristen's face. "There's nothing to tell. He gave me guidelines when I remodeled the house. I didn't have a clue where to start. Todd lent me tools and showed me how to use them."

"I don't think his admiring look had anything to do with your construction skills," Robyn said. "Is he married?"

"No. Well, I don't know too much about him."

"Then it's high time to find out," Jade teased. "I can't imagine letting a good-looking guy like that walk around unattached."

"It's getting late. I think we should start back," Olivia said. She stood to leave. Jade and Robyn followed. "We'll see you Wednesday, Kristen."

Robyn drove Olivia home before she dropped off Jade. When Jade started to get out of the car, Robyn stopped her.

"What do you think, 'bartering with my job', means?"

"I don't know. Evidently, Judge Gillette has in some way goaded Mitch. He wouldn't have shown him the pictures.

Mitch would have killed him, so the judge had to come up with something else to agitate Mitch."

"I don't think this is going to heal itself. I wish I could think of some way to help," Robyn said.

"Me too, but I don't know what. Unless Olivia and Mitch get together and talk this out, nothing will change. If we could only find out what went on between Mitch and Judge Gillette it might help."

"Mitch and Olivia love each other. Someone has to bring them back together."

"Good luck there. Mitch is angry and Olivia, hurt. I don't know how we can fix that," Jade said.

"In spite of Olivia's distress, we had a good day. I'll see you Wednesday night at dinner. Gotta go."

Robyn didn't go home. She drove to the back of Dr. James's office and parked her car. She walked to the apartment and rapped loudly on his door.

"What is it?" Mitch asked when he peered out the small window. "Do you have an emergency?"

"I would say so."

"Robyn? What can I do for you?"

"Can I talk to you, Dr. James?"

"What's on your mind?"

"Olivia."

His face darkened. "I don't care to discuss Miss McDougle."

Robyn pushed her way inside. "There are things you can't possibly know. Sit down, doctor. I've a story to tell you."

Robyn covered every detail. When she finished, Mitch buried his face in his hands.

"My God, it never occurred to me—you say there were pictures?"

"From this very apartment."

"The window. I had opened it earlier to let the breeze in."

"And someone waited outside to take advantage of the situation. Can't you see, Dr. James? Someone had you and Olivia followed."

"And all that crap Judge Gillette told me...I have to call her. I have to explain. The judge threw me under the bus and I let him get away with it."

"Be careful. I'm putting my friendship with Olivia on the line by giving you this information. If you tell her about the pictures, she'll know it came from me and if you mention it to Judge Gillette, you'll compromise whatever agreement he made with Olivia."

Mitch stood and paced the small apartment. "How on earth will I make amends?"

"Whatever you decide, don't let it go on too much longer. You're the doctor. Heal this before it's too late."

FORTY

The questions Jade, Robyn and Kristen continued to ask about Mitch made matters worse. As soon as Olivia thought she had a hold on her emotions, someone mentioned his name. Everyone had advice but no one had answers. There were no answers.

When Olivia returned home from Millsburg Saturday night, Aunt Etta asked if Mitch had attended the festival. Sarah said she saw him at the drug store and he looked, 'real sad.' One of them managed to mention his name in every other sentence.

Sunday afternoon, Olivia realized it was a contrived plot by Aunt Etta and Sarah to bring Mitch's name up in every conversation. In spite of Etta's and Sarah's good intentions, by Sunday evening, Olivia could no longer keep it together. She felt as if the walls were closing in, squeezing the very life from her. She couldn't breathe, couldn't think. She had to get out of the house and clear her head.

Maybe a long walk would wear her out and she'd finally get a good night's sleep. She attached the cell phone to her belt and put a small note pad and pencil in her pocket to jot down any new ideas she might have for her next editorial.

"I'm going for a walk. Don't wait up," she called to Aunt Etta and Sarah as she went out the front door.

A light wind cooled the August heat and Olivia felt comfortable enough to stroll to the other side of town and back. She reasoned it should give her a decent work-out.

Olivia couldn't believe how much some areas of Rexford had deteriorated. She leisurely walked on the side streets and came upon the three-story apartment complexes near the corner of Oak and Hawthorne. Rexford residents once referred to that part of town as the new addition. A developer had planned to build additional apartments in the area. Later the lots were sold and rezoned for single family homes.

She recalled the summer the apartments were built. Uncle Fritz took her along when he looked over the construction. She must have been seven or eight at the time. Olivia remembered feeling important as they trudged through the partially finished structures. Modern apartment buildings in Rexford caused everyone to become excited. They became a symbol of progress to the small town. Over the years the two buildings had become shabby and ill-kept. The untrimmed shrubs grew high and ragged. Trash and debris littered the grounds.

Olivia had walked past the first building when a flash caught the corner of her eye. She turned for a second look and saw a blaze rising from the back of the second structure. She grabbed her cell phone and called the fire department and then made a second call to Evan Henner. When he answered, she briefed him of the situation, gave the location and asked him to meet her there.

"I'm on my way," Evan said.

Olivia ran toward the burning building and screamed, "Fire," over and over again but her voice didn't seem to carry. She began to pound on doors. "Get out. The building's on fire." Blank stares from the residents amazed her. As her message registered, the tenants began to pour out of the downstairs units. She moved on to the second floor and banged on those doors. As she ran down the darkened hallway, two of the tenants scrambled to carry a disabled lady to safety. Others left the building with only the clothes on their back.

Olivia raced up the stairs to the third floor and fought her way through the rising smoke, thankful she heard the shrill of sirens blare in the background.

By the time she reached the final apartment in the back of the building, the smoke had turned thick and black. "Fire, you have to get out," she screamed and pounded on the door. No one replied. "Fire, fire. Please, you have to leave," Olivia yelled again. She turned to go back down the stairs when the door partially opened. A young girl holding an infant backed away as Olivia pushed her way inside. The door slammed shut behind her.

Olivia could see a look of fear frozen on the girl's face. She spoke softly, "We have to get out now. The building is on fire and it's not safe to stay inside any longer."

The girl didn't speak, but held the infant tighter, as if she feared Olivia would attempt to take the baby away.

"Let's go." She led the girl to the door. The metal knob seared Olivia's fingers and the door felt equally hot. Smoke seeped into the apartment from underneath the threshold. Olivia realized they could no longer use the stairs as an escape route. A sickening wave of fear flooded her senses but she had to remain calm and reassure the girl that they would be safe.

"What's your name?" Olivia asked.

"Melissa."

"How old is your baby?"

"Three, ah three weeks."

"Stand by the window. I'll stuff a rug against the door to keep the smoke out."

Olivia used her cell and called Evan. "I'm on the third floor in the southwest corner of the second building. There's a mother and a newborn baby here. The fire has spread to the stairway and we're trapped." She kept a steady voice although she could feel her body tense with growing panic.

"Got ya, Olivia. Hold on. Don't hang-up." He yelled to the Captain of the Rexford Fire Department, "My boss is on the third floor with a woman and her baby. She says there's no escape route from the apartment. The fire has spread to the stairwell. You'll have to bring them down on a ladder." He gave the captain their location. "Okay, Olivia. They're on their way."

Mitch James had arrived in time to hear Evan's message. His face paled as he grabbed Evan by the shirt. "Your boss? You work for the Press?"

"Easy doc." Evan removed Mitch's hands. "Yeah, I'm the Press photographer."

"Dear God, is Olivia McDougle caught in the fire?"

"She's okay. They're bringing the ladder around. She'll be out of there in a few minutes."

Mitch stared at the fire and listened to Evan's conversation with Olivia.

"Don't worry, boss lady. Watch the window for the firemen."

Before the fire crew could extend the ladder, an explosion rocked the building. By this time, both structures were engulfed in flames. Mitch watched helplessly as the firemen backed away.

"You still with us Olivia?" Evan shouted on the phone.

"We're okay, but the ceiling is crumbling and the room's thick with smoke. I'm taking the mother and baby to the bathroom. Let me know when it's safe to go back to the window."

"Roger. Stay put." Evan relayed the message to the chief.

The firemen beat back the blaze and once again raised the ladder to the third floor. Smoke billowed from the window as one of the men entered the apartment. The chief called to Evan, "Tell Miss McDougle my men are inside."

To protect them from the heat, Olivia dampened a towel, wrapped it around the girl's shoulder and draped another over the baby. After words of encouragement, Melissa reluctantly released the infant to the first fireman and he passed the baby to the second man on the ladder. He carefully carried the child down and handed it to Dr. James, who cradled the baby in his arms and held an oxygen mask close to the infant's face. The second fireman positioned himself on the ladder and coaxed Melissa out the window. He held on to her as they backed down the ladder together. Olivia attempted to follow, but was told to wait until someone returned for her.

Smoke filled the apartment, making it almost impossible to see or breath. A flash of fire licked under the door and the intense oppressive heat in the small room became almost unbearable. Terrified, Olivia soaked the remaining towels and covered herself.

Mitch sent the mother and baby to the hospital for observation and could now focus his attention on the third story window. His heart thumped with anticipation as he searched for a glimpse of Olivia. Worry sickened him as he watched fire shoot skyward from other apartments on the third floor. He prepared to climb up himself when a fireman went back for Olivia. Mitch watched with relief as they safely touched the ground. Before he could talk to Olivia, one of the firemen called him to the side of the building to tend to a critical victim.

Evan documented the entire rescue on film. "Ms. Editor, you're a hero," he teased Olivia.

"Some hero. The firemen had to rescue me."

It became bedlam on the ground. The chief shouted orders as they aimed extra hoses at the blaze. He alerted the Ottawa Fire Department to send extra ambulances to the scene.

Firemen began to bring victims from the other building to a make-shift triage set up on the grass. Fortunately, there were few serious victims, mostly smoke inhalation, minor burns, cuts and bruises. It became apparent that Olivia's early warning allowed most to escape unharmed.

Hamilton Bowers and a few of his men had arrived, cordoned off the area and directed traffic. That allowed the EMT's and Dr. James to attend to the victims without interference from onlookers.

It would have unnerved Olivia to be so close to Mitch if the situation hadn't been so frantic. She kept occupied with the job at hand. She called pastors from the local churches to find temporary shelters for those who lost their homes and belongings, and then focused her attention on interviewing the tenants. Evan followed her, snapping photos for the Press.

When the last ambulance left the scene, Mitch searched for Olivia. "Are you hurt?" He reached out to wipe blood from the side of her face.

"I'm fine. It's no more than a scratch."

"Olivia, I..."

She interrupted. "We have nothing to say to each other. I have no intention of allowing you to make a fool of me again."

His shocked look quickly faded. He didn't have time to stay and reason with her. Mitch got into his Jeep and drove to Lima General.

After Olivia gave a statement to the Rexford Fire Chief, she rode back to the office with Evan. She wrote the story while he developed pictures. The sun hadn't yet peaked over the horizon Monday morning when Olivia finished. She placed the article and photo on Millie's desk with instructions for her to call the fire department and inquire if they had determined the cause of the blaze. She also left a note for Julius to research the tax records and find out who owned the buildings, and if they were equipped with sprinkling devices.

When Olivia returned home, the dire events of the evening crowded her senses. Tears filled her eyes as she thought about the fire, the people who were injured and the danger that surrounded her…and Mitch. She wanted his arms to comfort her. She wanted to feel his touch, make love to him. The more she tried to put him out of her mind, the more he lingered there.

After a hot bath, she fell into bed and slept. But his image invaded her dreams.

***

At the hospital, Mitch had difficulty concentrating on his patients. By the time he returned to Rexford, he was exhausted and emotionally spent.

Thoughts of Olivia crowded his mind. The hurt look on her face told it all. She would no longer speak to him and seemed to shrink away from his touch. How could things have gone so wrong?

"Judge Gillette caused this. It's his fault that Olivia can no longer trust me." As soon as he said the words, he knew they were untrue. He owned the fault. He didn't think it through. He was too quick to believe Judge Gillette's lies. Mitch wondered what kind of man he had become to allow himself to use such poor judgment. He alone had shattered his relationship with Olivia.

After spending too much time feeling sorry for his actions, Mitch made a decision. He loved Olivia. He would do whatever it took to win her trust. He'd pull out all the stops and convince her they were meant to be together.

FORTY-ONE

The crisp autumn air turned the green leaves of summer into hues of red, yellow and orange. Fall had always been Olivia's favorite season. Had been. Now she didn't have a favorite anything. It became a chore to get up and get dressed in the morning.

Far beyond tears, Olivia wanted to scream, yell and pull at her hair. She couldn't bear to see couples hold hands in public or catch a quick kiss. She felt extremely jealous of the love Jade had for Ham. In her wildest dreams, Olivia couldn't imagine being so petty. The unfamiliar taste of self-pity became ever present in her mouth. That trait had never before raised its ugly head and she hated herself for it.

She feigned cheerfulness around Aunt Etta, Sarah and the staff at the Press. The charade wore on her like a too-tight shoe.

In addition to the disaster surrounding her personal life, Olivia faced pressure at the Press after the headlines and pictures recounted the horrific fire at the apartment complex. The story provided additional fodder for the ever-present Rexford rumor mill. Julius' probing uncovered the name of a city council member who owned the property and found the buildings were in violation of the fire code regulations. The paperwork had mysteriously disappeared while Judge Gillette sat on the bench. Once again Olivia came under criticism for exposing the information in her editorials, but any attempt to block her from revealing the underhanded tactics failed.

Judge Gillette sent a letter to the editor complaining that the Press took sides without reporting the true facts. The councilman who owned the apartments demanded Olivia's censure and urged the Press readers boycott the paper. It seemed ironic to Olivia that the alleged guilty parties used the Press for their forum and she wrote as much in her editorials. She also made a plea for clothing and furniture for the fire victims. One of the churches offered their basement as a gathering area for donated goods.

***

Jade, Robyn and Kristen, well aware of Olivia's personal dilemma, insisted she continue to meet with them for dinner on Wednesday nights. They warned they would accept no excuses for her absence and would come to her house and drag her to the Steak Grill if necessary.

Although Olivia tried to keep up with the conversation, she had little to add. And as much as the girls tried to encourage their friend, she felt demoralized, empty.

Olivia's attempt to set up an advertising blitz for Newton City proved unsuccessful. When she visited with the Newton City Council, they decided there wasn't sufficient time to organize anything this year. After much discussion, they put together an autumn hayride to take place early next October. Tentative plans included a train of hay wagons starting at one of the large pumpkin farms with stops along the way at local apple orchards and ending at the town hall for a barbecue and square dancing. When the city council reviewed the coverage the Rexford Press gave Millsburg, they became excited at the prospect of attracting neighboring communities to Newton City and assured Olivia they would work with her to set up a fall program. Olivia found a contributor to write news of

Newton City for the Press and promised the mayor to highlight their town events. They in turn would encourage subscriptions to the newspaper. Her apparent enthusiasm touched everyone at the meeting. A smile grasped her face as she interacted with the council members. Inside, her heart withered with pain. Olivia felt as if she were running on automatic pilot. Before she left, Olivia purchased a truckload of pumpkins to be delivered in time for Rexford's Halloween celebration.

Rexford's plans for the Halloween parade were set in motion. The route would start at the business district on Main Street and end at the high school gymnasium. A panel of residents would choose the best costumes in each age category and award trophies supplied by the Press. Rexford merchants agreed to set up tables and provide treats for everyone who dressed for the occasion. The PTA supervised games, including a pumpkin carving competition and apple dunking contests. While entertaining Rexford's young children, the event also kept them safe and off the dark streets. A dance for the high-school set had been scheduled for the evening.

Exhausted after an emotionally draining work week, Olivia slept in on Sunday morning.

"Miss Olivia," Sarah called. "Come quick."

"Aunt Etta," Olivia said aloud as she bolted from her bed and rushed out to the foyer. "What is it?"

Sarah held her sides, her belly jiggling with laughter. "I ain't never seen anybody get flowers delivered on Sunday. Would you look at this?"

A basket of fall flowers sat on the entry table.

Olivia blinked her eyes. "How nice of someone to send flowers to Aunt Etta. Is there a card?"

"Yes ma'am, but it ain't for Etta. It's addressed to you."

Olivia opened the card. "Olivia, I've been a fool. Will you forgive me? I love you. Mitch"

"No," Olivia screamed. "No, no, no. Sarah, get rid of these."

"What is it Miss Olivia?"

Olivia dropped the card and ran to her room.

"Oh my." Sarah nervously wiped her hands on her apron.

"What on earth is all the shrieking about?" Etta asked as she came out of the kitchen.

"It must have something to do with whatever's on this," Sarah picked up the card and handed it to Etta.

Etta grinned. "It's about time Mitch James came to his senses. Sarah, leave the flowers where they are. Maybe they'll remind a certain someone that people do make mistakes."

Monday morning Olivia sat at her desk reviewing notes for the next issue of the Press.

Millie brought her a cup of coffee. "Victoria Gillette has been given a court date. Julius noticed it on the calendar while he covered a DUI case in Ottawa Friday afternoon."

"When?"

"October 31st."

"Halloween?"

"Ironic, isn't it?"

"Who's assigned to the case?"

"According to Julius' notes it's Judge Matheson."

"Uh-oh."

"You got that right. Judge Matheson and Judge Gillette have bumped heads on several occasions."

"Do you think Gillette will request someone else?"

"That would be suicide. This isn't a felony. Julius told me this morning that Victoria will probably get a severe warning and perhaps have to pay the Zelman girl's medical bills. Extreme cases might result in a fine or jail time, but that's not likely to happen."

"Make sure Julius attends the hearing," Olivia said. "We need to stay on top of this."

Later, Millie signed for a flower delivery from the Rexford Florist Shoppe. "This is for you." She brought in an arrangement of yellow mums set among multi-colored fall leaves and cat-tails, and placed it on Olivia's desk.

Olivia swallowed the emotion that attempted to surface. "Please set them in the front office for everyone to enjoy," she said.

"Don't you want to read the card?"

Olivia took the card and asked Millie to close the door on her way out.

"Olivia, I'm reaching out to you. Please give me another chance. I love you. Mitch." Olivia tore it in as many pieces as she could possibly manage.

Balloons waited for her at home that evening followed by candy on Tuesday.

"Livie, you should fight with Mitch more often. I'm liking this," Etta told her.

Wednesday, when the girls met at the Steak Grill for dinner, the waiter brought a bottle of champagne to the table.

"Compliments from Dr. James," he told them.

Robyn searched the restaurant but Mitch was nowhere to be found. She inquired at the bar and learned Dr. James had phoned in the order. Kristen and Jade roared with laughter when Robyn announced they could have seconds if they wanted. Olivia was not amused.

"Come on, Olivia. Anyone can make an error in judgment. At least he's man enough to own up to it," Robyn said.

"It's too late," Olivia said. "I'm not interested."

"Help me out here, girls," Robyn said to Kristen and Jade.

Kristen winked at Jade. "Can you read the residue in the bottom of a champagne glass?"

"No, but if we order loose tea..."

"That won't be necessary," Olivia said. "I can tell you my future and it doesn't include Mitch James. Now, could we please change the subject?"

"I have news," Robyn said. "Greg may be coming home on leave in December. He e-mailed me last night. If it works out, I'll fly to Hawaii to meet him."

"That's wonderful. When will you know for sure?" Kristen asked.

"I should hear from him this week-end. I can't wait."

Everyone talked at once, everyone except Jade. The news troubled her. She could see a haze of disappointment surround Robyn.

After the dinner, Olivia turned down offers for a ride home. The walk in the clear cool evening air provided time to clear her mind. When she reached her porch, Mitch waited in the shadows.

"Olivia."

"What do you want?"

"I want you to hear me out."

"I believe you said everything the last time you stood here."

"I was wrong. Won't you give me an opportunity to explain?"

"It's too late. You've made your feelings perfectly clear."

He reached for her hand, Olivia stepped back. "Don't," she said. "Don't touch me. Don't come into my life again." She ignored the look of distress on his face.

"You can't mean it."

"I mean every word. I'll not get hurt again."

"Olivia, Judge Gillette told me…"

"I don't care what he said to you. You chose to believe him. You felt so comfortable with his story, you didn't bother to talk to me, didn't bother to ask what really happened. You made your choice, Mitch James, and now I'm making mine."

Before he could speak, she went into the house and closed the door.

FORTY-TWO

A re you sure? I mean, you won't let them put me in jail or anything. Like, I couldn't bear that. I swear, daddy, I'll kill myself if that happens."

"Don't be overdramatic, Victoria. You'll probably be assigned community service."

"Like at the Red Cross or the library? I could help the elementary school teachers with their reading program. That would be cool."

"Something along those lines. Now don't worry. The main thing to remember is to stay calm. Small town courts are very informal. There's no jury and probably no witnesses. The clerk will read the charges and you'll plead not guilty."

"That's it? Then we come home? I mean, I totally don't want to spend all day there."

"Pay attention, Victoria. Judge Matheson may or may not lecture you. No matter what he says, acknowledge the court with respect. He won't tolerate an outburst in his courtroom. Be contrite. Tell him just as you told me. It was a terrible mistake. The girl had been drinking before she arrived at our house. Billy brought her uninvited, and you had no idea she was underage."

"Yes, daddy. That's exactly what happened."

"Okay. Put on something conservative, nothing flashy. And smooth you hair back in a barrette or something."

Victoria changed her clothes three times, and removed the flashy jewelry she favored, before she finally came out of her bedroom wearing something they both agreed on.

Dorothy looked as if she had dressed to attend a funeral. She wore a plain black outfit with no accessories. Unable to control the tears that streaked down her face, her make-up smeared and gave her a grotesque, sad clown-like appearance.

"Oh for God's sake, look at you. Why don't you stay home? I don't need for you to make a scene with all that blubbering. You won't do Victoria any good and you'll more than likely draw more attention than we need," the judge growled.

In spite of the insult, a look of relief eased across Dorothy's face as she dropped to a chair in the living room and quietly waited for them to leave.

The judge drove Victoria to the Putman County Courthouse for her two o'clock appearance. They arrived early and took their place on a bench in the hallway, waiting for their case to be called.

At three, Judge Gillette caught the bailiff's attention. "How much longer will it be?"

"There's a complication in the case the judge is hearing now. It shouldn't be too much longer." When the bailiff walked out of earshot, he muttered, "I sure wouldn't want to be the next person up in front of Matheson today."

Fifteen minutes later, the bailiff called Victoria Gillette to the courtroom and swore her in. The court clerk read the charges and Judge Matheson asked for a plea.

"Not guilty, your honor," Victoria said.

Surprised to see the county attorney present, Judge Gillette recalled his own attorney told him representation would not be necessary. "You know the law," his attorney reaffirmed. "This case will probably be dismissed. The harshest punishment will garner a fine or community service. If I appear, they might make more of the situation than it merits." Henry glanced around the courtroom and was dismayed to find many spectators in attendance. Also, an employee of the Rexford Press didn't escape his notice.

The county attorney spoke, "This is a serious charge, your honor. Miss Gillette knowingly served liquor to a minor, Sandra Zelman. Miss Zelman suffered the early stages of alcohol poisoning and required emergency transportation to Lima General Hospital where she spent two days under their care."

"What do you have to say to the charge, Miss Gillette?"

"Your honor, I had no idea Sandra Zelman was underage. She came to my house with her cousin and they had been drinking prior to their arrival. I immediately asked them to leave."

Judge Matheson turned his attention to the county attorney.

"I have a witness who will testify that not only did Miss Gillette provide liquor, she encouraged the girl to celebrate the Fourth of July by pouring her a large amount of vodka in a glass filled with cranberry juice. She encouraged Miss Zelman to celebrate."

"That's a lie," Victoria started to raise her voice, then noticed her father's expression, and regained control. "That's not true, your honor."

"Are you saying Miss Zelman didn't have anything to drink at your residence?" The judge asked.

"No, I mean, well, she arrived drunk."

"Your honor, the EMT's who responded to the call at the Gillette residence, reported they found an empty vodka bottle next to Miss Zelman," the county attorney said.

"Did she bring the vodka with her?" the judge asked Victoria.

"Yes, no…I don't know."

"Your honor, Miss Gillette not only gave the liquor to Miss Zelman but allowed the minor to drink all she wanted. No one supervised the activities at the Gillette house during that party."

"You weren't there. You're making things up." Victoria's eyes flashed with anger.

"Oh, were your parents at home?" Judge Matheson asked.

"No. You're trying to confuse me."

"Were you drinking, Miss Gillette?"

"Everyone drank. Like, it was a party."

"Including Miss Zelman?"

"I don't know. Well, yes. She got sick. I mean, she acted unfriendly and didn't want to join the others. I couldn't be expected to watch her every minute."

"So you allowed her to drink all she wanted at your house." The county attorney pushed. "You made no attempt to take the alcohol from her, although you knew she was underage. Did you have an open bar, Miss Gillette? Could anyone off the street come in and imbibe?"

"What? No. That's not fair. I never invited that little snip to my party. It's not my fault she couldn't hold her liquor."

Judge Gillette hung his head and closed his eyes.

"Enough," Judge Matheson ordered. "Miss Gillette, it is apparent to this court that you served liquor to a minor. I could levy a fine but you show no remorse for your actions. I believe a few days in jail might get your attention."

"I can't go to jail. Like, I mean, you can't send me there. Daddy, do something," Victoria screamed.

Judge Gillette jumped to his feet, but the bailiff ordered him to remain seated.

"Miss Gillette is remanded to the county jail for the weekend and fined $500.00." Judge Matheson slammed the gavel down. "Call the next case."

"You can't do that to me. Do you know who I am?" She glared at the police as they put her in handcuffs. "It's your fault," she yelled at her father. "You promised me it would be okay." Her protests echoed down the hallway as they led her away.

Judge Gillette attempted to approach the bench on his daughter's behalf. Judge Matheson scowled at him, "One word from you and I'll send you along with your daughter." The bailiff led the inconsolable Henry Lee Gillette out of the courtroom. Tears dampened his eyes as he grabbed the doorframe to steady himself.

Judge Gillette couldn't imagine how he'd face Dorothy and tell her their only daughter would spend the weekend in jail. He knew Victoria could have been given more time due to her immature and rude behavior, but it wasn't her fault. The county attorney goaded Victoria and Judge Matheson didn't listen, didn't care. Humiliating the daughter of a former judge became Matheson's only interest. That bastard probably had a good laugh at Victoria's expense.

Once Henry Gillette regained control, he walked to the parking lot and slid into his car. He stared out the window, a broken man.

Olivia McDougle is responsible for this. She set it up and even sent a newsman there to record the proceedings. Then she can slant the facts the way she twists the rest of the news printed in the Rexford Press. The more he thought about the situation, the more distressed he became. Miss McDougle wasn't the one sitting in jail. His precious daughter, Victoria, took the brunt of McDougle's editorials. That despicable self-serving bitch shouldn't be allowed to get away with it. She had no respect for anyone.

The judge started the car and drove onto the street. Children strolled along the sidewalks, costumed like little ghosts and goblins, holding tight to their treat bags. He recalled the year Victoria dressed like a princess on Halloween. Sobs wracked his body and he pulled the car to the curb to collect himself.

He removed a flask of whiskey from its hiding place under a false bottom of his glove compartment and took a long healthy swig. The Halloween parade, set up by the Press, was scheduled in Rexford tonight. Maybe he'd dress for the occasion. He drained the contents of the flask and formulated a plan. Instead of heading home, he made a few stops and then drove on to his office.

***

At the Press, Olivia finished the last of her paperwork. "I'll lock up, Millie. I'm going from here to the gymnasium to help set up for the party."

"I'll join you as soon as I get Walt's dinner," Millie said. "This should be a fun and safe evening for the kids. You know, Olivia, you've done wonders for the town's young people. Once you started the ball rolling, everyone wants to become involved."

"I appreciate that. We've come a long way, the two of us. I couldn't have accomplished anything here without your help. I'll see you at the school."

Olivia made a few notes, and as she straightened her desk, she heard the front door open.

"Did you forget something Millie?" Olivia looked up from her desk. "Oh my goodness, a vampire. I'm sorry. We're giving treats at the school gymnasium after the parade. I don't have anything here." Olivia thought she had spoken to a child, but an imposing six-foot figure dressed in black loomed over her.

"I don't want a treat, Miss McDougle, but I have something to give you."

"I don't understand. I think you'd better leave."

"You'll get the message soon enough. I have a treat for you." An evil laugh erupted from under his mask. "Or maybe a trick."

"If you don't leave immediately, I'll call the police." Olivia picked up the phone only to have the overpowering figure grab it from her hands and slammed it across the room.

"It's too late for phone calls, sister. It's too late for you."

"What?"

Henry Gillette tore off his mask and pointed a gun at Olivia. His features appeared distorted, veins in his neck bulged and slobber dribbled from the corner of his mouth. Rage-filled eyes stared menacingly at her.

Olivia shrunk back in her chair, "Judge, consider what you're doing. We can talk this out."

"Talking time is over, lady. You're going to pay for what you did to my baby."

FORTY-THREE

Jade waited patiently until the last straggler left her beading class. They were a fun group of ladies and worked diligently on intricate beaded Christmas angels. Their enthusiasm and progress impressed her, but she was anxious to close the shop.

An unsettling sensation of sadness mixed with dread pervaded Jade's thoughts. She couldn't understand where the feeling came from and attempted to shrug away the dark mood as she cleaned the craft area and returned the supplies to the storage bins. Jade took one last look around the shop to make sure everything was organized, then locked the door and trudged upstairs to her apartment.

She wished Ham was there. He called earlier to tell her that everyone on the force had to work overtime as a deterrent to Halloween mischief makers. "Got to make our presence known," he laughed. "Lord only knows what the teen-agers will come up with this year."

She loved him unconditionally, loved his humor and his slow southern drawl. But most of all, she loved the way Ham showed his absolute affection for her. The thought snuggled around her heart as she warmed soup and prepared a salad for dinner. Maybe he'd surprise her and take a break later to join her for coffee. She had baked an apple pie that morning, Ham's favorite. The little things she could do for Ham gave her great pleasure.

Jade ladled soup into a bowl and set it on the table. When she reached in the cupboard for a package of crackers, Olivia's earrings caught her eye. Olivia left them on the counter when she spent the night. Something made Jade take them in her hand. *I must remember to return these.* As she fingered the small gold hoops, terror swept through her. The dreadful sensation that draped itself around her all day magnified itself a thousand times. *Why hadn't she foreseen this? Why hadn't she warned Olivia?* Her hand shook as she reached for the phone and quickly dialed. *Ham, where are you? Oh my God, please answer me.*

"Chief Bowers."

"Ham, this is an emergency."

"Jade?"

"Don't ask questions. Get over to the Press immediately. Olivia's in danger." Jade hung up before he could say anything. Next, she called Mitch. How could she explain her vision to him?

"Dr. James."

"There's been a terrible accident at the Rexford Press. Please get there as fast as possible. The police are on the way and I'm calling the EMT's." After Jade made the calls, she ran down the stairs and through the back alleys to Olivia's office, praying Ham had arrived in time.

As Ham reached the Press, he heard a shot ring out. He drew his gun and carefully eased his way through the front door. Voices could be heard coming from the inner office.

"That wasn't meant to kill you, Miss McDougle. I want you to experience pain before I end your life. I want you to suffer like my baby. You had no right to chastise her. You've ruined her life and now I'm going to ruin yours."

A searing pain had torn through Olivia's body. She gasped for breath as blood spurted from her chest. "No." Her last word rasped as a harsh whisper before her head rolled to the side.

"Drop it, mister. Drop the gun," Ham shouted from the front office.

The judge turned, his face contorted and his hand shaking violently. "What? Stay back or I'll kill you both."

"Holy shit," Ham said when he saw Judge Gillette holding the gun. "Put it down, Henry."

The judge turned and fired immediately, the bullet nicked Ham in the arm. Ham returned three shots in rapid succession. Ham learned long ago never to give an armed man a second chance. If Ham had to shoot, he would make it count. The judge fell to the floor, dead.

Mitch entered the front door just as Ham fired his gun.

"My God, what happened here?" he asked when he saw Ham clutching his arm. A stream of blood seeped through his fingers and ran down his sleeve.

"Let me take a look at that."

"I'm okay, doc. It's just a scratch. Gillette's dead. He shot Miss McDougle," Ham pointed to the inner office.

A sickening feeling engulfed Mitch. Judge Gillette's body was stretched across the doorway of Olivia's office. Mitch stepped over him to reach Olivia who was slumped sideways in the chair, her clothing soaked with blood.

Mitch couldn't allow himself to react with his heart. "Call Lima General and tell them to prepare for a gunshot victim," he shouted to Ham.

His emotions in check, Mitch laid Olivia on the floor, tore off her blouse and stopped the bleeding the best he could. Her eyes opened briefly and she grabbed his arm before spiraling into darkness.

Jade arrived, gasping for breath, followed by the EMT's. Bedlam took over the Press office. There had never been a fatal shooting in the small town of Rexford. Ham radioed for one of his deputies to help secure the area and then alerted Evan Henner to come as quickly as possible to take pictures of the crime scene. Tears flooded Jade's eyes, but she tried to keep her voice calm as she used Millie's phone to call Robyn. "I'm at the Press office. Judge Gillette is dead and Olivia's been shot. They're ready to take her to Lima General. Can you come?"

"I'll be right there. We'll follow the ambulance to the hospital," Robyn told her.

Jade made the second call to inform Millie and then turned her attention to Ham. "You've been hurt. Are you okay?"

He gathered Jade in his arms. "Yeah, I'm okay. How'd you know, gal? How could you possibly have known your friend was in danger?"

Jade looked into his eyes and knew she had to come up with a reasonable explanation. "Olivia and I were chatting on the phone when Judge Gillette barged into the office. I heard him threaten her, and then the phone line went dead."

Ham nodded. "This is God-awful. I mean the judge— Miss McDougle." He released Jade and clenched his jaw as one of the EMT's cleaned and bandaged his wound. "You'll need to go to the emergency room and get this checked."

"Yeah. I'll do that when I get time."

The other two EMT's, along with Dr. James worked to stabilize Olivia. Jade couldn't bear to watch.

"Ham, I know you can't leave until you sort this out, but I need to go to the hospital. Robyn is driving me there," Jade said.

"Call me when you hear anything," Ham said.

They stepped aside as the EMT's wheeled the gurney holding Olivia's lifeless body out the door and into the ambulance. Mitch rode with them to Lima General. Robyn waited for Jade at the curb in front of the Press building and they followed closely behind.

"Tell me what happened," Robyn said as they sped toward Lima. "I know you're holding back."

Jade went over every detail.

"You mean to say you got all that from touching Olivia's earrings?"

"I wish I could have foreseen this. I'm so worried."

"Do you know her condition?" Robyn asked.

"From the look on Mitch's face, I'd say it's not good."

"I called Kristen before I left the house. She'll meet us there," Robyn said as they entered the Lima city limits.

Tears filled Jade's eyes. "I should have foreseen this. All the signs said..."

"Don't do this to yourself. I'm relieved you were able to call Ham in time to keep Judge Gillette from finishing his mission. There's hope. We have to believe that." Robyn pulled into the hospital parking lot and parked the car. The two girls raced to the emergency room.

FORTY-FOUR

Within the hour, Kristen arrived at the hospital and checked with the information desk. The nurse on duty informed her Olivia had been taken to surgery. She joined Jade and Robyn in the waiting room.

Robyn's call to her had been cryptic at best. She said Olivia had been hurt and was transported to Lima General. During the drive to Lima, a hundred scenarios played in Kristen's mind, but in her wildest dreams she never expected to learn that Olivia had been shot, was in critical condition and may not survive.

Kristen held on to Jade and Robyn for support. The three girls took turns sitting and pacing for what seemed like hours. Every time the door opened they jumped, hoping for good news. A few minutes past seven Mitch joined them.

"She's alive but her prognosis is not good," he said. Strain pulled at his eyes and the color had drained from his face. "This hospital has some of the best surgeons in the state. If any one can save her..." he let the words hang.

Kristen cried softly, Robyn grew deathly pale.

Jade put her arm around Mitch. "I feel sure she'll pull through. Olivia's a fighter."

"Thanks, Jade. If you hadn't called when you did, she wouldn't have had a chance."

"But she does. Don't forget that for a minute."

Mitch raked his fingers through his hair, "They allowed me to watch, but they won't let me help. I don't know what I'll do if I lose her." He fought the tears that rimmed his eyes. "I wanted to let you know what was going on and ask if anyone told Etta."

"Mom went over to stay with her and Sarah," Robyn said. "I'll call them with an update."

"I want to get back," he said. "I need to be in there."

"Did you mean what you said to Dr. James?" Kristen asked Jade when Mitch left the waiting room.

"If you're asking if I know anything, I don't. But I have to believe she'll make it through this. We all do."

They tried to maintain positive thoughts. While Kristen went for coffee, Jade called Ham on his cell phone and gave him the latest details.

"We're still at the Press office, tying up loose ends. "It'll probably be after midnight before I'm finished with this mess," Ham told her as he watched Evan Henner take the last of the crime scene photos. The hearse waited at the curb to transport Judge Gillette's body to the local funeral home until the county medical examiner could come to Rexford.

"Ham, make sure you take care of the wound on your arm."

"Yeah gal, don't worry about me. Save your concerns for Miss McDougle."

Three hours later, Mitch returned to the waiting room and told the girls Olivia had survived surgery, but was listed as critical. "I plan to stay with her in the ICU. There's nothing else you can do. You might as well go home and get some rest. I'll call if there are any changes."

They asked Mitch to contact Jade. She'd keep the others posted. Robyn and Kristen had to work in the morning but Jade didn't plan to open her shop.

After assuring each other that Olivia was in good hands, the girls went to their cars. Kristen drove out of the hospital parking lot first and went on her way to Millsburg. Robyn followed her as far as Rexford where she dropped Jade off at her apartment. Then she drove to the Anderson's to give Etta the latest news. She made every effort to put a positive spin on the information, assuring Etta that Mitch would stay with Olivia and call if her condition changed. By the time Robyn drove her mother home, she felt completely drained.

FORTY-FIVE

Ham, thank God you're here," Jade said when she opened the door to her apartment.

"I had to see you, gal. Anymore news on Miss McDougle?" he asked.

"She's barely holding her own. Dr. James is with her."

"Figured he'd stay. I gather something's going on there."

"He loves her. They had a misunderstanding and he feels guilty on top of everything else."

"That's tough. How are you holding up?"

"I'm more concerned about you? How's your arm?"

Ham grimaced and rubbed the bandage with his hand. "Sore. First time I've been shot." He attempted a laugh. "Should have been a little quicker on my feet, I guess."

"Let's hope it's the last time. Did you have a chance to go to the hospital?"

"Nah, I'll try to get over there sometime tomorrow. Got 'Suits' from the county seat coming in the morning to talk about Judge Gillette's death and Miss McDougle's shooting. I've got paperwork up my kazoo. It's a real can of worms."

"Be sure you take care of your arm. You don't want it to become infected. I could make a warm compress and..."

"Sit down gal. I think we need to talk."

A sickening feeling of dread bubbled from the pit of Jade's stomach as she sat stiffly on the sofa.

"When Gillette pointed that gun at me, I thought I was a goner. Good thing my appearance unnerved him and he missed. It got me to thinking. I need to consider my future."

Jade braced herself. Ham was going to tell her their affair had ended. She struggled to control her voice. "Ham, I..."

He held up his hand. "Let me finish. I've given this a good deal of thought. I don't like the way things are between us."

A sigh escaped although Jade had clinched her lips. She thought her heart would break. On top of everything else, Ham was leaving her. She could hardly hear the words he said.

"I feel I'm wasting my life. It's time for me to make a decision."

Jade's hand flew to her mouth to stop the cry that threatened to escape.

"Jade, I don't want us to be apart anymore. I want to move in with you."

Relief and then utter joy softened her face before a sense of logic took over. "What will people say? You're the chief of police and Janie's been gone less than three months."

"Gal, Janie wouldn't have wanted me to grieve too long. Besides, I don't give a rat's ass what anyone has to say. I know I loved her and we had a good marriage. Now it's time to move on. I want to share the rest of my life with you."

"Hamilton Bowers, are you proposing?"

Ham got down on one knee in front of Jade. "I reckon I am. Will you marry me, Jadene Kendall?"

"I'll marry you. You know I'll marry you."

Ham stood and took Jade in his arms. "Gal, I didn't know, but I sure was hopin'."

Jade pushed back. "We'll have to wait until Olivia recovers. I don't want a cloud hanging over us."

"As soon as she recovers," Ham agreed. "Meanwhile, let's get the blood tests and license. I don't want to take the chance you'll change your mind."

Later, Jade lay in Ham's arms listening to the steady rhythm of his breathing. She had no doubt of her love for him. She kissed him lightly before she slipped out of bed and went to the kitchen to call the hospital. No change. She picked up Olivia's earrings again hoping for a sign. Nothing. She considered reading the cards but knew she couldn't concentrate. Overcome with grief, she put her head in her hands and sobbed.

"Jade, honey, you don't have to cry alone."

"I didn't hear you come into the kitchen. I'm so afraid for Olivia."

Ham enclosed her shaking body in his arms. "You never have to do anything alone again, gal. I know how much you care about your friend. Want me to make coffee?"

"It's late. I guess not."

"Then come back to bed. I'll rub your back. I love you Jade." He smiled as he led her back to the bedroom. He loved her. He could finally say those words without feeling guilty.

FORTY-SIX

The surgeon examined Olivia and then conferred with Mitch. "There's no change, Dr. James. She's holding her own. I wish I could give you better news."

"Before surgery I wasn't sure she would survive. I'm thankful she's progressed this far," Mitch said.

The surgeon nodded. "There's not anything you can do now. You need to get some rest."

"I'm fine, but I feel so helpless."

The surgeon put his hand on Mitch's shoulder. "The next twenty-four hours will tell..." he didn't finish. He left Mitch alone with Olivia.

Mitch pulled his chair close to the bed and watched Olivia breathe with the help of a ventilator. He brushed his fingers lightly against her face. She felt cool to the touch. The only sound in the room came from the robotic beep of medical equipment. Mitch took Olivia's hand and tried to think of the right words to say. He spoke from his heart. "Sweetheart, you're the love of my life. Please don't leave me. I can't bear to think of my life without you. You have to fight." He brought her hand to his face, no longer holding back the tears that spilled freely from his eyes.

"I didn't know about the pictures or that Gillette had threatened you. When he told me you traded a news story for my job, I remembered how my ex-wife attempted to manipulate my life. She hated Rexford. Her plans of a posh lifestyle by marrying a doctor disintegrated when I settled in a small town. She had delusions of living the good life in Philadelphia. She went behind my back and arranged for a position with a prestigious medical firm there. She went so far as to forge my signature on a letter of intent."

Mitch realized he was rambling, but he needed to tell her everything he felt. He had to rid himself of the overwhelming guilt. Mitch watched for a reaction. Olivia didn't move.

"I didn't care when Gillette threatened to withhold the remaining funds the council had set aside to pay for my loans, but when he laughed and accused me of hiding behind your skirts, I allowed my pride to get in the way of my common sense. God help me, I believed him when he told me you tried to bribe him. I have no excuses, Olivia. I only know that I love you and I'm so very sorry." Mitch rested his forehead on the edge of the bed. He dozed off and on, waking each time the nurse entered to check the machines attached to Olivia.

***

Friday morning, printed in huge black letters, the Rexford Press headlines shouted, "PRESS EDITOR SHOT." A picture of Olivia plus an article written by Millie covered the rest of the page. Millie detailed Olivia's background in advertising and listed all of the local programs and events she initiated with the full sponsorship of the newspaper.

The staff scrapped the next two pages and ran a complete account of the circumstances surrounding the shooting of their editor. The morbid story and crime scene photos, showed the black robe and vampire mask worn by Judge Gillette. The author methodically pieced together the judge's steps on the day of the shooting, from the time he left home until he attempted to murder Olivia. Millie held nothing back.

In a separate article, Millie ran the short story Robyn Martin told her of Gillette's attempt to blackmail Olivia. Then she accurately reported the blood-alcohol content found in the judge's system. Millie made sure she described every detail of the sinister side of Judge Gillette, including the fact that he had threatened Olivia on two previous occasions.

Although Jade Kendall's name had been withheld, the Press reported a tip was called in to the Rexford Chief of Police, warning him of a disturbance at the Press office. He arrived in time to hear a shot fired and discovered Judge Gillette, with a gun in his hand, standing over the seriously wounded editor of the Press. Chief Bowers ordered the judge to drop the gun. Judge Gillette turned and fired point blank, wounding Chief Bowers. The chief returned fire, killing Henry Lee Gillette.

Julius Mendon wrote an account of Victoria Gillette's day in court and her subsequence sentencing to jail time. He restated the events of the Fourth of July party at the Gillette home.

The fire chief wrote an account of the apartment complex fire, stating how Olivia saved many lives by going from apartment to apartment to warn the occupants. He also reported that Miss McDougle insisted her part of the tragedy be downplayed, instead, asked him to focus on the plight of the tenants. Millie's clever use of the photo Evan Henner snapped of a fireman helping Olivia down the ladder with the blazing buildings in the background added startling drama to the story.

Kristen sent in a piece to the Press informing the readers how Olivia's outreach to Millsburg opened the lines of communication between the two towns. Millie included a picture of the mayor of Millsburg shaking hands with Olivia at the Corn Roasting Festival, to highlight the article. Letters from residents of Millsburg and Rexford regarding Olivia's contribution to the communities completed the story.

The Press ran off extra copies and by late Friday afternoon, they had sold out. Phone calls, letters and flowers inundated the Press, the Anderson home and the hallway outside of Olivia's room at Lima General Hospital.

FORTY-SEVEN

S orry to disturb you doctor," the floor nurse said. "A Miss Jade Kendall is in the waiting room and asked if she could have a word with you."

Mitch looked up and hesitated.

"Don't worry. I'll be happy to stay with Miss McDougle while you're out of the room."

Mitch stood and stretched. He took the time to recheck Olivia's chart.

"Dr. James, you need a break. Grab a cup of coffee. I promise I won't leave until you return."

Mitch nodded grimly.

"Any change?" Jade asked when Mitch entered the waiting room.

He shook his head. "She's still the same."

"You look exhausted. Did you get any sleep?"

"I doze off and on. I'm afraid to leave her alone."

"Sit a minute. I brought you something to eat." Jade handed him a box of food she prepared.

"I'm not really hungry."

"Eat. You won't do her any good if you get sick."

"You sound like the doctor," Mitch managed a slight smile. He finished the sandwich and coffee Jade gave him and put the apple in his shirt pocket to eat later. "That hit the spot. I appreciate it, Jade. You're a good friend."

"I know I'm not allowed to go in the ICU but would you promise to clip this to Olivia's gown?" Jade produced a four inch delicate pearl and glass beaded angel. In the angel's hands, she attached a miniscule basket which she sealed with a silver thread to conceal its contents.

"Olivia loves my beadwork. Maybe it will help. Everyone needs an angel sitting on their shoulder to watch over them."

"I will, I promise. I pray to God something will help. She hasn't moved." Tears began to fall from his strained eyes. He raised his arm and wiped them with his shirt sleeve. "I'm so terrified for her...for me. There's nothing I can do but wait."

His honesty touched Jade to the core. She didn't hesitate to put her arms around him. "She'll make it, Mitch. Olivia will pull through."

"Thanks, I needed to hear that." Mitch kissed Jade on the cheek and returned to Olivia's room. He held the angel for a few minutes before he clipped it onto the shoulder of Olivia's gown.

***

Jade's grandmother was a healer and that gift had been passed down through generations of Kendall women. Other members of her family were quite proficient at the practice, but Jade's talent leaned more toward extra-sensory perception.

The herbs used in country medicine could not readily be found now that the woodlands were cleared for housing developments, and some of the plants her grandmother had used were extinct. Jade had saved and stored some of the more exotic herbs in the back room of her shop and sealed them in air tight jars to protect their potency. That morning, she used her grandmother's special healing recipe for calming nerves and alleviating pain. If Mitch clipped the angel to Olivia's shoulder, Jade felt sure the aroma of the herbal mixture would reach her senses. This remained the only option Jade had until Mitch permitted her to sit with Olivia.

FORTY-EIGHT

Lowell's Hardware," Todd gave the usual greeting into the phone.

"Hey Todd, this is Bob Burner. Wonder if you'd do me a favor?"

"Sure thing. What do you need?"

"It's about Miss Beckford. I know you have become friends with her and, well, I'm concerned."

"I'm listening."

"A couple of her students came to the office and told me they thought she might be ill. When I questioned them further, they agreed she seemed upset and teary. I'm tied up all afternoon. I scheduled a conference with parents of a student who needs my assistance to arrange special-ed classes. There's no way I can cancel. Could you make an excuse to stop over to Miss Beckford's house and see if she's okay?"

"Be glad to."

"Thanks, Todd. I owe you one. Let me know if there's anything I can do or..."

"I understand. I'll talk to you later."

Kristen was in the kitchen about to make tea when a knock on the door interrupted. She had the kettle clutched in her hand as she opened the front door. "Todd, I didn't expect you."

"Sorry to bother you Miss Kristen. I've finished making the piece of molding to fit the gap in the hallway. I came by to help you install it."

"I, I can't." Suddenly, pent-up tears streamed down her face.

"What is it?"

Kristen's normal calm demeanor crumbled. Between deep, uneven breaths, she told him about Olivia. "She treats me as family. Now, when she needs my support, I can't be with her. The school has scheduled parent-teacher conferences for my classes tonight."

Although they had never as much as touched in the two years Kristen lived in Millsburg, Todd didn't hesitate to take her into his arms while she sobbed uncontrollably. She seemed so small and vulnerable it took his absolute resolve to keep from kissing her tears away. Instead, he held her tightly, thankful for the opportunity to provide an outlet for her distress.

When Kristen first came into the hardware store and asked for assistance with remodeling the old house she purchased, Todd was bowled over by her quiet beauty. He and his father loaned her tools and helped her plan out the construction step by step. Todd came to the house at least once a week to see how she was doing and assisted with the heavy work. Kristen let him know early on she wasn't interested in anything other than friendship, much to his dismay.

Todd Lowell was a perceptive, patient man. The first day she came into the hardware store, he noticed the look of sorrow deep within her eyes. Although Kristen had a good sense of humor and her melodic laughter sang out with ease, an ever present, underlying sadness surrounded her. He couldn't imagine what tragedy had occurred in her life that would cause this beautiful woman grief. She changed the subject anytime he asked about her family. Todd didn't push. Sooner or later Kristen would realize how much he cared for her.

"I'm sorry Todd. I shouldn't have burdened you with my problems."

"Miss Kristen, you couldn't possibly be a burden. Let me call the school principal and cancel your evening meetings and then I'll drive you to Lima. You're in no shape to go alone."

"I can't ask you to do that."

"You didn't ask, I volunteered." Todd hesitated before releasing Kristen from his arms, but stepped back before he made her feel uncomfortable. "You make tea. I'll make the call."

Todd called Bob Burner and told him Miss Beckford had a personal emergency and asked that he reschedule her appointments. He didn't indicate they had spoken earlier. Then Todd sat at the kitchen table with Kristen and waited until she composed herself.

"I don't know what to say. I'm sorry for the way I reacted. Olivia invited me into her life, introduced me to her friends, Jade and Robyn and made sure I was included in their Wednesday night get-togethers. She's the first true girlfriend I've made since moving here. She felt comfortable enough to turn to me when she had a problem, but now I'm completely helpless."

"Your friend had a tough break. I believe you should be there, if only for a while. It'll make you feel better. I walked here from the store and need to get my car. I'll be back in fifteen minutes."

Todd returned for her and within the hour they approached the outskirts of Lima. Kristen sat quietly as they made their way through the rush hour traffic. Todd's square jaw tightened as he manipulated the route leading to the hospital.

"Watch it," he said to Kristen as he slammed on the brakes when another driver cut him off. "Sorry, are you okay?"

"I'm fine," Kristen said.

This is why I don't live in the city anymore. I enjoy the slow pace of Millsburg."

"I thought you always worked in town with your father."

"Dad owns two hardware stores. The one in Millsburg is also a lumber yard. I worked there as a teen-ager but after high school I decided I wanted to go to college and get a business degree. After graduation, I became enthralled with the city and found a job in Chicago. Before long, the excitement wore off and I found I craved the slower pace of a small town.

"Dad divides his time between the two stores. I handle the accounting for both, but mostly stay in Millsburg. I know everyone here. It's comforting to walk down our streets and be called by name. I know I'm settled."

"But you never married?"

"Haven't found the right girl."

Kristen changed the subject. "You really didn't have to drive me here. I'm so sorry to have imposed."

Todd grinned. "And miss this opportunity to be alone with you? It's my pleasure, ma'am."

Uncomfortable silence filled the car. Fortunately, directional arrows pointing to the hospital came into view. They pulled into the parking lot and made their way to the ICU.

Robyn and Jade looked surprised when Kristen arrived with Todd Lowell, the handsome young man they met at the Millsburg Corn Roasting Festival.

Kristen explained she was too upset to drive and Todd volunteered. "How's Olivia?" She quickly changed the subject.

"Mitch came out a few minutes ago and said she has begun to move slightly. I hope that's a good sign," Robyn said.

"He called the surgeon. They're both in the room with her now."

"Have you ladies had anything to eat?" Todd asked.

"We haven't thought about it," Jade said.

"Let me round up something." He left before they could protest.

He returned with two large bags from a fast food restaurant. "I got a little of everything. I'm sure you can find something you like." He let the girls rummage through the food, glad he went heavy on the salads. He brought chocolate shakes in place of coffee and while he didn't expect them to go for the fries, they giggled like teen-agers as they dumped ketchup on the greasy sticks.

"You broke the tension, Todd. We appreciate it," Jade told him.

"And for the food," Robyn added.

Todd took a sandwich from the bottom of the bag, along with one of the extra milkshakes and carried them to a chair in the corner of the waiting room. He pulled out the book he brought with him and attempted to keep a low profile while the girls talked freely. And talk they did.

"I think Olivia has turned the corner," Mitch said when he entered the waiting room. "She still has a long way to go, but the prognosis is looking better." The strain on his face had diminished somewhat.

Todd glanced up from his book and gazed at a relieved Kristen as she hugged her friends. The bond the three girls seemed to share amazed him. After spending a few minutes reassuring Olivia's friends, Mitch returned to the ICU. Jade and Robyn, comforted by the news, prepared to drive back to Rexford. Todd decided not to say anything until Kristen suggested they leave. He didn't want to appear impatient, and he relished the opportunity to study the high school teacher. Her beauty was a given, but more than that, she possessed a sense of class.

Kristen was different from anyone he'd ever met. She clearly came from a well-to-do family, but seemed content to do the difficult physical work on her house. He could tell she had never used a tool of any kind in the past. Her grit and determination amazed him. The smile that crept across her face when she mastered a remodeling project brought him more pleasure than she could ever imagine.

He sometimes left things at her house as an excuse to return. She was always pleasant but reserved. Today, for the first time, she revealed her personal feelings.

"Todd?"

"Sorry. What did you say?"

"You were in another world. I said I'm ready to go."

"Right. Would you like me to get the car?"

"Don't be silly. I'll go with you." Kristen looped her arm through his and they walked together to the elevator.

The ride back to Millsburg gave Todd another chance to cross the barrier Kristen built around herself as the conversation flowed between them. He hoped it was a sign of better times to come.

"Would you like to come in for coffee?" she asked when he pulled into the driveway.

"That would be great, if it's not too much trouble."

"It's the least I can do. Besides, we've never taken the time to become acquainted."

A smile washed over Todd's face. *Thank you God.* He parked the car and walked around to open the passenger side door. He hoped this would be the beginning of a deeper friendship with Kristen. One not limited to building projects.

FORTY-NINE

Saturday afternoon, Robyn brought her mother and Etta Anderson to Lima General. Although Mitch called Etta everyday to keep her posted on Olivia's condition, he discouraged her from coming to the hospital. He thought it better that she stay home under Sarah's watchful eye. As Mitch waited for their arrival, he worried about Etta's reaction at seeing her only niece on a ventilator.

Etta surprised him as she sat beside Olivia's bed. "Is she truly out of danger?"

"I think she's making progress. This morning the surgeon said she should be breathing on her own within the next few days."

"You been home?"

"I couldn't leave. I had Maxine cancel my appointments until I could arrange for Dr. Hartman to take over. He'll be at the office Monday morning."

"You look terrible. I think you need some rest."

"Thanks," Mitch laughed. "Now who's the doctor?"

"You can't take care of Livie if you're exhausted."

"I hope she gives me the chance to take care of her." Mitch rubbed his hand over his unshaven face. "In my wildest dreams, I couldn't imagine Judge Gillette going this far. It's completely out of character."

"I could tell you things about Henry Gillette that would change your mind about what he was capable of, but I agree, I never thought he'd attempt to kill Olivia. Something terrible must have happened to drive him over the edge."

"Jade told me Victoria behaved badly in court and the presiding judge sent her to jail. That could have made him snap." Mitch didn't mention the Judge's attempt to blackmail Olivia. Some topics were better left unsaid.

"Lord, he loved that girl. That might have done it, but still, it's hard to believe. He had to know he wouldn't get away with murder."

"Thank God Jade notified the police and me. If I hadn't arrived in time..." he bit his lower lip. "I don't even want to consider the results."

Family members were permitted to visit ICU patients for ten minutes every hour. Although Mitch allowed Etta to stay as long as she wanted, Etta stood and wrapped her arms around Mitch briefly. "I'm ready to go home. You take care of her."

"I don't plan to do anything else until she tells me otherwise."

"Mitch is with her," she told Robyn when she returned to the waiting room. "Could you take me back to Rexford?"

Robyn shrugged and looked at her mother. "I'll get the car and meet you downstairs."

They met Jade and Kristen at the elevator.

"How is Olivia?" Jade asked.

"Mitch says she's improving but she looks terrible," Etta said.

"That will change. I'm glad you were able to come, Mrs. Anderson," Kristen said.

"Thank you, dear. I feel better now that I've seen her and know Mitch is taking good care of her."

As the girls sat in the waiting room, Jade mentioned that Etta seemed preoccupied.

"She might be in shock. Maybe we should talk to Mitch."

"Did I hear someone mention my name?"

"Mitch, you startled me," Jade said. "We spoke to Etta and she seemed distracted. Is she okay?"

"Etta usually puts up a good front. I think this has totally destroyed her. Once Olivia recovers she'll be back to her old self. She managed to tease me when she was in ICU. I'll call her later today and reassure her."

"Are you saying there's been an improvement?"

"The surgeon said as much. I have to tell you it could have gone either way. There were days I didn't believe she'd pull through. She still hasn't acknowledged my presence." Sadness covered his tired eyes. "I'll let you two go in for a minute. You can't stay, but let her know you're here. I hope she'll react to your voices."

Jade and Kristen spoke to Olivia, each encouraging her to get better. They told her Robyn visited her earlier, but took Etta back home. Although Olivia didn't stir, the girls felt better seeing her. Mitch thanked them for all their support and returned to sit with Olivia.

After returning to Rexford, Etta became a woman with a mission. As soon as Robyn and her mother left, she had Sarah pull the car out of the garage.

"Where are we going?"

"To the Gillette house."

"Are you sure you want to do this, Etta?" Sarah asked when she pulled into the Gillette's driveway.

"I am. Wait in the car. I won't be long, but I need to talk to Dorothy before anymore time passes."

Dorothy Gillette made no effort to conceal her shock when she opened the door and saw Etta Anderson standing on the porch.

"You're the last person I expected to see. What are you doing here?" Her voice held an edge.

"I came to say how sorry I am for the terrible events of the past few days. How are you holding up?"

"How do you think I'm holding up? Henry is dead and Victoria is completely destroyed. I feel as if this nightmare will never end."

"Where is Victoria?"

"They released her as soon as they heard. She should have never been put in that awful situation in the first place. Your niece...ah," Dorothy took a deep breath. "I don't know what Victoria will do. She refuses to come out of her room."

"Let me talk to her."

Dorothy stood aside and indicated a closed door at the end of the hall.

Etta rapped lightly and then went inside without waiting for an invitation. "Victoria."

"What are you doing here? Get out of my room. Get out of our house."

Etta let her rant. She sat quietly on a chair beside the girl's bed and waited until Victoria spewed all the venom she could about Olivia McDougle.

"Like, aren't you going to say anything?"

"When you're finished."

"You have a lot of nerve coming here. My father's dead."

"And my niece is in critical condition. You and I can't change that. What we can do, is come to terms with it. We won't ever know what happened at the Press office, but your mother needs you now and you can't hide out in your room. It's time for you to step up and do what you can to help with funeral arrangements."

Victoria put her hands over her ears, "You don't understand."

"Child, I understand more than you know. Your daddy doted on you. He gave you everything you wanted. When things didn't go your way in court, he snapped. You can't do anything about that, but you can help your mother put her life together. Think of someone beside yourself, Victoria."

"I can't." Her voice dropped to a whisper. "I can't."

"I know it's hard, child. You have to go on with your life. You'll never get over your loss, but you'll learn to live with it."

Victoria looked at Etta, her eyes swollen, her face drawn. "Is she gonna be okay, your niece, I mean?"

"I hope so. Etta's face softened and she put her hand on Victoria's shoulder. "Now get out of bed and fix your face. Let's comfort your mother."

Victoria did as she was told without grumbling, probably for the first time in her life. Etta spent a few more minutes consoling Dorothy Gillette, before she had Sarah drive her home.

FIFTY

While the surgeon stayed in the room with Olivia, Mitch took the opportunity to go to the resident's locker room at Lima General to shower. He borrowed a set of scrubs and then checked in with Maxine to discuss his patients. By the time he returned to ICU, the surgeon had removed the ventilator and watched carefully as Olivia breathed on her own.

"She's recovering from surgery, but she hasn't regained consciousness. I can't find a medical reason for that. I suspect it could be trauma. We'll keep a close eye on her. I'll stop in later," the surgeon told Mitch.

After the surgeon left the room, Mitch sat in the chair next to Olivia's bed. "You're going to be okay, sweetheart. It's over." He took her hand. "It's time to wake up. It's time to come back to me."

Olivia remained motionless. Her skin felt cool and remained pale. Her red hair hung limp around her face.

Mitch continued to reassure her. "I love you, Olivia. I love you with all my heart. I'll do anything to prove it. Please allow me to make amends for my bad behavior."

Mitch changed his approach. "Jade, Robyn and Kristen have been here every day. Jade made a beaded angel for you. I clipped it to your gown. Robyn brought Etta yesterday. Do you remember?" He watched for a reaction. Olivia remained still.

"Last Friday night, Todd Lowell drove Kristen here. Jade told me you and Robyn met him at the Millsburg festival. Everyone's praying for your recovery. You have great friends."

He rubbed ice chips on her lips. "I know your throat is dry. If you wake up, I can give you a sip of water." He closed his eyes, trying to think what else he could do or say to stimulate her back to consciousness.

"I don't know what I'd do without you. I've loved you from the first day I met you in Etta's house. I thought you were with Home Aid, remember? I made excuses to come back to the house to see you. Talk to me, Olivia. Tell me you forgive me."

He felt a slight pressure from her fingers as he held her hand to his face. "You hear me, Olivia. I love you." When she didn't move again, he thought it might have been an illusion. Mitch sat quietly and watched her breathe.

"Dr. James, take a break. It's time for Miss McDougle's bath and I need to change the bedding," the nurse said as she brought fresh linens into the room.

Mitch stepped outside, stretched and sighed. He felt helpless. Maybe Olivia didn't want to talk to him. He couldn't blame her. He sat in the waiting room, hung his head and cried.

Jade found him there. As soon as she touched his shoulder she knew Olivia would recover, but was aware Mitch had issues to resolve. She sat next to him and spoke softly. "You're exhausted. If you give me permission, I'll sit with Olivia while you get some rest. I promise to have you paged if there's any change at all."

As much as he didn't want to leave, he agreed. He hadn't slept more than a couple hours at a time since they admitted Olivia into the hospital. He gave Jade his beeper number and introduced her to the nurse as Olivia's sister. "She'll stay with Miss McDougle while I catch a few hours of sleep."

"About time you took care of yourself," the nurse said. She brought Jade a pillow to put in the chair beside Olivia's bed. "If you need me, call."

Jade had waited for this opportunity. She reached in her purse, brought out a small bottle of oil and dampened her fingers with the contents. With a light touch, she rubbed it on Olivia's temples. She whispered a few words and waited. Soon Olivia began to stir.

"Careful, Olivia. This isn't going to heal you but it sure will make you feel better. Don't open your eyes yet. Think about all you've heard the last few days. I'm sure you're aware that your man Mitch hasn't left your side until today when I insisted he get some rest. He hasn't slept for days. Don't give up on him. That guy loves you. I've never seen anyone so devoted.

"The judge shot you, do you remember? He also shot Ham in the arm. That proved to be his big mistake. Ham didn't take kindly to someone throwing bullets in his direction. Listen carefully, Olivia. Judge Gillette is dead. He can't hurt you anymore." Jade watched her friend. Color began to edge its way onto Olivia's face. Her eyelids fluttered ever so slightly.

"Now, about your Aunt Etta. After she visited here on Sunday, she had Sarah drive her straight over to the Gillette house and made Victoria face up to her responsibilities. Etta has a lot of spunk. Sarah told me there was no stopping Etta once she made up her mind. When I read Judge Gillette's obituary in the Lima News, I could feel changes in store for Victoria and her mother. I envisioned a new address. There's something unsettling going on there, but I can't seem to put my finger on it."

Olivia wrinkled her nose.

"And speaking of new starts, you should have seen Todd Lowell watch Kristen in the waiting room the night he drove her here to visit you. That boy's smitten. I don't think Kristen is aware of it yet, but she'll get the message loud and clear. You could have knocked Robyn and me over with a feather when they came in together. He's a prince of a guy. Went out and brought enough fast-food back for a dozen people, because he didn't know what we liked to eat. We gave the nurses in the ICU the extra sandwiches." Jade held Olivia's hand to see if she could feel any movement.

"Now let me see what else. Oh, Millie did a three page story in the Press, complete with pictures on the events of Halloween night. They retraced the judge's steps from the time he left the Putman County Court house, until he paid you a visit. Ham discovered that Henry Gillette stopped at a liquor store in Ottawa and then a variety store, where he bought the rubber mask. Then he drove to his office to pick up his gun and the black robe he wore while he presided on the bench. Ham concluded the judge planned to kill you and then blend in with the crowd at the parade so no one would notice. I'll tell you how Ham caught him in the Press office later.

"I know you hear me." Jade rubbed Olivia's hand. "It's difficult for you to take in all that happened, but my friend, none of this was your fault. Henry Gillette harbored a mean streak. You learned enough about him from Robyn's mother to know how manipulative and down right vindictive he could be. He felt he could control everything and when he couldn't convince you to twist the truth, he lost it. I have to tell you, it was bound to happen. His importance had begun to decline in Rexford. The 'good ole boy' network is becoming a thing of the past."

Olivia's eyes blinked, not quite open but Jade could see she had made an effort.

"That's it, Olivia. You're coming back. You don't have to fight it anymore. Take your time and I'll tell you about Ham and me. He proposed. He wants to marry me, can you believe it? Sometimes I'm able to predict what will happen to others but this came as a complete surprise to me. He's ready to move into my apartment. He sold his house last year to pay for Janie's medical bills and has been living in a room over the drug store. I told him we'd have to wait until you recovered because you promised to dance at my wedding. I'm holding you to that."

Jade smiled when she noticed Olivia lift her chin.

"You know those extra rooms I have in my apartment? I've turned one of them into a study for him. He hasn't seen it yet, but I know he'll appreciate a space of his own. Olivia, he's so down to earth and caring. I can't begin to tell you how much I love him. I can't wait to officially be his wife."

Olivia moaned softly.

"Quiet now, the nurse is coming. We need to let Dr. James get a few more hours sleep. We'll wait until she checks on you and then finish our conversation."

"How's she doing?" the nurse asked as she took Olivia's pulse and blood pressure."

"She's been quiet. I think she's looking better, don't you?"

"She does seem to have regained some color. Push the call button if you want anything." The nurse hurried on to her next patient.

Jade took her friend's hand. "Olivia, you're going to be okay. You'll be home before you know it."

FIFTY-ONE

Voices faded in and out. Oh God, the pain. Olivia wanted to cry out but she couldn't move, couldn't remember what happened. Mitch. She felt his presence...smelled his aftershave. Doctors probed and prodded. It seemed surreal. She wanted to sleep. Her throat throbbed, her side felt as if it were on fire.

Olivia realized she was in a hospital but couldn't remember how she got there or why. Maybe an accident? It became quiet again and then Mitch spoke softly and took her hand. She felt his tears. Was she dying? She felt an angel sitting on her shoulder. It calmed her as she melted into darkness.

Mitch told her he loved her. His voice slurred and she felt his head rest on the side of her bed. How long had she been there?

Time had no meaning. Waves of pain were followed by the depths of nothingness. The terrible discomfort in her throat had subsided but it felt so dry it burned when she tried to swallow. She felt ice on her lips. She wished for more, but couldn't speak and once again she dropped into the deep whirlpool of sleep.

Now Jade sat with her. Where was Mitch? Did he give up on her? When Jade's fingers touched her temples, the pain subsided. The welcome feeling of relief surged through her body. Olivia couldn't remember what happened, couldn't keep straight what she heard. Everything confused her. Jade said Judge Gillette shot Ham. Is Ham okay? He must be. She said they were going to be married. Is it too late for Mitch and me? Have I pushed him away for the last time? I love him so.

A tear leaked from Olivia's eye and ran down the side of her face.

"Dr. James. You need to come to Olivia's room. I believe Olivia's coming around," Jade said when Mitch answered his page.

Mitch raced to the ICU. "Olivia, sweetheart," he said as he leaned over her bed. "Welcome back. I love you. You're going to be fine." He brushed her hair back from her face and kissed her lightly. A wide grin burst across his haggard face.

Olivia blinked her eyes against the light. The ICU room became crowded with activity.

Jade stepped aside and slipped out of the ICU, satisfied that her mission had been accomplished. She located a phone in the waiting area and called Etta, Robyn and Kristen with the news. She suggested they not visit tonight but come for a short visit tomorrow. Jade wanted Olivia's first hours to be with Mitch. At last, she called Ham to tell him she was on her way home.

Early evening, the surgeon checked on Olivia and then spoke to Mitch. "She had me concerned. This is a good sign. I believe we can move her to a private room." He asked the ICU staff to arrange for the transfer.

Mitch felt uneasy leaving Olivia alone and requested a cot be placed in her new room for him. He knew the hospital was full and the night-shift nurses, stretched to the limit.

Mitch followed as they rolled Olivia's bed down the hallway and onto the elevator. He waited patiently while the nurses settled her in the private room. After everyone left and they were alone, a sense of dread blanketed him. What if she remembered their disagreement and asked him to go? He didn't think he could stand the pain.

"Mitch."

"I'm here," he pulled a chair next to her bed.

"Can you stay awhile?" Her voice rasped with dryness.

"Sweetheart, I didn't plan to leave unless you threw me out." Mitch heaved a sigh of relief as Olivia closed her eyes and slept. She wanted him there. She forgave him. Not ready to turn in for the night, Mitch settled in a chair next to her bed and watched the love of his life.

Once Olivia regained consciousness, the long road to recovery began. Mitch spent as much time with her as possible, encouraging her to take those first few steps. After morning rounds at the hospital, he sat with her to make sure she ate lunch and then drove back to Rexford to attend to his patients. In the evenings he returned to Olivia's room to stay the night on the cot next to her bed. He read to her, told her about his day, and also explained how very much he loved her.

***

Mitch asked Dr. Hartman to continue on as a temporary associate at his practice. The young doctor gladly accommodated. His first year out of residency, Dr. Hartman found it difficult to secure a full-time position with a general practitioner. He worked part-time at a clinic and picked up a few extra hours as an on-call doctor at Lima General. He hoped for a chance to put down roots and convince Dr. James to make the offer permanent.

FIFTY-TWO

Robyn begged off when Jade asked if she wanted to ride with her to the hospital. "I talk to Olivia every day. I have some personal things to take care of here," Robyn said.

Robyn hadn't told anyone about the e-mails she'd received from her husband. Early September Greg wrote of plans to come home for Christmas. Lately, the tone of his messages sounded cool and detached. He wrote more about the weather than anything personal. When she questioned him, he mentioned a heavy work load and stress. Then he said he planned to re-enlist, something he swore he'd never do. He stopped his monthly telephone calls and then sent an e-mail stating that he received orders to go to a secret temporary relocation and would not be able to contact her for several weeks. All the hopes and dreams Robyn harbored burst as she read between the lines. Her earlier suspicions of another woman seemed true.

Everything about Robyn Martin screamed practical. Her job at the bank, the clothing she wore as well as her work ethics. She thought Greg shared her dreams to save money to buy a house and start a family. Greg's agenda had changed. Now, he spent his entire paycheck every month instead of sending money home. Robyn realized she had to take care of herself. In October, she withdrew money from their joint savings account and placed it in her mother's safe deposit box. She explained to her mother that Greg had lost his wallet, his bank card and all of his identification and she wanted to make sure no one could access their account. Then she closed their joint checking account and began to pay bills with cash or money orders. Strength replaced grief as Robyn put everything in her name.

A check from Greg arrived at the bank in an attempt to withdraw all of their money. When the bank manager brought it to Robyn's attention, she told him of her failed marriage. He sent it back marked account closed. By the time Greg received the returned check, he would have also received divorce papers from Robyn. He didn't contest the proceedings.

As Robyn looked back at her life with Greg, she had to wonder if they shared a marriage based on love or lust. It pained her to think in those terms. She chalked it up to her attempt to create a sense of belonging, to feel wanted and safe. Whatever the emotion, she failed miserably.

Under normal circumstances, Robyn would have poured her soul out to Olivia. They had become so close since Olivia's return to Rexford, they both felt free to discuss anything and everything. Now that Kristen and Jade were at their last thread of worry, Robyn didn't think it fair to add her marital problems to the loop. Besides, nothing more could be done at this point. Robyn felt completely alone.

She told her mother of the divorce but let her know she didn't want to discuss it further. Robyn's tone advised Mary Margaret not to pry.

"What are you doing here?" Robyn asked Jade when she walked into the bank before closing time. "I told you I wasn't going to visit Olivia tonight."

"I know what you said, but I believe you should reconsider. Besides, I don't want to drive there alone."

"Where's Ham?"

"He's working. He has a new man he wants to break in."

"I'm not sure I'll be very good company."

"Robyn, I know what you're going through. I read it in your tea leaves months ago."

"But you never said anything."

"I told you enough at the time. There's such a thing as too much information. I saw the rift between you and Greg and I detected another woman hovering in the background. I hope you took my advice about money."

"I did. It's so painful I can hardly stand it."

"What I didn't tell you is that you will soon meet your true love. He worked his way through school, taking a few extra years to achieve his goals. He's kind and caring. You'll know he's the one the minute you meet him."

"Jade, I don't want to hear it. I feel heartsick and betrayed. I'm thoroughly disgusted with men."

Jade smiled knowingly, "Enough for now. We'll grab a quick dinner on our way to visit Olivia. She'll know something's wrong if you don't show up."

Kristen and Todd were in Olivia's room when Jade and Robyn arrived.

"I met you in Millsburg, Miss McDougle. I hope you don't mind that I tagged along," Todd said.

"I'm glad you came. It's nice to see you again."

Todd stayed a few minutes and then excused himself and went to the waiting room to allow the girls to visit.

"C'mon Kristen, give," Robyn said.

"I don't know what you're talking about." Kristen's ivory complexion flushed with a slight tinge of color.

"I knew he was more interested in you than remodeling your house," Robyn teased.

"He's a friend. That's all. Let's talk about you, Olivia. You're looking so much better," Kristen said.

"Thanks, I've been walking every day to build up my strength. The surgeon says I might be able go home by the end of the week if I keep improving. I can't wait."

"That's good news. It's about time, we miss you," Jade said.

"There's something I want to talk to you about," Olivia said.

Jade nodded. "We'll discuss it when you get home."

When the girls ended their visit, they found Mitch with Todd in the waiting room. "I'm glad you all came," Mitch said. "Olivia worries if she doesn't see or talk to you every day. I'm concerned about her. I don't believe she's come to grips with what happened."

"But she knows," Robyn said.

"I've told her, but she doesn't seem to realize or accept the fact that Judge Gillette is dead. She mentioned yesterday that she dreaded the thought of dealing with him again."

"Give her time," Jade said. "Once she gets in her own environment things will fall into place."

"I hope you're right. She still feels threatened by the judge. I haven't pressed it. She needs all her strength to recover," Mitch said.

"Do we need to worry about Olivia?" Robyn asked Jade on the drive back to Rexford.

"We need to be there to support her."

"You're not telling everything you know."

Jade sighed. Her gift or curse, whatever you wanted to call it, caused her anguish. How could she enter Olivia's mind and free her from the demons?

"Jade?"

"Once she's home it will be okay, trust me."

FIFTY-THREE

A new restaurant opened in Columbus Grove. We could stop for dinner on the way home," Todd said as he held the car door open for Kristen.

"I'd like that."

He started the car and pulled out of the hospital parking lot and merged into the downtown traffic. "You're beginning to feel more at ease with me."

"You've always made me feel comfortable."

"I'm not so sure about that."

Kristen bowed her head slightly. "I'm afraid I didn't communicate very well before. I felt shy around you."

"I can't imagine why. I'm a pretty straight forward guy."

"You are, but I didn't know a thing about tools or remodeling. I felt intimidated.

Todd nodded and pulled into a parking spot in front of the Red Onion. "Let's hope this place lives up to the recommendation I received from a customer last week." He opened the car door for Kristen and held her arm as they went inside. There were plenty of tables available. "We either missed the rush or the food isn't as good as I was told. Let's hope it's the former."

"I'm sure it will be fine. A new place always takes time to build up a clientele," Kristen said.

"Welcome to the Red Onion," the hostess said as she showed them to a table and gave them menus printed on a card shaped like an oversized red onion. Ceramic onion-shaped pitchers, mugs, cookie jars and bowls all with onions painted on them sat on the pot shelves lining the restaurant walls. Pictures depicting different kinds of onions dotted the walls.

"Now this is intimidating," Todd said as he looked around the eatery.

Kristen laughed, "To say the least, it's unique."

They ordered the chef's special and made small talk over a glass of house wine while they waited to be served.

"I'm worried about Mitch's remark," Kristen said.

"Regarding Olivia's denial of Judge Gillette's death?"

"Yes. What do you think?"

"Your friend's been through quite an ordeal. I don't know too much about medicine, but Jade could be right on the money. Once Olivia returns home, things will fall into place."

"I hope that's the case."

The waitress brought plates overflowing with food, with a basket of beer-battered onion rings for them to share.

"I'll never be able to eat all of this," Kristen said.

After they finished, they agreed the meal was exceptional.

"Dessert?" Todd asked.

"Not for me, thanks."

Todd paid the tab and escorted Kristen to the car. He noticed she seemed more relaxed and open in his company. Conversation flowed on their way back to Millsburg.

"Would you like to come in for coffee?" Kristen asked when Todd pulled into her driveway.

"Thanks. I'd like that."

Aside from driving Kristen to the hospital to see Olivia, they had been together on three different occasions. Todd had taken her to an art museum in Toledo one Sunday afternoon and bowling in Findlay on a Friday night. Small towns weren't the ideal place to become a twosome too quickly. Local gossips would have them married, or Kristen pregnant before the month was over, if they were seen too often in Millsburg.

Todd decided it was time to bridge the gap and ask Kristen a few personal questions. As they sat at the kitchen table, he took a breath and jumped in. "Of all the places to teach, what brought you here?"

"I wanted to start my career in a small town. Once I settled in Millsburg, I loved the closeness of the community."

"But you haven't mentioned a family in the area. Do you miss being near them?"

Kristen studied the handsome man sitting across from her. How much should she tell him? Would he possibly understand her past? She paused a moment and chose her words carefully. "Todd, I don't have family. I moved here because I lost everything and everyone I loved in my life."

"I don't know what to say." He set his cup on the table and walked over to her. "I didn't mean to embarrass you." He put his hand out to her, hoping against all odds she'd respond.

Kristen rose to meet him and was swept into his arms. The kiss that took years coming sent chills through her. Then she buried her head in his shoulder. "I know you deserve to know about me. It's difficult to talk about but if we want to continue to see each other..."

Those were the magic words. Before she could finish, Todd cupped her face in his hands and kissed her again. He closed his eyes in quiet thanks. "I want to know about you, but I don't want to make you uncomfortable. Let's take it slow."

"You're so sensible." Worry creased her face as she weighed the consequences. "I'm afraid after you hear about my past you might not want to spend time with me."

"Kristen, there's nothing you could say that would change the way I feel about you. I've loved you from the first day you came into the store." He kissed her again.

She could feel his heart beating, or was it hers? She pressed close to him, abandoning all her inhibitions. It felt so right, so freeing. But she knew she had to tell him before they lost their way and then he changed his mind.

Her father was a murderer and she was the result of an adulterous affair. Those words weren't easily said to a man who displayed nothing but goodness and decency in everything he did. He was polite and kind and obviously had no scandals in his background.

Kristen pulled back and led him to the sofa in the living room. "You have to know. We can't begin a relationship with secrets." She sat beside him with his arms around her shoulder, thankful he couldn't see her face as she spilled all the horror of her past. She couldn't bear it if his look changed from affection to pity.

When she finished, the room hung heavy in silence. Then Todd said, "I have to leave."

Kristen's thought her heart would break. She didn't allow the tears that glistened in her eyes to escape and bit her lower lip to keep from screaming. "I understand. I realize the events of my past changes the way you feel about me." It took all of Kristen's will to keep her voice steady.

"Honey, you have no idea what's going through my mind. I'm so sorry I made you uncomfortable. You went through hell. No wonder you were reluctant to see me as anything other than a friend. I should have waited until you were ready to tell me about your past. I shouldn't have pressed the issue.

"If I don't leave right now, I'd carry you off to the bedroom we so carefully remodeled last summer and I wouldn't be able to control my desire. I'd make love to you forever. I want to be with you so much my heart is bursting from my chest, but I know you're fragile and vulnerable now. I don't want to take advantage of the situation."

"You mean..."

"I mean, I love you more, if possible. Kristen, I love you, not your past. You had no control over your family and their problems. I love who you are today. I want to become a permanent part of your life, if you'll let me."

Relief surrounded Kristen. Todd said he loved her. It sang over and over in her heart. She wanted him to stay, to be with her forever.

Todd stood and walked toward the front door. Kristen followed and watched as he put on his jacket.

"I'll call you when I get home. Let's make plans for tomorrow night." He held her close and kissed her passionately and then whispered, "And every night from now on."

FIFTY-FOUR

Two weeks after Olivia entered Lima General the surgeon signed her release. Mitch borrowed Etta's car to bring her home and then stayed as close to her as moss on a tree. He insisted that Etta put a rollaway cot next to Olivia's bed.

"Sarah's here," Etta protested. "She can see to Livie."

"I know, but I'll feel better if I'm here in case of an emergency."

"Humph. If I didn't agree, you'd probably break in through a window. Why don't you marry her and get it over with."

A broad grin hugged Mitch's face. "I'm trying, Etta."

That night, Mitch attempted to apologize again. Olivia would hear none of it.

"I should have chased you all the way back to your apartment to hash it out," she said.

"And I needed to trust you enough to tell you exactly what happened."

"We both have a lot to learn about relationships. Promise we'll never do that again. If there's a misunderstanding, we'll talk it over."

"Baby, I don't plan to have anything but love and affection for you. I'll never doubt you again." His soft kiss caressed her lips. He whispered, "I can't wait to make love to you again."

The rollaway wasn't used. Mitch held Olivia in his arms until they both fell asleep.

***

Ham came along with Jade to visit Olivia at the Anderson house the next evening.

"Where's Mitch?" Jade asked.

"At the office. He needed to catch up on his paperwork. Let's sit in the den. Can I get coffee or a drink?"

"We're fine," Jade said.

"Gal, you sure look a whole lot better than the last time I saw you. I didn't think you'd make it," Ham said.

"Jade told me you were shot. Are you all right?" Olivia asked.

"Yes ma'am. Compared to what you went through, I had little more than a scratch."

"I don't know how I'm going to face Judge Gillette after all this. I don't believe I can handle him."

Ham started to say something but Jade nudged him. She walked over to the door and closed it.

"Let's talk about that," Jade said. "Exactly what do you remember?"

"It comes and goes in a haze. I recall getting ready to go to the Halloween party at the school when someone came in the front door of the Press. I thought Millie had forgotten something but it wasn't her."

"Who did you see, Olivia?"

"I don't know. He wore a mask and was dressed completely in black."

"Think about it. What happened next?"

Olivia started to cry. "The man screamed at me. Then I felt a terrible pain. Mitch came."

"And what else?"

"I can't remember."

Jade pulled her chair close to Olivia. She took a pendant from around her neck and allowed it to swing slowly in front of Olivia's face. "I want you to watch the stone. It's an opal and if you concentrate on it, you will become completely relaxed. Don't move your head. Allow your eyes to follow the stone. You are safe and at ease."

Olivia's eyes followed the opal, mesmerized by the changing colors as the light reflected off it.

"You're at the Press office. Someone came in and confronted you. What is he saying?" Jade asked.

"He said I ruined everything. Told me it was my fault."

"Now what is happening?"

"I'm trying to reason with him. His face is contorted and he's screaming at me. I tell him to leave."

"Go on, Olivia, what do you see?"

"He's taking off his mask and throwing it to the floor. Oh no, he has a gun. He's pointing it at me."

"Olivia, you won't feel any pain. I'm going to take your pain while you tell me what's going on."

"An evil leer covers the man's face as he points the gun at me. Oh my God. He shot me. He shot me in the chest."

Jade turned white as Olivia's pain swept over her. Ham gasped and reached for her but Jade held her hand out to stop him. "I'm okay," she whispered and then continued, "Olivia. What do you hear?"

"Chief Bowers is in the outer office, demanding the man put down the gun. The man said he would kill us both."

"Think, Olivia. What happened next?"

"No. No-no-no."

"It's okay. You're safe now. You can tell me."

The man shot Chief Bowers and then the chief fired back at him. I think I'm dying and I didn't get the chance to tell Mitch how much I love him."

"Who shot you, Olivia? You must tell me."

"I can't. He'll come back. He said first he'd cause me pain and then he'd kill me."

"Olivia, don't be afraid. You see his face clearly now. Who's threatening you? Tell me his name."

Deep sobs shook Olivia's body and tears streamed down her face. Almost in a whisper the name fell from her lips. "Judge Gillette."

"Listen to me. You will awake and remember everything. Judge Gillette is dead. Ham shot and killed him in your office. He can't hurt you again. It's over and you won't dwell on it any longer. You can get on with your life." Jade touched the side of Olivia's face and she opened her eyes with a look of surprise.

"Well, I'm glad we got that over with. How do you feel?" Jade asked.

"Free. I feel as if a burden has been removed from my soul. It's true, Judge Gillette is dead. Chief Bowers, you saved my life. How can I ever thank you?"

"It's Ham, gal. The one who deserves your thanks is Jade. She alerted me in time."

"Jade, how did you know?" Olivia asked.

Fortunately a tap on the door interrupted the answer.

"What's going on?"

Olivia rushed to Mitch's arms. "Mitch James, I love you. Are you ever going to marry me?"

A look of surprise followed by total joy took over his face and he held Olivia close to him. "Tonight, tomorrow or whenever you say, sweetheart."

"I think it's time for us to go," Jade told Ham.

Olivia and Mitch were locked in each other's arms and didn't seem to notice as Jade and Ham left the house.

"What went on in there, gal?" Ham asked as they walked to the car.

"Sorry you had to see that. Are you going to be uneasy around me now?"

"I guess I'll know enough not to keep secrets from you," he laughed. "Do I want to know what other talents you have?"

"You don't."

Ham put his arm around her. "Then let's make use of that marriage license."

"Are you serious? When?"

"How 'bout first thing in the morning? We'll drive over to the county seat, unless you want to do something fancier."

"Ham, all I want is for us to be together."

"Gal, that's exactly what I had in mind."

FIFTY-FIVE

"Maybe we should wait until after the first of the year to set a wedding date." I want to make sure you're healthy. I couldn't stand it if all the excitement and planning caused you to have a relapse," Mitch told Olivia as they sat on the sofa in the living room.

"You're talking like a doctor. I've been home from the hospital for over a week. I'm getting stronger every day. I don't want to wait a minute longer than necessary. Let's elope. Can't we run off to Las Vegas or anywhere?"

Mitch's eyes crinkled. "Baby, I like the way you think, but I don't believe Etta would appreciate not participating in her only niece's big event."

"I know you're right. We can discuss it with her, but I want you to know I'm not going to waste anymore time debating this. I've made up my mind."

Mitch pulled her close to him. "I love you. Let's talk to her."

Etta put her hand on her hips when she heard the news. "You're absolutely, positively not going to elope. I want to throw a wedding the likes of which Rexford has never seen before."

"Aunt Etta, that's not necessary," Olivia protested.

"Oh, but it is. You have to give me at least six weeks to get it all together."

"I'll give you one week. Forget the wedding preparations. Throw us a big party instead."

"Livie, don't you want a white gown, the bridesmaids, flowers and everything else that goes with it?"

Olivia put her arms around her aunt. "I only want Mitch."

"Have you thought this through? You can't move into Mitch's small efficiency apartment. Where will you live?"

"I'll find a rental," Mitch said. "I'm sure there's something available in town."

"Humph. You'll move upstairs. There are four rooms and a bath on the second floor and I'll have carpenters convert one room into a kitchen and refurbish the outside entrance," Etta told them.

"I can't ask you to do that," Olivia said.

"Livie, it will be completely private and besides, I have ulterior motives. It'll be reassuring to have a doctor in the house."

Olivia offered a compromise. "Today is the fifteenth of November. Thanksgiving is coming. We could combine the two to make one grand celebration."

"Livie, I've dreamed of the perfect wedding since you were a child. Please don't deny me this small pleasure. Allow me time to plan. Consider Christmas day." The look in Etta's eyes melted Olivia's heart.

"We'll discuss it," Olivia said. "Meanwhile, I'll take Mitch upstairs to look at the rooms."

"There's plenty of space. Try to picture it clean and furnished," Etta pushed.

"Are you sure you'll feel at ease living here?" Olivia asked as they surveyed the area.

"I'll be absolutely content anywhere I live, as long as you're there. I love you, Olivia, and Etta has been my favorite patient and staunchest supporter since I opened practice in Rexford. I believe we could settle in here without a problem. What about you? How do you feel about a Christmas wedding?"

"I guess I can wait until then, but you're moving in here tonight, understand?"

"Yes ma'am."

***

On the front page of Friday's Rexford Press, in bold letters, the headline read, EDITOR ENGAGED TO MARRY. The notice followed, Mrs. Loretta Anderson announces the engagement of her niece, Olivia McDougle to Dr. Mitchell James. The couple will be married on Christmas Day. The article told of Olivia's move back to her hometown from New York City, and gave statistics about Mitch's medical career.

On the back page of the same edition, Miss Jadene to Mr. Hamilton Boyers, were among the names listed under recent marriages.

Millie called Olivia with the news before the paper went to press. Quick phone calls to Robyn and Kristen put plans in motion. By the time Jade and Ham returned from a visit to Jade's parents in northern Kentucky, the girls had a reception party organized.

Etta invited Jade and Ham to the Anderson house for a quiet dinner, explaining that she worried about Olivia. "She hasn't left the house. Maybe a visit with friends would encourage her. Mitch will be here by six. If you come at seven, it will give him a chance to shower before we eat."

Jade agreed that she and Ham would come to cheer Olivia and persuade her to get out of the house and maybe spend time at the Press. They arrived on time and Olivia acted surprised to see them.

As they sat at the table, guests began pouring in. Jade blushed and Ham's grin took over his entire face.

The Anderson house rocked with music, people and lots of food. Etta bloomed with pleasure. She and Fritz entertained large crowds on a regular basis before he died. Watching Aunt Etta's joy, Olivia realized how selfish she was to deny the aunt that raised her, the pleasure of preparing a memorable wedding for her only niece. Olivia decided to stop dragging her heals and participate in the planning.

A week later, an anonymous letter addressed to the editor of the Rexford Press put a damper on those plans. Millie called Olivia and read it to her over the phone.

"Olivia McDougle cannot marry Dr. Mitchell James. He's legally married to Lily De Molante. Annulment papers were never filed."

"Where was it postmarked?" Olivia asked.

"No postmark. I found it in the mail drop at the office this morning." Millie told her. "I wouldn't have bothered you but if it's true, you and Mitch will have to deal with it. Do you want me to call the police?"

"I can't imagine what they could do. Would you make a copy and drop it off to me on your way home from work tonight?"

"Sure thing."

"Anything else I should know?"

"Nothing to concern yourself about. I believe we have everything under control." Millie quickly added, "Feel better and hurry back. You're needed here."

"Thanks. Watch for any follow-up letters and be careful in handling them. Put the original in a folder and put it in the safe. I'll talk to Mitch tonight and see what he says. Meanwhile, let's keep this between you and me, for now. It's probably a sick prank."

Mitch swore under his breath when he read the copy Millie had dropped off to Olivia. "I wish she hadn't worried you with this. She should have called me."

"I'm not made of glass. I can handle the truth."

"Olivia, there's no truth here. The court granted me a divorce over two years ago. I have the papers in my safe deposit box at the bank. Whoever sent this is assuming they know what went on in my life."

"Who would do this?"

"We have to ask, who knew Lily's maiden name. The first person that comes to mind is Judge Gillette."

"We know that's not possible. Could it be someone from the city council or the committee who brought you here? Maybe a partner or secretary from Gillette's law firm."

"We can eliminate the law firm employees. They'd have nothing to gain. I would have received an official document from them if it were true, not an anonymous letter stuffed through a mail chute."

"Who else would benefit? What possible motive could there be for anyone to send the letter?"

Mitch rubbed his chin as he thought about it. "Lily has a brother who wasn't thrilled and delighted with our break-up. He made his feelings known in a phone call when Lily left and returned to Philadelphia. He told me in no uncertain terms, he didn't believe in divorce or annulments. Still, I can't imagine he would make a trip back here to hand-deliver an unsigned letter. Let's wait and see if this person sends any follow-up notes."

"I hope this is the end of it. I don't want anything to spoil our happiness."

"Have you told Etta?"

"No. I asked Millie not to say anything at the office either. Only the sender, Millie, you and I are aware of the letter." Olivia shook slightly as she attempted to maintain control of her emotions.

"Baby, I'm so sorry." Mitch held her close. "Don't upset yourself. Tomorrow morning, if you're up to it, we'll go to the court house and get our marriage license and blood tests. We should continue with our plans, not let some nut-case mess with our lives."

"I feel fine. I've decided to go back to work. I need to get out of the house."

"Good. Limit yourself to half days and if you feel the least bit tired, come home."

Olivia kissed him. "Yes doctor. I believe I'm ready for other activities too."

"Sweetheart, I've been waiting to hear you say those words. Hold that thought until tonight."

FIFTY-SIX

Mitch asked Ben Hartman to join his medical practice in Rexford. He realized he didn't have the time to meet the needs of his patients, and continue holding the free clinic in Worthville. He had talked it over with Olivia and they both agreed it wasn't about money but their time together. She would hire another part-time clerk at the Press, and Ben would pick up the slack and take over the night office hours and most of the hospital visits. Mitch offered Ben the use of the efficiency apartment until he became established. If Mitch's practice expanded in the future, they could turn the apartment into more office space.

Ben worked his way through medical school taking two extra years to obtain his degree. A completely dedicated young man, he looked the part of a serious physician. He wore a white medical jacket to cover his shirt, tie and dress pants. His shoes were always polished to a shine. Mitch, who usually wore a dress shirt tucked into Levi's, and his most comfortable sneakers, told Ben he wouldn't hold the fashion statement against him. The young doctor began to appreciate Mitch's sense of humor.

***

Wedding plans were in full swing at the Anderson household. Everything seemed to come together and fall into place except the purchase of the perfect dress.

"I've looked everywhere. I can't seem to find one I like," Olivia complained. "I want something unique and outstanding."

"Livie, we could go to Dayton or you could fly to New York," Etta said.

Olivia made a face. "New York is one place I don't care to see again."

"Miss Olivia," Sarah said. "Don't know if I should say anything, but..."

"Do you have a suggestion? Anything you can bring to the table will be appreciated. I don't know where else to look."

"Could you maybe, draw a picture of what you have in mind? I ain't never used a pattern in my life, but if I see it, I can make it." Sarah went to her closet and pulled out her best tailored suit for Olivia and Etta to look over. "I saw something close to this in the window of a department store in Lima. You can see the way it's made."

"You did this? I can't believe it's hand sewn. Sarah, you've done a professional job." Olivia fingered the silk lining. The hand-sewn stitches were small and perfectly even. "Do you have any more hidden talents?"

Sarah blushed. "I learned to sew at an early age because my family couldn't afford to buy store-bought clothes. I found I liked designing things that no one else had."

Olivia called Jade. "Can you come to the house?"

"You don't have another surprise party waiting, do you?" Jade asked.

"No, nothing like that." Olivia explained what she had in mind.

When Jade arrived, the four of them put their heads together and after many sketches, came up with the perfect design for both the wedding gown and the attendant's dresses.

Olivia called Robyn and Kristen to tell them her choice of colors and described the general design. Once everyone was in agreement, Jade drove Olivia to Toledo to buy fabric.

At the end of the day, they returned to the Anderson house armed with bolts of fabric. Etta suggested they turn the den into a sewing room and informed Mitch the closed door meant it was off limits to him until after the wedding.

"Does that mean I have to wear a dress coat with my Levi's?" he teased.

"It means you and your best man and ushers will have to make a trip to the tuxedo rental store," Etta declared. She gave him definite instructions on what to reserve.

By the middle of November, the basic dresses were finished and everyone worked on the hand sewing.

***

A few days before Thanksgiving, Olivia prepared to walk to work. The crisp, cool air felt refreshing and sidewalks were clear as the snowfall of the week before had melted.

"Don't forget your gloves," Sarah called to Olivia as she walked to the front door. "And your scarf. It will be cold by the time you're ready to come home tonight."

Olivia shook her head with amusement. Sarah acted like a mother hen, looking after her chicks. "Got them. See you later." She walked out to the porch and discovered a box, wrapped in black paper with a white skull painted on the side, leaning against the porch banister. She bent down to pick it up but jumped back when she noticed wires dangling from an open corner. Olivia trembled as she stepped away. Slowly she reached behind for the door knob and backed inside the house and closed the door.

"What is it, Olivia. You look as if you've seen a ghost. Are you feeling okay?" Sarah grabbed hold of Olivia before she fell to the floor.

"Etta, call Mitch. Olivia has fainted," Sarah called as she helped Olivia to the bedroom.

Mitch was driving home from Lima General when Etta reached him on his cell phone. "Now don't panic. She felt dizzy and is lying down." She didn't tell him about the delivery.

In minutes he pulled into the driveway and sprinted up the front steps to the porch. Etta met him there before he tripped over the package. "There are wires coming out of the corner," she told him. "Olivia saw it when she started out for work this morning."

Mitch took hold of Etta and literally dragged her inside. "I'll check on Olivia. You call Ham and stay away from the front door."

"I'm fine," Olivia protested. "I'm afraid I over reacted."

"I want you to take it easy today. These threats have gotten out of hand. Etta's calling Ham."

"Do you think that's necessary? It's probably a hoax."

"Sweetheart, when someone sets a box on our porch that looks like a bomb, it goes beyond hoax. Maybe Ham can get to the bottom of this. He should be here shortly. I need to give him a copy of the letter also."

"It's in the top drawer of the dresser. I'll get it."

"You lie still. Olivia, I can't bear the thought of anything happening to you."

Ham came around to the side door as Etta requested. "What's going on here, Ms. Anderson?"

"I hope it's only aggravation, but you'll have to judge for yourself."

Mitch met them in the foyer and showed Ham a copy of the letter the Press received.

"How is Olivia taking this?" Ham asked.

"Okay until the latest incident." He opened the door and pointed out the box.

"Did you go out the front door this morning?"

"No, my car was parked in the garage. I went through the breezeway."

"Etta, when was the last time you opened the door?"

"It's been a few days for me. Sarah swept the porch yesterday morning when she got the mail. If someone left it there, she would have noticed."

"I suspect it's nothing, but better safe than sorry. I have a vest and insulated gloves in the patrol car. I'll grab my hook and drag it out to the street."

"Are you sure you want to do that?" Mitch asked.

"I can't imagine someone would've put a bomb on your porch and set it to detonate twenty hours later. The way it's wrapped, the person would have had a death wish to bring it up the steps and lean it against the banister, especially if they programmed it to blow up if it's moved. Whoever did this meant it as a warning. Someone set out to scare you. The way this box is constructed seems almost juvenile. Have any idea who'd want to threaten you or Olivia?"

"We immediately thought of Judge Gillette. Of course, that's not possible."

Ham scratched his head. "Not unless he did it from the grave. Meanwhile, let me get the box off your porch and then we'll talk. I want all of you to stay back from the front of the house just in case. Where's Olivia?"

"In the front bedroom."

"Get her out of there for now. This will only take a few minutes."

When Ham approached the porch from the front of the house, he wore safety glasses, the bulletproof vest he kept from his days with the Ohio State Highway Patrol, and a heavy coat. He hooked the box and as he lifted it the bottom broke open. A brick with wires wrapped around it fell to the ground. He dropped the hook and picked up the evidence and placed them in the trunk of his car. Then he went back inside the Anderson house to tell them they were safe."

"Now let's get down to business," Ham scowled. "Is Olivia able to join us?"

"I'm here. I don't plan to stay in bed another minute." She sat beside Mitch at the kitchen table. "What do we do now?"

"The first thing I suggest is to put motion lights around the property. Keep the porch light on at night and also at the side entrances of the house. I don't expect you'll have anymore surprises here but be careful. Second, we need to determine who has a vendetta against either of you. A disgruntled subscriber? A patient? You have any thoughts about who it could be?"

"We've talked it over and over. Neither of us can come up with a name other than my ex-wife's brother, but he lives in Philadelphia."

"There are all kinds of crackpots out there," Ham said. "Go through your patient files and see if anyone stands out. Olivia, see what you can come up with at the Press."

"I'll discuss it with Millie. We can sort through the letters to the editor. Most of them are either signed or relate to a specific incident. Off the top of my head, I can't think of anything out of the ordinary," Olivia said.

"Give me the information on the ex-brother-in-law. I'll run a check on him. So far the perp has been harmless, but don't let your guard down. I'll try to get prints off the letter and the box. Also, I'll make sure a patrol car drives by the house on a regular basis."

"Ham, the original letter is at the Press office. I'll call Millie and tell her to give it to you," Olivia said.

After Ham left, Sarah poured everyone a cup of coffee.

"Don't you have to go to the office?" Olivia asked Mitch.

"I don't want to leave you alone. I'll let Ben handle things today."

"You definitely will not stay home with me. We won't allow this to keep us housebound. Drink your coffee and then you can drop me off at the Press on your way to the office. I'll call you when I'm ready to return home."

"Baby, you have a lot of grit. Have I told you today how much I love you?"

"Not nearly enough. Now let's get going."

FIFTY-SEVEN

W e've been invited to the Anderson house for Thanksgiving dinner. Etta said the entire wedding party is coming along with Robyn's mother," Jade told Ham.

"That's quite a crowd. Should I buy some wine or dessert?"

"Etta insisted we bring absolutely nothing, but she did tell me that Mitch is giving Olivia an engagement ring.

"The one you designed?"

"Yes. I'm so excited. I can't wait to see her expression when she opens the box. She thinks Mitch ordered it from a jeweler in Toledo and is waiting for it to be delivered."

"Gal, you never cease to amaze me. I'll add designing jewelry to the many things I'm finding out about you."

Jade raised her eyebrow. "Don't you worry. I have all sorts of abilities you haven't discovered yet. I never want you to take me for granted."

"Gal, that won't ever happen. Everyday with you is an adventure. You keep on astounding me."

"And I intend to keep it that way. Surprised, astounded, amazed and in love with me."

Ham chuckled at the devilish look in his wife's eyes when she answered him. He sat quietly for a few moments before he spoke. "You know, I'm looking forward to getting to know that fella from Millsburg."

"You mean Todd Lowell?"

"Yeah. I know Robyn from the bank and Kristen has been to our apartment many times but I've never been introduced to Todd or Mitch's new assistant."

"Ben Hartman? He was at the hospital once when I visited Olivia. He's very professional, both in his dress and manner. Not a bit casual like Mitch."

"You like him?"

"I think so. He's a little stiff, maybe reserved is a better word. I chalked it up to the fact that we just met."

"Interesting."

"What do you mean?"

"Oh, nothing. Just seems unusual that Mitch would hire someone so different since they have to work together. Do you know where he comes from?"

"Okay, Mr. Detective. What's going on?"

"Gal, it's my nature to nose around. I promise I won't ask any questions on Thanksgiving. I'll behave and enjoy my new friends. I haven't been to a family celebration in a lot of years. I'm looking forward to this dinner." He wrapped his arms around his wife. "I love you, Jade."

Ham couldn't stop thinking about the threats Olivia and Mitch had received. He'd make it his business to find out about everyone they knew, friends or not.

Thanksgiving brought clear skies and cool weather. Robyn and her mother were already at the Anderson's when Ham and Jade arrived followed close behind by Todd and Kristen.

"Where's Ben?" Jade asked.

"He had to answer an emergency call. He said he'd try to make it later, but I expect he'll be tied up at the hospital for most of the night," Mitch said. "Meanwhile, let me pour the wine. Sarah said dinner will be ready in a few minutes."

While Jade, Kristen and Robyn surrounded Olivia, Mitch filled their glasses. Mary Margaret and Etta talked together about the upcoming wedding and caught up on the events of their lives.

Ham took advantage of the opportunity to sit on the couch next to Todd and strike up a conversation. In a matter of a few minutes, Ham had enough information to run a check on the Millsburg hardware proprietor, if necessary.

"Dinner is served," Sarah announced as she placed a silver platter heaped with sliced turkey in the center of the table. After everyone had found their place at the table, she started back to the kitchen.

"Not on you life, Sarah," Etta said. "You're part of our family. Get a plate and come right back here and sit with us."

"Sit here by me, Miss Sarah." Ham stood and held a chair for her. This gave him the ideal opportunity to talk with the housekeeper without raising any suspicions. "I want to sit next to the person who prepared this feast," he teased.

Sarah started to protest, but the look on Etta's face told her it would do no good.

They had finished dinner and were waiting for some of Sarah's famous pies when Mitch tapped his wine glass with a spoon. "I want to propose a toast. Lift your glasses to Olivia, the love of my life."

"To Olivia," everyone echoed.

Mitch dropped to one knee, removed a small box from his pocket and presented it his bride-to-be. "Open it sweetheart," Mitch said.

"Oh my gosh, this is the most elegant ring I've ever seen," Olivia said as she slipped the diamond and emerald engagement ring on her finger. "How did you know that emeralds are my favorite of all gems? I've never seen anything so unique. Who designed it?"

"Etta helped with the choice of stones, and Jade designed and crafted it. I hope it's what you wanted."

"It's breath-taking, Jade."

"This makes it official, sweetheart. You can't back out now." Mitch wrapped his arms around her.

"Nor can you," Olivia said.

Sarah and Etta were in the kitchen heaping whipped cream on generous wedges of pumpkin pie. Mary Margaret busied herself pouring fresh coffee when the front door chimes rang out.

"I'll get the door," Olivia called to Sarah. "Maybe Ben has made it in time for dessert."

"I have a delivery for Miss McDougle," a teenage boy said when she opened the door. He handed her a package, turned and hurried down the porch steps.

"Mitch, you sent me flowers." She tore away the outside ribbon and opened the box.

"Stop, I didn't send you anything. Mitch hurried to Olivia's side."

Ham jumped from his chair and snatched the box from a surprised Olivia's arms, but not before she saw the contents. The box was filled with roses, brown and shriveled with age. They were tied with a soiled, faded black bow. Olivia grasped the enclosed card. Tears fell from her eyes as she read the note. The words, made up of cut out newsprint letters, displayed the cruel, cryptic message.

"Beware. Anyone who dares attend your wedding could end up as dead as these roses."

Ham carefully took the card from Olivia's hand and studied the threat. "From the look of the print, the letters were probably clipped from the Lima News." He wrapped his dinner napkin around it and slid it into his pocket, hoping to find identifiable prints.

"Who delivered these, Olivia?" Ham asked.

"A young man. I've never seen him before."

Ham raced out the door in time to see a tall, slim boy walking down the street. Ham moved swiftly for someone his size and weight. He caught the teen-ager off guard and tackled him to the ground.

"What the hell's the matter with you mister? Have you lost your freakin' mind? Get off me before I call the cops."

"I am the cops." Ham pulled the kid up by the collar and pushed him against a tree. "Spread 'em." Ham checked for weapons. "You have any ID?"

"I ain't got a driver's license, but my picture ID is in my wallet." He started to reach but Ham grabbed his hand.

"Where?"

"In my back pocket."

Ham pulled the wallet from the kid's pocket and flipped it open. He eyed the picture and then the boy before handing it back.

"What's this about? I ain't done nothin'."

"You make a flower delivery to the Anderson house?"

"Yeah, so?"

"Don't give me an attitude, smart-ass. Where'd you get the box?"

"Some dude paid me ten bucks to deliver it."

"What did he look like?"

"Like I paid attention. Just some dude."

Ham lost his patience. "Listen up, wise guy." He put a firm grip on the kid's shoulder and glared at him while he fired a series of questions. "How tall was he? What was he wearing? Any scars? Think hard or we'll take a trip to the station. It might be a couple of days before I get back to you because of the holiday."

"Jeeze, don't get so hyper. I don't know. He was a little shorter than me, maybe 5'7" or 5'8". I couldn't see his face. He wore a dark parka with a hood, and yeah, he wore boots. I remember the boots because there ain't no snow or nothin'."

"Where'd you meet him?"

"I was hangin' at the bowling alley. They had a half-price special for Thanksgiving. My friends left earlier and this guy stopped me when I came out the side door. He handed me the box, the address and the money."

"Tell me everything he said?"

"Something about the florist bein' too busy tonight and he needed the flowers delivered for a special event."

"What kind of car did he drive?"

"I don't know. It was ten bucks, man. I took the money and brought the box to the address on the card. I didn't see him leave. Honest, I don't know what's goin' on. I'm tellin' ya the truth."

Ham took out his notebook and pencil and pushed them toward the young man. "Write down your name, address and phone number. Don't screw with me, kid. Make sure everything's correct. If you think of anything else, call the number on my card, got it?" Ham shoved it in the boy's jacket pocket.

The kid finally realized the seriousness of the situation and wrote down the information Ham requested.

"Now get out of here before I change my mind and throw your sorry ass in jail," Ham said in his best, bad-cop voice.

"Yes sir," the kid answered. He turned and ran down the street.

Ham thought about the teen-ager as he walked back to the Anderson house. "He didn't have anything to do with this. It was a case of being at the wrong place, wrong time."

While everyone did their best to comfort Olivia, Etta and Mary Margaret brought out trays of coffee and the pie.

"Let's not allow this incident to spoil Olivia's and Mitch's engagement. That's exactly what the sender wanted to do," Etta announced.

Todd stood and held the chair for Olivia before he joined Kristen at the table.

Olivia forced a smile. "I agree. It's over. It's time to enjoy dessert."

Sarah put the box holding the dead roses in a plastic garbage bag for Ham. She swept up the dried crumbling flakes from the floor while Ham took Mitch aside.

"Someone paid the kid to deliver the package. I'm convinced he didn't know anything about the contents or who gave it to him."

"We're back to square one. This is insane," Mitch raked his fingers through his hair. "I'm not sure Olivia can stand anymore of this stress. I don't know how to protect her."

"Mitch, I don't think this crack-pot is aiming to harm either of you, but he's hell-bent on making you uncomfortable."

"Well, he's succeeding. I feel completely helpless. Olivia won't go through with the wedding if she believes there's the slightest danger to anyone who attends."

"Tell you what. Let's bring this to a head before the big event. How about a very open engagement party? Maybe do something at one of the restaurants in town. Announce it in the Press. It might bring the perp out in the open and we can put a stop to this nonsense once and for all."

"You'll have plenty of protection?"

"I'll arrange for some of my men to be present outside and in and hire a few off-duty cops from Ottawa to supplement my force. You'll be well covered."

Mitch rubbed his hand across his chin. "It might work."

"Run it by Olivia and let me know in the morning," Ham said as he put a reassuring grip on Mitch's shoulder.

"I'll talk to her about it later tonight. Let's go back and join the party." Mitch began moving in that direction. "Olivia is upset enough without discussing this anymore tonight."

FIFTY-EIGHT

Olivia arranged the engagement party, without telling anyone but Millie, what was really going on. They had time to put Olivia and Mitch's picture on the front page of Friday's paper along with the details of the celebration and to reserve the Steak Grill for the Saturday evening event.

"Are you sure about this, Olivia?" Millie asked.

"I'm not sure about anything anymore. Whoever is attempting to terrorize Mitch and me is doing a good job. We have to trust Ham's judgment. He assured us everyone will be protected."

Mitch and Olivia had decided on an open house cocktail party. The notice read, "Friends of Olivia McDougle and Mitchell James are invited to celebrate their engagement at the Steak Grill from seven until nine." The date was included.

The Philadelphia Police informed Ham they had been unable to interview Lily's brother because he left the city to go on a hunting trip. They had no information regarding his location or when he would return. They faxed a picture of Joseph De Molante to the Rexford Police Department, along with pertinent statistics about his height, weight, hair and eye coloring. Ham had copies made and handed them out to his staff.

Mitch and Olivia had prepared a list of people who had previously said something derogatory about the medical treatment they had received from Mitch or wrote letters critical of Olivia's editorials. Neither of them could pinpoint anyone on the list they felt would cause the threats.

They decided in advance that Etta and Sarah would stay home. Mitch worried about Etta's ongoing heart problems and on the outside chance that something dramatic happened, it wouldn't be good for her.

The stage had been carefully set, and the plans completed. Ham hired three off-duty cops from the Ottawa Police Department, along with his own men, to mingle with the crowd. He had a uniformed cop patrolling the parking lot to watch for anything suspicious.

"Looks like we covered all the bases," Ham said to Mitch. "I want you and Olivia to stand near the back of the room. That will give my men the time to check everyone who enters before they have a chance to reach you.

During the evening, Ham and his men purposely, but politely, brushed against those guests on Mitch and Olivia's list, to check for concealed weapons.

Well-wishers came and went without incident. After an hour, Ham had decided his plan failed to turn up the person or persons who had threatened Olivia and Mitch.

Jade found Ham milling around in the crowded room and caught him by the arm, "What's going on? You haven't sat with me for more than two minutes all evening."

"Gal, I can't tell you about it now." He gave her a quick hug. "Please go back and stay with your friends. I'll explain later."

When Victoria entered the restaurant with her mother, Ham immediately gave Mitch a 'heads-up.' Mitch grabbed Olivia and held her close beside him.

"We should have guessed. It's so obvious. Victoria is the person we're looking for," Olivia whispered. "Aunt Etta told me how bitter she was, and how she blamed me for her father's death. How could I have forgotten that conversation?"

"She's immature enough to do something like this. Stand a little behind me. I don't want her to get too close to you."

Ham motioned for one of his men to come around behind Victoria to stay within reach when she approached them. Ham positioned himself beside Olivia, ready to react to anything she might attempt.

Victoria had dressed in a black silk form-fitting dress, and carried a large brown leather handbag that conspicuously mismatched her outfit. Her make-up, as usual, appeared thick and over-done. She tied her hair carelessly on top her head with a rubber band. Wisps of lose hair escaped and clung to her neck and around her face. Several bracelets dangled from her wrists and clinked noisily when she moved.

"I wanted to give you both my congratulations. Like, I hope you're, you know, happy and all."

"Thank you for attending our celebration, Victoria," Olivia said.

"We appreciate your good wishes," Mitch added. He could feel Olivia shaking at his side and kept a firm hand on her arm.

Victoria looked around the restaurant. "Did you invite any single guys?" She noticed one of Ham's men mingling near the bar. "Guess I'll introduce myself to that hunk." She placed her purse on a table beside Olivia, and smoothed the skin-tight dress over her hips before she headed in his direction.

The undercover cop lunged for the bag when he saw small black wires protruding from the clasp. He turned to run for the door before a frantic Victoria stopped him. Ham had pushed himself in front of Olivia and Mitch.

"What's the big idea? What are you, like a purse snatcher or something?" She grabbed the bag from the cop's hand. "I can't believe you'd pick up someone's purse right in the middle of a party. She opened the handbag and checked inside. "Thank goodness you didn't wreck my iPod." She carefully pulled it up to examine it more closely, the ear-buds dangled from her hand.

A look of relief swept over Mitch's face while the red-faced cop mumbled apologies, saying he thought his wife had left it there. Then he quickly left to mingle among the party guests.

"Why would you invite someone like that to your party? That guy should, like, be in jail. I told my mom we shouldn't come but she insisted we get out of the house." An indignant Victoria stalked off with her purse tucked firmly under her arm and continued on her mission to meet the single men in the crowd.

They were about to call it a night as almost everyone had left the party, including Kristen and Todd. A few stragglers hung onto the bar for the last of the free drinks when a scream rang out, breaching the festive ambiance of the occasion. Before anyone had the opportunity to react, the sound of a gunshot pierced the air. The bullet splintered the mirror behind Mitch and Olivia and sent shards of flying glass in all directions. Mitch pushed Olivia to the floor and shielded her with his body.

By the time Ham reached the back of the room, he found Mary Margaret Gleason holding the weapon in her hand.

Mitch looked up and said, "Dear God, it's Robyn's mother."

Olivia couldn't believe what he said. "It can't be. Are you sure?"

"Mrs. Gleason has the gun. Stay down, baby. Wait until Ham gets control of the situation."

The police converged on the scene. Ham, about to arrest Mary Margaret on the spot, stopped when suddenly one of

Ottawa's cops brought a struggling Dorothy Gillette into the restaurant. "I saw her fire and run toward the door. This lady," he said pointing at Mrs. Gleason, "grabbed the gun. She's not the shooter."

Ham allowed Jade, Robyn and Victoria to stay at the back of the restaurant with Mitch and Olivia. He cleared out the remaining guests while he debriefed the officer and Mrs. Gleason. Mary Margaret couldn't control her trembling body.

"It's over, Mrs. Gleason. Take a few minutes to compose yourself and then tell me what happened. First, you'd better give me that gun. We wouldn't want it to go off again." Ham tried to put her at ease.

Mary Margaret dropped the gun in Ham's hand as if it were made of hot coals. "I came out of the restroom and saw Dorothy. At first I thought she was pointing her finger, but then I realized she was aiming a gun at Olivia. I tried to shove her hand toward the ceiling. After she fired, I wrestled the gun from her. Oh my God, I hope no one was hurt."

"Son of a bitch," Ham muttered as he looked at Dorothy Gillette cowering against the arresting officer. She spoke incoherently, talking to the judge as if he stood next to her.

"You'll be okay now, Henry. You don't have to hit me anymore. I've taken care of everything. We're in control again, just like you've always said. Control is power." She mumbled something about not telling anyone about the estate he stole from the family of one of his clients, and babbled on about the graft he received from some of the councilmen.

In the back of the room, Robyn held Victoria as they watched Ham put the handcuffs on her mother. Victoria, wide-eyed with astonishment, couldn't speak.

Mitch asked Jade to stay with Olivia as he went to check on Dorothy Gillette. "She's lost all track of reality. I'll call for an ambulance to take her to the psychiatric ward at St. Marks in Lima," he told Ham.

Ham agreed and arranged for one of his men to ride along with the EMT's.

"We never considered Dorothy," Ham told Mitch as they waited for the ambulance. "When you think about it, she's shorter and heavier than her daughter. She could have passed for the man who paid the kid to deliver the flowers."

"You're right. I was hung up on my ex-wife's brother, although I couldn't imagine how he could have managed without being noticed in town. Dorothy Gillette didn't make it on my list of suspects."

"Damn, I don't want anymore excitement for the rest of the year," Ham said.

"Amen to that," Mitch agreed.

Mitch put his hand on Mary Margaret's shoulder. "You saved our lives. I don't know how Olivia and I can ever thank you."

"I happened to be at the right place, so to speak. When I saw Dorothy point that gun, I had an automatic reaction. If I would have had time to think about it, I probably would have fainted. I'm sure no hero. I believe I'd like to go home now."

"Sit down and relax a few minutes. I'll get Robyn."

"You knew something was up and you didn't tell me." Jade confronted Ham after the EMT's put Dorothy into the ambulance. "Maybe I could have helped."

"I know gal, but I didn't want you involved. It would have been your nature to do something to stop it and we wouldn't have found out who was behind this until too late. You've told me that you can foresee events, but not always the details." Then he told Jade the whole story.

"I saw an older woman pointing at Olivia when I read her tea leaves. We decided it was Etta pointing her in the right direction. Ham, I should have given it more credence. I should have..." Jade began to cry.

"You can't blame yourself. I'm the one who has to take responsibility. I honestly thought this whole thing was a vicious hoax. I didn't want anyone to disrupt the wedding and believed we'd catch the prankster. I never meant to put Olivia or Mitch in danger."

Jade kissed him. "You did what you had to do. It turned out okay. No one got hurt, but Mitch and Olivia will remember this engagement party for the rest of their lives."

Ham started toward the front of the Steak Grill to dismiss the extra men when he stopped short, slapped his forehead and turned back to his wife. "Damn, you read tea leaves too? What else do you, ah, never mind, ignorance is bliss."

When Mitch went back to find Olivia, she had her arms around Victoria, comforting her. He shook his head. "Olivia McDougle, you are truly a remarkable woman. You never ceased to amaze me. I'm one lucky man."

Robyn and her mother took Victoria home with them that evening. "After all, she's my half-sister. She has no one else," Robyn whispered to Olivia. "Hopefully we can change her narcissistic nature. She's not a bad kid, just a bit obnoxious and downright spoiled."

FIFTY-NINE

Etta rented the hall and reserved the church. By the first week of December, Olivia had mailed the invitations. As time grew closer, last minute details seemed to pile up. Olivia's emotions wavered between that of the serene bride-to-be and the anxious frantic, 'I'll never get this done in time,' wedding planner. Mitch's obvious delight grabbed hold of his face and wouldn't let go. He organized a few surprises of his own.

***

Christmas Eve at the Anderson's was joyful, peaceful, with a little nervous energy thrown in for good measure. The porch dazzled with multicolored lights dangling from the eaves. A wreath of cedar boughs, pine cones and bells hung on the front door. Decorated trees sat in the corner of the living room and in the foyer. The entire house had been decked with holly and bright red ribbons. Mistletoe had been positioned at the top of every doorway. Large pots of poinsettias encased in red and silver foil were placed on stands in every room.

"I believe we've covered every nook and cranny," Sarah said as she set platters of decorated cookies on the end tables in the living room.

"You've done a wonderful job," Olivia agreed. Her smile matched the holiday glitter.

Olivia, Mitch, Etta and Sarah held hands around the dining room table before dinner and wished each other the best for Christmas, for their wedding and all the days and years to follow.

That night after persistent protests, they banished Mitch to a spare room in Ham and Jade's apartment. Early the next morning Jade, Kristen and Robyn gathered at the Anderson house. Kristen fixed Olivia's hair while Jade did her make-up. Robyn helped with the dress, joking that it took all three of them to get this wedding underway.

Olivia couldn't believe how nervous she felt. "I don't believe I'll be able to walk down the aisle. I can hardly stand without shaking."

"After all you and Mitch have been through, we'll get you to the altar if we have to carry you," Robyn assured her.

"Is everyone ready?" Etta asked when she came into the study. She looked elegant in a mint green, floor length dress with a matching brocade coat. The beaming delight on her face brightened the room.

They piled into a limo and were driven to the crowded church. Etta used the front entrance where Todd Lowell waited to escort her down the aisle, while the girls went to the back of the church and waited in the choir room for their cue.

Ham delivered Mitch to the church and made sure he took his place at the front of the altar. Mitch looked a bit pale, but handsome in his black tuxedo with the red cummerbund as he waited for his bride-to-be to be lead to the front of the church.

The organ sounded and Kristen led the way, followed by Jade, both wearing dark green velvet fitted jackets over silk green plaid strapless floor length dresses. Then Robyn, the maid of honor, made her way to the altar, clad in the same style, but her jacket was deep red. The striking ensembles caused a buzz in the audience. The wedding march sounded and the crowd arose to see the bride escorted by Hamilton Bowers.

Olivia wore her auburn hair piled in loose curls atop her head, fastened with pearl combs. Dainty sprigs of holly and berries adorned her veil. A waist length, long sleeved white velvet jacket covered the strapless, pearl encrusted satin gown.

When Ham and Olivia reached the pew where Etta sat, Ham stepped aside and allowed Etta to take his place. Etta beamed as she had the long awaited pleasure of giving her niece away. Ham took his place next to the men.

As Etta brought Olivia to the altar, Mitch thought his heart would surely burst. Olivia's red hair glistened. Her pale complection glowed with barely a hint of color on her cheeks. Her dress looked like something out of a fairy tale. Her bouquet of red poinsettias and white roses quivered slightly as she walked toward him. Mitch almost choked with pride.

The vows were repeated and Mitch kissed his bride. Dr. and Mrs. Mitchell James were introduced to the applauding guests as he lifted her in his arms and kissed her again.

When they gathered for pictures, Robyn met the best man, Dr. Benjamin Hartman, for the first time. Their eyes held on to each other's a little too long, and Robyn knew instantly that this was the man she had waited for. Jade's infectious laugh erupted as she winked at her friend.

Mitch had quietly talked Etta out of the elegant reception she had organized, and swore her to secrecy about his new plan. In place of the string quartet, he substituted a Blue Grass band from Worthville and instead of pheasant; they served chicken fried steak from Jolts. Olivia couldn't believe her eyes when they entered the hall. Her mouth open, and she was unable to speak as she gazed around the room.

"Are you disappointed?" Mitch asked, not sure what to make of her reaction.

"I don't know what to say. You're the most amazing man in the world."

The reception was met with a gleeful reaction from the guests. Everyone seemed to enjoy the change of pace from the usual stuffy wedding parties and joined in the dancing, and of course, the food. The reception was a great success.

Before the evening was over, Jade couldn't help but notice the quiet conversation between Robyn and Ben, and how close Todd held Kristen when they danced.

"You look like the cat who swiped the mouse's cheese," Ham told her. Want to tell me what you've been up to?"

"I'm sure you don't really want to know," Jade teased.

"You're right. It's that ignorance, bliss thing again. Come on gal, let's dance the night away."

Mary Margaret Gleason introduced her friend, Robert, to Mitch and Olivia. "We've been seeing each other secretly for years. I didn't want to stir-up more gossip in town. Robyn met him last month and told me that life was too short to hide our affection. She insisted I bring him to the wedding."

Millie and Walt stood on the sidelines and enjoyed Olivia's day. She whispered to her husband, "I knew the minute I met her, she would make the Press a success. Now, she and Dr. James will continue to serve the community." Walt shook his head, but didn't comment. His wife had a short memory of the first weeks Olivia became editor of the newspaper.

A beeper sounded and Mitch reached for his pocket.

"Not tonight, of all times," he said. A frown creased his forehead.

Olivia's smile clung as if frozen to her face. She was determined not to show her disappointment as party-goers gasped. Mitch walked toward the double doors and flung them open. Sarah had called Mitch's beeper to notify him that his Jeep, loaded with luggage that Sarah had packed, sat outside. The crowd roared with laughter when Mitch tossed his beeper to Ben, went back to his surprised wife, grabbed her coat and carried her out the door. They drove off to spend their honeymoon at an undisclosed location. No one heard from Dr. and Mrs. James for the next two weeks, but their future life held many unexpected surprises.